Climate Change

(A Nina Bannister Mystery)

by

T' Gracie and Joe Reese

For information, email **Cozy Cat Press**, cozycatpress@aol.com   or   visit   our   website   at: www.cozycatpress.com

COZY CAT
P R E S S

ISBN: 978-1-939816-64-1

Printed in the United States of America

Cover design by Paula Ellenberger
http://www.paulaellenberger.com/

1 2 3 4 5 6 7 8 9 10

To the cozy mystery writers of the world:

May they and their cats forever prosper!

CAST OF CHARACTERS
(listed in alphabetical order)

Garth Amboise: one of America's most prolific young writers, but not the easiest man on earth to deal with.

Molly Badger: a would-be cozy writer haunted by a dark secret.

Nina Bannister: heroine of the Nina Bannister mystery series. Heads to The Candles in search of a few days' peace and quiet, and soon finds herself sent into Abbeyport on an errand of vital importance.

The Cozy Pussy-Cats: they arrive thirty-strong in elegant, hand-designed cat carriers—and the fur begins to fly!

Harriet Crossman: executive director of the AGCW (American Guild of Cozy Writers), she is charged with maintaining structure and order amid a flood of threats to her beloved literary genre.

Professor Brighton Dunbury: author of the Drusilla of Sestos cozy series; the professor re-kindles an old romance and hands Nina a vital clue.

Sylvia Duncan: high-ranking executive at HBO; she is charged with making a life-changing—and dangerous—decision.

Margot Gavin: proprietor of The Candles Bed and Breakfast. Allergic to cats.

Maybelle, Annabelle, Mildred, and Ben: unimportant characters. Don't worry about them.

Jim and Pat Hershey: the country's most beloved husband and wife cozy-writing team. (They look SO CUTE together!)

Suzy Maples: beauty contest queen. Her exotic Siamese cat, Miss Whiskers, has an unfortunate liaison with the plantation house cat, Sluggo.

Sarah Morgan: Does not exist.

C. R. Roberts: woman body-builder-writer. Her cozy heroine, Patty Parity, is a fierce advocate for women's rights.

The Smathers Sisters: writers of paranormal romances (as well as cozies); they are the first American writers to introduce inter-creature sexual intercourse.

Abbeyport Police Chief James Thompson: almost driven to a mental breakdown by the last Writers' Convention at The Candles, he has vowed never to deal with the profession again. Events, however, dictate otherwise.

Rebeccah Thornwhipple: she and her heroine are both in their early nineties. She is almost thrown out of the AGCW for writing works with too explicit erotic content.

Mark Twain: as himself.

PROLOGUE

Nina Bannister, occupant of a haunted room, awoke at six o'clock in the morning, the canopy of a huge four-poster bed stretching above her, mythological figures staring menacingly either at each other or at her—it being far too early to decide exactly which.

She missed her cat Furl.

She missed having to kick his little yellow and white body off the northeast corner of her bed back in Bay St. Lucy. She missed snarling something bad at him as he plopped to the floor and rrraaawwd back at her, his words meaning, in cat, "All right, all right, so where's breakfast?"

She missed her morning's walk along the beach.

What could one walk along if one lived in a plantation house such as this one, tucked away in the middle of Mississippi?

The River?

But it was two miles away and separated from her by dense pine forest and prehistoric undergrowth.

So there was nothing to do but slip out of the bed— parachute out, really, because the hardwood floor of the room had been built at least a foot too low from the surface of the mattress itself—and, having hopefully neither sprained an ankle or shattered a foot, totter over to the huge thing on the far wall that was either a burnished mahogany vanity or a court house.

She looked at herself, saw nothing particularly new nor frightening—though it must be said, nor particularly encouraging either—then padded back across the room to the stately chair on which she had piled both her jeans and the gray, black, and tan sweatshirt with the snarling Mississippi State bulldog on it—and, as it were, dressed.

The sweatshirt seemed to engulf her.

It was as though she had been eaten by the bulldog, and was now inside it.

Yesterday she had bought the thing, during the first small shopping spree ventured upon by her and Margot as they entered the town of Abbeyport.

Time, time—

Yesterday, is that all it was?

And where exactly had it begun, this strange venture that was supposed to be a pure vacation but that now promised to be—what?

No way to know, no way to predict, not just this morning anyway.

But as for where it had begun, why, that was easy when one thought about it.

It had begun under the blackest of all skies, with crabs sizzling in the equally black pot, and she herself talking of hurricanes (the real ones, not the ones from Pat O'Brien's in New Orleans) and of Sarah Morgan, flaming red-haired Sarah, who, Nina knew, would have been one of her best-ever friends—

—had Sarah Morgan not been dead.

Such a pity.

CHAPTER 1: HOW TRIPS ARE PLANNED

The whole thing had started on a Friday evening in late August.

What a terrible time of year.

The tourists were leaving the town, which meant death for the merchants, and school was starting, which meant death for the children.

Those of them unfortunate enough to have birthdays in the last week of the month received not toy planes and guns and animals and dolls and video games, but bottles of paste and packages of number two lead pencils.

One might as well not have been born at all.

This particular night though, given all the circumstances which seemed stacked against it, was going surprisingly well.

Margot Gavin had arrived that morning on her monthly visit to town and had spent the morning gabbing with Nina and fussing about her shop Elementals, moving a vase from here to there and being doubly certain that none of Nina's lighthouse paintings had found their way onto the walls.

Then the two had split up. Margot had stayed in the office to catch up on paperwork, and Nina had betaken herself, garbed in rags and flip flops, down to the stone jetty, where she'd spent two hours crabbing.

She had then made the rounds to the various liquor stores, laying in gin for Margot and a bit of white wine for herself.

Some piling up of driftwood then, a nap, her ritual watching of the sunset and appearance of the first stars—for tonight was no moon—and, a bit later on, the starting of the fire.

She had constructed—or rather Tom Broussard had constructed for her—a ramshackle metal framework from which the big black kettle could be hung, and beneath which driftwood dried by the July and August suns could be kindled.

So that, by the time the sky had become as black as the kettle and the waves had begun their nightly moaning cadence, she could dump her sack of crabs into the bubbling water and watch their color change to fierce red and hear Margot say:

"Those crabs are so red. They remind me of Sarah Morgan's hair."

There was very little leeway in casting about for a reply to this, since only one response was possible. That being of course:

"Who is Sarah Morgan?"

"Was."

"Who was Sarah Morgan?"

"Our ghost. The ghost who haunts The Candles Plantation. Far and away, the best bed and breakfast ghost in Mississippi."

"Really?"

A shake of Margot's head:

"Of course 'really.' A 'false' ghost story would have no point. No one would listen to it."

"Well, I'm ready to listen then. Tell me about Sarah Morgan. Here, let's get some of these crabs on your plate. You just have to tear them apart you know."

"I know. You promise me that they don't feel pain when you boil them like you just did."

"I'm told it's a soothing experience for them."

"All right. Then I shall devour my share. First though, I want to read you something."

She reached into the huge purse of dull gray and cracked leather which lay beside her like a dead manatee.

"What have you got there?"

"A letter."

"My God, I'd almost forgotten that such things existed."

"They don't any more, but they apparently did in 1864 when Sarah wrote this one."

"She couldn't just text?"

"The Union troops controlled the Internet. According to historians, they perpetrated a great deal of identity theft."

"Yes. Of course, the Confederate States of America had done some of that too, for centuries, in order to get their cotton picked."

"Let's not quibble. Ooh, these little morsels are good!"

"I catch only the finest specimens. So go ahead, read. Is there enough light by the fire?"

"I think so. I feel Sarah's spirit is here with us, and she'll brighten up the fire if need be."

"Would Sarah's spirit like a crab?"

"If it does, I'm sure it will just help itself. Here, though. Let me unfold this. Aha. Now, listen:"

She read:

"Oh, they are coming! God grant us the victory! They are now within four miles of us, on the big road to Bayou Sara. On the road from town to Clinton, we have been fighting since daylight at Redbridge, and have been repulsed."

The wind, Nina noticed, was coming stronger off the ocean, but it was still not strong enough to move a ludicrous number of stars that had spilled out across the sky.

Margot squinted through her glasses and continued to read:

"Fifteen gunboats have passed Vicksburg, they say. It will be an awful fight. Colonel Grant badly beaten at Redbridge. No matter. With God's help we'll conquer yet! Again! The report comes nearer. Oh they *are* coming! Coming to defeat, I pray God. Only we seven women remain in the house. The General left this morning, to our unspeakable relief. They would hang him, we fear, if they should find him here. 'Mass' Gene has gone to his company. We are left alone here to meet them."

A momentary pause to let this sink in, so that Nina might take a moment to evaluate the prospects of seven women against a major portion of the Army of the North. Then the reading went on, as, of course, the Civil War went on, as it has always done in the state of Mississippi, and it will always continue to do—Appomattox be damned—until the end of time.

"If they *will* burn the house, they will have to burn me in it. For I cannot walk, and I know they shall not carry me. I'm resigned. If I *should* burn, I have friends and brothers enough to avenge me. Create *such* a sensation! Better than being thrown from a buggy. Only I'd not survive to hear of it!"

Silence save for the wind, the waves, and the breaking up of the crabs, which the two women were violently devouring.

"What happened?" Nina could not help asking.

Margot shook her head:

"What happened was exactly what Sarah Morgan had predicted. A mortar shell—it must have been only a few hours after the passage was written—hit the East wing of the plantation and set it on fire. The blaze was put out before it could consume the rest of the building. But they were not able to get Sarah out. She perished in the fire."

"She must," asked Nina, "have been very old at the time, and unable to walk down the stairs?"

"No. She was a young woman. But she'd been thrown from a horse the week before—I'm told she was an ardent horsewoman—and had sustained a broken leg. The men had carried her upstairs, the soldiers protecting the house. But those soldiers were gone now."

"Why didn't the women leave too?"

"That simply wasn't done. There would have been no place safer, not for a woman with a broken leg."

"Why couldn't she go to the town nearby? What is it called? Abbeyport?"

"It was hardly a place in the road at that time. No, the Southern ladies simply had to depend on the gallantry of those troops that might be invading. Sarah was in a bad position. She probably would have been spared ill treatment—I'm told the rest of the ladies were—but there was that chance mortar round. Yankee soldiers arrived soon after and put out the fire. They wanted the place as a headquarters, of course. But—well, that's the story. Or at least part of it."

"And so Sarah is now—"

"Yes, Sarah is a ghost. She has always refused to leave her house. She is said to appear from time to time on the front balcony, her hair blazing in red flames. She appears infrequently, and to any new owner of The Candles, some few weeks after the plantation has changed hands. And always in the same room, that room being in the center of the house, directly over the main entrance. Your room, actually."

It took a bit of time and crab to let this last phrase soak in.

"My what?"

"Your room, Nina. The room where you'll be staying. Tomorrow night, actually."

"I thought I'd be staying in my room tomorrow night."

"Why would you want to do that?"

"I don't know; maybe because I live there?"

"What a lame reason!"

"All right; so what are the reasons for my sharing a room at The Candles with fire-headed Sarah?"

"Why, because I'm inviting you, of course! Nina, you were at the plantation on the day of our wedding."

"And a beautiful wedding it was, too. No ghost as I remember."

"No, Sarah apparently always allows for a bit of 'living in' before she makes her appearance. But, at any rate, you keep saying you're going to visit us."

"I know, Margot. But I was a little busy in Washington. And then before that I had to go to Austria to break up an international art smuggling ring. And there was the horrid mess with the deep water drilling rig Aquatica—"

"I know."

"Pick pick pick the little everyday details of life. Errands here, murders there—"

"And you never seem to get time to do what *you* really want to do. Well, this time things will be different. Goldmann is in New York on business, and we have no guests booked into the place all next week. We would have it to ourselves. We would do nothing but take it easy. Stay in bed until ten, make ourselves a little coffee, enjoy the absolute perfect stillness of the woods around the place. Come on, say you'll come."

Nina thought about it.

Why not?

She was still tired from her month in Washington, and even several weeks at home had been insufficient to get her old energy back.

Maybe this was what she needed.

Jackson Bennett's daughters could come and feed Furl.

They could simply close Elementals for a few days.

"And," she said, thinking aloud now, "there's the hurricane."

Margot leaned forward:

"What hurricane?"

"Hurricane Clarence."

"Hurricane who?" asked Margot.

"Clarence."

"That's the dumbest hurricane name I ever heard."

"I know," said Nina.

"I think they should go back to naming hurricanes after women."

"That's sexist."

"I know, but it doesn't matter. I'll give them my name, sexist or not. Better Hurricane Margot than Hurricane Clarence. At any rate though, what's the story with this storm, other than the fact that it sounds like a bookkeeper?"

"I heard about it today on the weather. It's apparently just now forming out in the Gulf. It's started to move, though, and they expect it to head toward Texas."

"How does that affect you here in Bay St. Lucy?"

Nina shook her head:

"It means rain, heavy rain. Again! This is like the fourth hurricane we've had to deal with this season. More than ever before. Some say it's due to climate change or global warming or whatever. And I always find that depressing, just sitting in the shack, not being able to Vespa around town or walk on the beach."

"All right, then! Nature is speaking to you! Come up and be my guest! We'll have our own little Woodstock!"

"You envision Woodstock; I envision Girl Scout Camp. And by the way, the two had more in common than you might guess. Especially sixth grade."

"Okay, then, if that's what it will take, we'll make s'mores on a campfire out by the river."

"You're talking me into it."

"Oh goodie! We'll leave for Abbeyport tomorrow afternoon. It's a three hour drive, we'll be there by nightfall."

"Now you do have to promise me I won't meet Sarah Morgan."

"No such promises. I do promise you though, that if you do meet her, you'll have a lot in common."

"What?"

"All she did was take on the Union Army. Compared to the battles you've fought in the last year or so, that's small potatoes."

And so Nina was decided.

She always enjoyed Margot's company.

And she was sure to enjoy the quietness and serenity of The Candles.

And she would not see any bizarre and supernatural creatures.

And she found herself in these thoughts for the rest of the evening.

Not knowing that she was completely wrong about every one of them.

CHAPTER TWO: ABBEYPORT

Margot had made the drive from Bay St. Lucy north to Abbeyport—the nearest village to The Candles—so often that the nearest and most straightforward route up through Mississippi had become somewhat boring to her. This time, purely for variety, she drove directly west into Louisiana, crossed the Mississippi at St. Francisville, and meandered north through Louisiana, glimpsing the great river as often as possible, and passing through towns such a Vidalia, St. Joseph, Talulah, and Lake Providence.

The small local road she chose was two-lane and blacktop, bordered on each side by impenetrable walls of yellow pine, and punctuated at five- to ten-mile intervals by smaller villages and communities, each of which consisted of house trailers, small houses, larger houses, the village mansion, the downtown, the village mansion on the north side, large houses, the McDonalds, the Wal-Mart, small houses, house trailers, and once again the forest.

Margot's driving proved to be the only safe and reasonable part of her personality, and so Nina was able to unclench her fists after only thirty or so miles, and concentrate on finding something to listen to on the radio.

There were political talk shows railing against the government; there were sermons and wild-voiced ministers warning about the upcoming end of the world; there were sports babble shows describing the wonders of high school running backs who, though only sophomores at present, were still being wooed openly by not only LSU, where loyalty dictated that they should go, but also, terrifyingly, Ole Miss.

There was a show advising people what to do with their 401K's.

There was a National Public Radio show that dealt with the ancient art of quilt making in Southern Croatia.

Scan, scan, scan—

Finally there was a channel from which emanated a strange sort of static with which Nina was not familiar. It frightened her, and she wondered if something had gone suddenly wrong with the electrical system of the Volkswagen.

"What is that?" she asked Margot.

"What is what?"

"That static."

"It isn't static; it's Led Zeppelin."

"It's what?"

"Led Zeppelin."

"Is that a kind of electrical malfunction?"

"No, it's a rock band."

"You're kidding."

"Have you ever heard an acid rock band?"

"Margot, I've lived in Bay St. Lucy all my life. When and where would I have heard an acid rock band?"

"I don't even want to go into that. Keep scanning, though."

"You don't like Led Zeppelin?"

"I don't like their lead guitarist."

"What's wrong with him?"

"I went to bed with him. The first thing he did was—"

"Stop."

"Okay, but I still remember his—"

"Stop, Margot."

And Nina continued to scan stations as one community melted into another and the main square court houses began to run together in her mind, all of them guarded by a granite confederate soldier with wide-brim hat, a rifle, and an angry glare.

"There. Listen. Is that another rock band?"

"No. That's actual static."

"It's so amazing to me. How you can tell the difference?"

"Well, drugs help."

They were entering another town, the name of which Nina had not noticed. Margot slowed the car, then braked for the first signal light in a series of Wendy's, Taco Bells, Arby's, Kentucky Fried Chicken, Shell Gasoline, Whattaburger, and a building that said State Farm Insurance.

Almost as a matter of reflex Nina, child of the Gulf Coast, let her eyes scan the skies. Still crisp blue but different. The wisps of clouds a bit higher, farther apart, lacier and almost diaphanous, as though she were imagining rather than seeing them; and the blue, the deep eternal and frightening blue, now tinged with something else, some other non-color, as though God had injected into it a drop of flavoring.

At precisely 4:15 p.m.—Nina noted the time on the dashboard clock, because something momentous seemed about to happen, and she wanted to know when—they topped a small rise and noted by the roadside a sign that said:

ABBEYPORT FERRY, ONE MILE

Then Margot turned slightly to the right, wove her way through a grove of pines, made a harder turn left, and there before them lay the Mississippi River.

The sight of it created in Nina the same feeling that always overwhelmed her when, after an absence of some days, she returned to and glimpsed again the ocean.

"Wow," she found herself whispering.

A child-like thing to say.

But then, elemental things always drew her back into childhood.

She might not appreciate Led Zeppelin but she wasn't dead, either.

There it was, almost as wide as the sea itself, placid and winding, a barge floating far to the north, another one disappearing around a bend to the south, the sun's rays glittering on water that seemed, from this distance, absolutely motionless.

The narrow road descended, a little steeper now, a turn here and there—down to a pier, toward which could be seen chugging a ferry boat with no cars on it.

Weekdays, thought Nina.

No traffic.

"We could," said Margot, sliding the car into the narrow land that said, 'Autos board ferry here,' "have come up the interstate and over. I thought it might be fun to go over with the ferry."

The Volkswagen reached the river's edge where the ferry's mooring had been set up. It stopped, motor still running, while the ferry chugged toward it and cut its engines, drifting along toward the shore.

Nina could not stop looking first to the left, where one barge had finally disappeared, and now back northward. There, just coming into view, almost at the middle of the river, was a ghost ship.

There were ghosts on the plantation; all right, so there were ghosts on the river, too.

It seemed to be an old paddle wheeler, gaily painted in red white and blue, smokestacks puffing, a few passengers tiny in the distance, posed like miniature dolls along the rails of the quarter deck, and, every few seconds, its whistle tooting to the upcoming town—in this case, Nina assumed, Abbeyport—that miraculous warning: STEAMBOAT'S COMING!

"Will you look at that, Margot?"

"Yes. It's a pleasure line from St. Louis down to New Orleans. The ferry we're about to take is one of the few still crossing the river. Mostly they've been replaced by bridges. But on the other side there's a portage point where the steamboat stops. You can get on it and go all the way down to New Orleans, or you can just go a few miles, ten or thirty, I forget which, and then catch another boat back upriver. There's a restaurant, of course. A band, shows—all that kind of thing."

Nina watched the scene spread out before her, but, as the ferry neared, her mind distanced, and she found herself standing on the Texas Deck with Mark Twain. He was a young Mark Twain as he stood there by Nina, not the white-haired man in the white suit that had come to characterize him, but a resolute young cub pilot, determined to learn the ways of the river. They watched as wavelets scudded out across the stream, belying or indicating shoals, invisible currents, snags just beneath the surface; they checked the boilers, remembering that one had blown up just below Cairo only a day before, sinking the boat in mid-river and drowning all on board; and they squinted into the sun, just able to make out a small island not too far from shore, where a little boy and a big black man, a runaway slave, cooked their simple meal on a small fire and set about changing American literature forever.

"The sky looks ever so deep," Nina found herself saying, softly, knowing that neither Sam Clements nor Huck nor Jim would hear her, but sensing that they, like her deceased husband Frank, existed as real and not imaginary ghosts, and would never leave her as long as she simply remained receptive to them—"ever so deep when you're looking up into it, and you're on a raft."

"What did you say, Nina?"

"Nothing. Just muttering."

"The ferry's here. We'll pull up now."

A man who appeared to be the exact opposite of Mark Twain—who appeared more like a gasoline attendant except that there were no longer any gasoline attendants—jumped from the cabin of the ferry, walked briskly toward the bow of the boat, and loosened a chain, allowing Margot to drive forward. She continued to edge on, following the man's hand waving instructions, as the car moved toward the bow and the boat began to pull away from the pier, creating a twin movement that had always delighted the ten-year-old Nina.

A few moments later they were standing on the ferry rail, leaning out slightly over the Mississippi. They could see the current moving beneath them now, forcing them south while the chugging engines of the ferry resisted, and the boat, headed north, wound up compromising with nature and drifting east toward Abbeyport. The steeple and roofs of the town gleamed white over the pilot house of the ferry.

The air, unusually fresh for August, had now subsumed into it all the aromas of the river, and felt delicious.

Nina was shaken from her reveries by the blaring of the ferry's whistle, and a brisk command to start the Volkswagen's engines, a command followed by Margot so that the little car was puttering away nicely as the ferry docked.

The chain fell in front of them, they edged forward, upshifted, gained speed, and, finally, found themselves driving along the main street of Abbeyport.

"My God," said Margot, "will you look at this?"

"Yeah," was all that Nina could say.

"One of the reasons I thought you might want to come with me, Nina, was to get away from Bay St. Lucy and let yourself be surrounded by something absolutely different."

"This is new all right!"

And they did in fact feel as though they had entered a world completely different from little Bay St. Lucy, gulf-side artists' and fishermen's community. In the first place, the population of Bay St. Lucy was 2,367 people. Here the population was—or so announced a large green and gold city limit sign showing the ferry boat approaching and the town backed up against the river—2,581.

So that was different, right from the start.

But as the Volkswagen headed down the central street of town, the other differences continued to mount up.

Here, for example, just at the west end of the broad avenue—which, as was the case with Bay St. Lucy's main thoroughfare, was called "Main Street"—was a shop called "Expressions by Claire." In Bay St. Lucy that exact position was occupied by the shop called "Clay Creatures."

How strange!

But it continued.

Farther along, instead of Joyce's Shells and Gifts, they saw Maggie May's. The Social Chair had been replaced by Uptown Interiors. The Blue Crab Gifts Gallery had become River Breeze. Where Moor-Haus Antiques would have stood in Bay St. Lucy, they saw before them Art Alley in the Pass.

Then came, instead of Aloha Gallery, a shop called Let's Make Up Gifts.

One could actually list it.

Whereas in Bay St. Lucy there would have been:

Just Flowers

And

M & L Gifts

And

Tuesday Morning

And

Your Gift Cove

And

Gratitude

—here there were:

Inside Out

And

Stephanie's Stuff

And

Cool Breeze

And

Jayne's Novelties

And

Rustic Rail

(Where they actually went inside, and where Nina bought a Mississippi State sweatshirt with a snarling bulldog on it.)

And—

—well, it just went on and on.

"Can you believe this place?" whispered Margot.

"How could anybody live here?" answered Nina.

Finally they made their way into "Obob's Coffee Shop," since one of the waitresses who worked there also helped out during busy weekends at The Candles.

They sat at a white wrought-iron table, from which Nina could see the street and Margot, sitting opposite, could see back into the interior of the shop. Beyond the actual coffee bar was a larger garden, ferns hanging everywhere, clay pots and framed riverscapes peeping out through the foliage.

A hefty, florid, and red-faced woman emerged from this area. Margot began to speak to her.

"Hello, Lizzy! Hey, I want you to meet my—"

But she was interrupted.

"Margot, where have you been?"

The woman, Nina could tell, seemed terrified.

She was then joined in the café's main room by a second woman.

This woman was the exact opposite of the first.

Whereas the first—'Lizzy,' Margot had called her—was hefty and ruddy-skinned, she was small and shriveled and sallow.

"Hi, Maybelle! I want you to meet my—"

Same response.

"Margot, where have you been?"

Margot stared back at the two horrified faces for a time, then stammered:

"Down in Bay St. Lucy. I go down there every month."

"Nobody could reach you!"

"But why did anybody need to?"

Both women had now surrounded the table. Their eyes were dark and furrowed, their mouths agape:

They seemed to speak as one:

"Margot, they tried to call you. Everybody tried to call you!"

"I didn't get any calls!"

"Margot," said Nina, sensing the trouble because of knowing Margot, "check your cell phone."

Margot took the small plastic thing from her monumental purse and looked for an instant at the dark screen before saying quietly:

"It's dead."

"You have to charge it every now and then, Margot."

"I know, but—"

"That's why," said the two women, again in unison, "nobody could get through to you."

Margot put the phone away and continued to stammer:

"But what in heaven's name is the matter?"

The bigger of the two women pushed her way in front of the more weasily of the two and fairly shouted:

"Margot, you have to get out there!"

"Why?"

"Because, because, because—"

What in God's name is going on? Nina found herself thinking.

"Has there been an accident?"

Fierce shaking of heads:

"You just need to get out there. Fast."

"A fire?"

"I'll call Mildred and them and tell 'em you're coming!"

"But if I could just know—"

"You just need to go. Thank God you're here, anyway."

"But I—"

"Go! Go now!"

And they did.

CHAPTER THREE: THE WORST THING IN THE
WORLD THAT COULD POSSIBLY HAPPEN

Highway 34 crept out of Abbeyport to the north like
something sinister, as though it had much to hide. Vast
forests loomed around and over it, still protecting Southern
troop movements from low-hovering helicopters, both those
belonging to the Federal Army and those belonging to local
radio stations and police departments.

"What do you think is going on, Margot?"

"I haven't the faintest idea. The next few days are
supposed to be completely open. No guests are booked in."

"Who is at The Candles now?"

"Four or five people at most. Our head cook, Mildred.
The handyman who takes care of small plumbing problems,
wiring issues. It's an old place, things go wrong. Two or
three girls to help them out. But, as far as I remember, the
arrangement was for them to spend today getting the place
cleaned and in shape—then they were supposed to head into
town and take the next few days off."

"Apparently it didn't work that way."

"Apparently not. But I can't imagine what might have
happened."

"A fire you think?"

Margot, gripping the steering wheel hard, pursed her lips
and shook her head:

"I think Maybelle or Lizzy would have told us. Same
with an accident."

"They didn't seem to be able to say anything."

"No. They were just panicked."

"Maybe they saw Sarah Morgan."

Margot said nothing to this.

And Nina could see nothing but the blacktopped road
before them and a strip of sky now pale and colorless—for

the weather was certainly presaging a change, though not an imminent one—bisecting the tops of the pines like a ribbon tying the world of forest and Volkswagen neatly together.

There was no traffic, nor had there been since they passed the three-story brown brick Magnuson's Funeral Home which was, appropriately, the last building to be seen in Abbeyport, when one left the city heading north.

The only other part of the world worth noting was a narrow channel of algae-covered and brackish brush-water that inundated the ditch just to the right of the road's shoulder. This body of water—it had no name, for it was both too narrow to be a bayou and too stagnant to be a creek—seemed to represent a totally failed Mississippi River, a great natural artery blighted at birth and doomed to remain eternally what it was at the present: a breeding ground for mosquitoes, a sanctuary for fallen limbs, and a haven for turtles, frogs, and snakes too frightened to enter moving water.

"Here's the turn-off, Nina. Whatever is going on out here, we'll know it soon."

"Where's your road? I don't see it."

"Up there, fifty yards to the right."

"That's your sign?"

"Yes, what's wrong with it?"

"It's not a sign, Margot, it's a prank."

"Now if you're going to be picky about everything—"

Nina did not want to be picky about everything. But this little sign? A prank it could certainly have been, because it was the farthest thing possible from the elegant billboards she'd seen for several miles past advertising The Waverly Plantation, or Emerson Manor, or Oak Grove Estates, or the other grand structures of Mississippi and Louisiana and Georgia and Alabama that celebrated a magical world long since vanished.

This particular sign—which would have been a foot square if it had been cut that precisely—seemed no more than the end flap of a pasteboard box with the words The Candles poorly drawn across it with dark blue paint.

This was not Nina's greatest concern though.

Her greatest concern was the road—lane—trail—path—paved concept—Mind of God—that turned abruptly away from the already perilously narrow Highway 34 and snaked menacingly into a dark and massive wall of timber that, but for the trail's questionable existence, would have seemed completely impenetrable. They bumped over a segment of railroad tracks unconnected to any other north or south tracks, seemingly leading nowhere.

"What are these tracks for?" asked Nina.

"At one time the grandfather of a previous owner preserved them as remnants of a narrow gauge spur that had, years before, rumbled by The Candles. Every owner before us collected anything you could imagine."

"This is your entranceway?"

"You're being picky again."

"But it's so, so—"

"So what?"

"It's so very 'there's not much of it,' you know?"

"That doesn't make any sense."

"It's just—little."

"So are you."

"I know, but big busses full of tourists aren't supposed to be able to run over me."

"They're not supposed to run over our entrance trail, either."

"So how do people get out here, anyway?"

"We bring them out in limousines, from Abbeyport. It's the kind of thing that differentiates us from the big touristy plantations."

"What, people can get to those places and they can't get to yours?"

"If you're going to keep on like this—"

"All right, all right. I'll be quiet. I'm just worried about what's going on."

"Me too, Nina. But whatever it is, I don't think it has anything to do with how narrow our little lane is."

Margot turned carefully onto the narrow, mud and gravel lane, Nina scanning the sign as they passed within a foot of it and wondering what vacation Bible school class had made it as an hour's introductory project—and the forest, which was now wrapping around them like a green pine-coned and needled blanket, burst into *The Hallelujah Chorus* as sung by tree frogs and cicadas.

Undergrowth subsumed them.

They crept on: fifty yards, one hundred yards, half a mile—

—until finally they were no longer in a forest but in an enormous children's book, light filtering supernaturally through unseen cracks in limbs and trunks and leaves and pine-paraphernalia all about them.

But somehow, there, just fifteen steps or so immediately to the right, there, behind an enormous tree trunk that had fallen naturally or been knocked down by a bolt of lightning or toppled by fire from one of Sherman's cannon—there, head up now and gazing at them with elemental curiosity and completely ill-advised trust—was a deer.

"Wow," whispered Nina, falling back on her natural wit and verbal elegance.

"Yeah," co-whispered Margot.

It was like George Bernard Shaw conversing with Oscar Wilde.

"That's a deer," observed Shaw.

"Yeah," reposted Wilde.

And the two of them, great minds both, sat there in the woods for a time, simply staring into the face of this light brown mottled animal, who, ears pricked upright, could have been a statue, save for the scarcely perceptible rising and falling of its flanks.

Finally it walked away, disappearing into the undergrowth.

There was nothing to say about this entire encounter, the stock of appropriate verbiage—said stock consisting of 'wow' and 'yeah'—having been used up.

So Shaw and Wilde did nothing but put their car into gear again and meander along their way, the right front tire's dip into a perilous pothole magically offset by the left rear tire's ascent upon a big flat rock.

The sky, Nina noticed, had changed and was changing even more.

Pre-hurricane sky.

The sun had become a colorless disc.

It made Nina uneasy.

As though something bad was going to happen.

"These late eclipses in the sun and moon portend no good to us," she whispered. "Love cools, friendship falls off, brothers divide, in cities mutinies, in countries discord—we have seen the best of our times. Machinations, hollowness, treachery, and all ruinous disorders follow us disquietly to our graves."

"What are you talking about?" asked Margot.

"That's Shakespeare. *King Lear*."

"How can you remember that stuff?"

But Nina merely shook her head and said:

"How can you not?"

At that point the road turned abruptly to the left—almost 45 degrees. Its narrowness made such a turn impossible at four miles per hour, perilous at three, dangerous at two, and possible only at one.

This then was the speed at which Margot took it, so that a minute had passed before they found themselves looking due North instead of due East.

And there, ten feet in front of them, the road was blocked by a yellow metal gate.

The gate consisted of three bars, perhaps ten feet in length, an inch or so in diameter, and soundly welded to equally yellow posts cemented into the ditches.

Precisely in the center of the gate hung a sign, not much more sophisticated than the one announcing The Candles, but newer.

It was white and not brown.

Two feet square instead of one

And painted with red paint instead of blue.

On it, quite plainly, had been printed the words:

CANDLES IS CLOSED FOR THE WEEKEND

"All right," whispered Margot. "That's just what it's supposed to say. We're closed for the weekend, and for the whole next week."

"How can we get through the gate?"

"I have a key."

"Well, maybe you better—"

The words 'use it' did not follow, though, for there was no need of them.

A figure was making its way through the undergrowth.

"That's Ben Danielson, the caretaker/handyman."

It could have been Ben Danielson, Nina found herself thinking, or it could have been The Scarecrow from *The Wizard of Oz*, so gangly was it, so loose of joint, so ragged and hay infested.

And so worried looking.

The Scarecrow reached the gate, leaned over it, watched handfuls of straw and other vegetation fall out of its war surplus clothing, and rasped:

"We didn't know how to get you, Ms. Gavin!"

"I was down in Bay St. Lucy! I told that to Mildred! I thought I told it to you, too, Ben! I thought I told everybody!"

"Yes, Ma'am. I remember hearing you say that. But we didn't know how to get in touch with you."

"What's going on? We stopped at Obid's in Abbeyport. Lizzy and Maybelle said to get out here as fast as possible!"

"Yes, ma'am! Yes, ma'am!"

"So what's happening? Has there been an accident?"

Two blackbirds flew low over Ben Danielson's big black shapeless hat, were frightened of it, and fluttered on.

"Not really an accident, no ma'am. We could have dealt with that all right."

"A fire?"

"No ma'am. Wiring's all safe, I done told you that."

"Then what?"

"We couldn't get a hold of you."

"Yes, I know. My cell phone is—well, not operating right."

"Because you don't charge it," said Nina, quietly.

"Be quiet," said Margot, not so quietly.

"We knew you was down on the coast. But we couldn't––"

"I know, I know. Just open the gate, Ben. We'll drive on up to the house."

Ben did open the gate, which was a marvelous feat, Nina remarked, for a creature devoid of tissue and dependent on the stalky remains of harvested grain.

Margot drove through.

"They'll be waitin' for you once you get up there. They been tryin' all morning to get you but––"

"I know I know", shouted Margot at the rear view mirror, accelerating slightly and cursing not so slightly.

"Well," said Nina, "at least we know they tried to get in touch with you."

"Yes. And we're going to know why, too. We're almost there."

And they were.

Forest forest forest––

Sharp turn to the right––

––and there it was.

The Candles.

All they had to do was cross a perilous little wooden bridge which spanned a fast-moving creek about ten feet wide.

"Is that bridge safe?" asked Nina.

"It is now."

"What does that mean?"

"It means it wasn't always so safe. We had to have it worked on."

"When?"

"Just after it collapsed with one of the limousines. Thankfully the water in the stream isn't too deep. The ladies––"

"Ladies?"

"Yes, a group from the D.O.C."

"What's that?"

"Daughters of the Confederacy. Anyway, they got pretty wet. But we managed to get the thing settled without a lawsuit. The bridge is fine now."

"I want to go home."

"Nonsense, you worry too much. Come on, just close your eyes and we'll be on the other side before you know it."

Nina closed her eyes as tightly as possible, and gripped the arm rest beside her.

In no more than six hours they had crossed the rattling-timbered bridge.

"Thank God," she whispered.

She opened her eyes.

And there was the main building of the plantation, all spread out before them.

As Margot pulled into the driveway and parked the car, Nina found herself struck again by the non-magnificence of the structure that surrounded her. She remembered the Robinson Mansion from Bay St. Lucy. This was the exact opposite. The Robinson Mansion, both in its original state, its run-down state, and its now resurrected state, had been built to intimidate. Its arches, windows, balconies, trellises, canopies, chandeliers, gutters, shutters, and butteries—all looked down on something, even if they had been built at ground level so that nothing could, at least physically, be beneath them.

It did not matter; everything was beneath them anyway.

Wherever one was in or around the Robinson Mansion, a part of it was frowning.

This building smiled. Every part of it. The color of its exterior walls—a soft and mellow off-peach which was the precise color of slanted sunlight on a late Friday afternoon— this color smiled. The broad porch smiled at the white and motionless rocking chairs which sat upon it, while they smiled, in turn, at the dilapidated outbuildings, which smiled at the rusted farm machinery and antiquated carriages that sat within them. And from the well in the middle of the back yard, its wooden frame apparently on the point of disintegrating with age and dropping into water far beneath ground level, the bucket which hung gleaming in the mid afternoon sun—from the very moss-covered stones rising above this well, there emanated a kind of benevolence, as though coming out of the deep earth itself, seeping over the lawns and fall gardens, and settling quietly at dusk into the not very recently mown grass.

Margot and Nina got out of the car.

There was no movement anywhere, no sound, except for birds chirping in the trees.

Then, finally, something came around the house and began approaching .

Nina turned quickly.

She saw a white form lumbering toward them, its tongue, like an obscenely red garden hose, hanging halfway to the ground and spraying saliva as though it were an extremely slow flying crop dusting plane with long white hair.

The animal looked occasionally from side to side but kept its attention riveted for the most part on a particular patch of ground that happened to be beneath it at the time, and that needed both watering and stepping on.

The dog sidled up to Margot, who laid one of her broad hands upon its much broader back, the effect being something like a cargo plane landing on an aircraft carrier.

"Borg," she said. "I don't know how old he is, or why he was named that. He just came with the place."

"Ms. Gavin!"

Nina realized, upon hearing this exclamation, that the house had been strangely inverted on its grounds, or that, more precisely, the grounds had been inverted around the house. Because the driveway she and Margot had approached the building on had led them to the back of the plantation and not the front entrance.

So that the creature now making its way toward them— woman, not dog—was coming out of the back door and clattering over the back porch.

Clattering was exactly the correct word.

For if Ben Danielson—handyman, plumber, etc.—was the scarecrow, this woman was the Tin Man.

Her body was composed of two metallic cylinders, each covered over with a thin film of skin-colored paint, the entire assemblage bouncing along a series of interlocking cans that functioned as legs.

"Mildred? Mildred, what's happened?"

Mildred kept coming, rattling off the porch now and onto the grass, which, had it not already been browned by the late August heat, would certainly have been crushed to death by the half-ton weight of each of her feet.

"We couldn't get hold of you!"

Margot, who had already heard this statement now from two or three hundred other people, tried to hide her exasperation by taking a few futile steps toward the building.

"I've been down in Bay St. Lucy! You knew that, didn't you?"

"Yes, but we tried to call you there, and you never answered."

"I forgot to charge my cell phone! What's going on?"

"We tried to get hold of you, but nobody answered!"

"I forgot to charge my cell phone!"

"You see, we called you. But we couldn't get no answer!"

"I forgot to charge my cell phone!"

"We kept trying to call you, but…"

"What," asked Nina, realizing that she would be driven insane by even one more repetition of the same lines, "is the matter?"

Everyone—Mildred, Margot, Borg, and several other younger people who had appeared on the eight-foot wide blue-painted board porch that surrounded the house—stared at her.

The world stopped.

"This," said Margot, starting it again, "is my friend Nina."

Thousand one thousand two—

"You see we tried to—"

"Let's go inside, Mildred," said Margot.

And they did.

So that a few minutes later they were, at least three of them were, sitting around a small breakfast table in the kitchen, adjacent to the entrance hallway. This house seemed topsy-turvy to Nina, with the front door really opening to the back of the place.

It was a homey room though, she thought.

All the stuff for baking. Pans hung neatly on the walls. A stove tucked into the corner. A big open-faced clock smiling down on them from the west wall.

And Margot, taking a deep breath, then exhaling calm words with the same demeanor she would have used to exhale tobacco fumes, when she still smoked.

"I know, and Nina now knows too, that you have all tried to contact me. I'm sorry that I did not have my cell phone on. It's clear that something has happened. It's also clear that the plantation has not burned down, because we are sitting in it right now, as we speak. It's also somewhat clear that no one has died, since there are no police cars, no ambulances, and no yellow tapes marking a crime scene. So what, Mildred, the heck is going on?"

The holes that were 'face' in the upper can of Mildred that was 'head' dilated slightly and flashed, leading Nina to wonder where her power source was.

"You said it wouldn't happen again, Ms. Gavin! You promised us. You promised all of us. You did!"

There were at least four other people, all teenagers, three girls and one boy, who were flitting about just outside the kitchen, ascending and descending the stairways, carrying pasteboard boxes, frowning, almost running into each other, running into each other, cursing softly, and looking over their shoulders as if expecting the nearest door to them to open and disgorge trouble.

"What wouldn't happen? What did I say wouldn't happen?"

"Those people!"

"What people?"

"We tried to call you but—"

"Mildred—"

Air hissed into the larger can that was Mildred's thorax.

She let it do its work inside her machinery, then allowed some of it to escape through a ventral screen, and went on repeating herself:

"You said you wouldn't let them come again!"

"Who?"

"You promised all of us that—"

"Who?"

"Because after the last time, when they—"

"Who?"

"And we begged you. We was all gonna quit, right then and there, but—"

"Who?"

Somebody tripped on the stairs, fell down a few of them, cursed as a box of dishes shattered, cursed again as she or he—it was pretty much indistinguishable at this point—got up and kept doing whatever was being done, and then tripped again.

"It was yesterday. About six in the evening."

"All right. Now we're getting somewhere. What happened yesterday about six in the evening?"

"We had everything all cleaned up and locked away. Lights was off. All the doors and windows locked up good."

"Right."

"We were all getting ready to head into town. Two cars was here to take us."

I wonder, Nina found herself musing, *if we will ever come to the end of this story? If we will ever find out what really happened? Or if we will simply sit here almost finding out, hearing a bit more and a bit more of the build up to it, until we die. People die. We ourselves are dying. What if the Lord has not given us sufficient time to get to the heart of this, the substance of it? What if we are taken before we are enlightened?*

Will God tell us when we get to Heaven?

Here is who killed Kennedy, and here is what really happened at Candles in that late afternoon in August.

These things Nina found herself wondering.

Until finally Mildred said:

"We was about to walk out. And the phone rang."

"Aha!" said Margot.

'Aha' mused Nina.

"I picked it up."

"And then you put it to your ear and then you put it closer to your ear and then you said hello and then you waited a second and then…"

I'm going crazy, she thought.

"And who was it," asked Margot, "who was calling?"

"That man from Chicago."

"What man?"

"The man who does the bookings."

"Ah! Amidon Phillips!"

"That's him! He said he'd been trying to contact you but–—"

"Go on, Mildred. What did he want?"

"He was real excited. Said he had great news. Great for The Candles. Lot of money involved."

"Okay, and this is bad why?"

"He said we needed to get in touch with you quick because they was coming day after tomorrow. Only that's tomorrow now, because the rest of that night and all day today we've been trying to call you but—"

"All right, so what is this thing that was supposed to be great for Candles?"

"They booked a group in, Ms. Gavin."

"A group?"

"Yes, Ma'am."

"But you were supposed to have a few days free. This was everybody's vacation!"

"I know, Ma'am. We was all expecting it. Was ready to go into town. But the phone rang and—"

"All right, all right. He booked a last minute group in. I'm sorry about that, Mildred. I wish I could have talked to him and tried to talk him out of it. But it's a group and they'll pay money and we'll have bonuses to pay all of you. Surely it can't be so bad."

"It's not that, Ms. Gavin. You know we don't mind workin.' Even at short notice. We never let you down, not that I can recall. You need a meal fixed, we come out and fix it. Something breaks, we fix it."

"I know, you've all been wonderful, and Candles is lucky to have you. So I don't see why this particular group should——"

"You told us they wouldn't never come again. Never. Not after that last bunch in June."

"But I don't—"

Margot stopped in mid-sentence, as though her mouth had been clogged.

"Oh God," she whispered. "Mid-June. You don't mean—"

The woman across the table from her nodded, the machinery which was her physical being screeching and moaning softly as though in need of oil.

"Yes, Ma'am. It's writers."

"Oh, no. Oh, no."

"You told us it would never happen again, Ms. Gavin."

"But, I—Amidon—how could he—"

"A lot of us wanted to quit after that last bunch. We could take the painters and the actors and the singers and the fiddle players and all those others out of Chicago and New York City. They wasn't so bad. They made funeral music all the time and got paint on the curtains and tried to make little jokes that nobody could understand—but not everybody has a proper upbringing, and parents to teach them about the real world. So we could understand them and not let 'em worry us too much."

"I know."

"But them writers—"

"Mildred, I—"

At this moment, a young and haggard-looking once-blonde, now dirty straw-blond girl stuck her head in the kitchen door and, having apparently overheard part of the conversation, half shouted:

"We're still trying to get those scrambled eggs out of the carpets!"

A teen-aged boy stuck his head over her shoulder:

"The dog ain't really right yet! I don't know what they did to Borg!"

Mildred attempted to shoo the two away:

"Go on about packing up, you two."

"Tell her we're through! Tell her we won't—"

"I'm telling her! I'm telling her!"

The kitchen door closed.

Mildred continued, quietly, as though reciting a dirge:

"Them people—you see them just walking along, not talking with each other like real people would but—seeing things in the air, making little waving motions, muttering to themselves—"

"Well, Mildred, they're writing things, they're making things up."

"What are they seeing, Ms. Gavin? Who they talking to?"

"No one knows that except for other writers, Mildred. And, of course, they aren't really mentally stable people to begin with—"

"Yes, Ms. Gavin."

"So it's best to leave them alone."

"Then why they coming here? Why they all want to get together?"

"I don't know. I just don't know, Mildred."

"Why can't they leave folks alone?"

"I don't know that either."

"I called the police, you know."

"The police?"

"Yes, Ma'am. Soon as I knew they was coming. Officer Thompson—you remember James Thompson—he said, after last time, that we ought to never have a bunch like that out here again, and to let him know as soon as possible if one was coming."

"So what did he say?"

"Oh, he was real mad. He said to keep them out of town."

"Can he send any people out here to Candles?"

"Oh, no, Ms. Gavin. He said we was on our own. He said two of his people from last time still wasn't the same. And that woman officer is teaching school now."

"I'm so sorry about what happened to her."

"And Ben—Ben still can't figure any of it out. How they got that big wagon into the upstairs bathroom—"

"Well, it was hot and—"

"You know the County Board of Health says we still can't use that room down in the basement."

"You haven't told them, have you?"

"Oh, no, Ma'am!"

"Thank God!"

Nina saw a shape in the doorway.

It was Ben, the scarecrow, gesturing for Margot.

"Excuse me, Mildred. I have to talk to Ben."

"You do what you have do, Ms. Gavin."

Margot rose and walked toward the door, then through it and out onto the porch.

Nina followed, not wanting to be left alone with Mildred, and thus in danger of hearing again that all of them had attempted to contact Margot, but had been unable to.

She was, she realized, probably never again going to forget those lines.

Once on the porch she saw Ben move closer to Margot and whispered:

"They coming again, aren't they?"

"Yes, it appears so."

"All right then. I done the best I could for you, Ma'am. You know there wasn't much time. We only found out about this yesterday. But I done the best I could for you."

"In what way? What are you talking about?"

"I used all my contacts. Two guys I know in Pottersville, and one in Crossland. But in only a day and a half—"

"I still don't understand—"

"About thirty pounds, I was able to round up and have shipped out here."

"Thirty pounds?"

"Pot, Ms. Gavin. Weed. We put it all in that big trunk up in the attic. The one with the Rebel flag painted on it."

"There's thirty pounds of marijuana in the attic?"

"All I could get my hands on, given the short notice. It might get you through tomorrow night, but after that—I don't know what you're going to do."

"I'd forgotten—"

"Yes, Ma'am. Last time we had sixty on hand but when that ran out—well, that was when they started going after the dog."

"I remember now."

"He was a good dog, too. Just kind of lumbers around now."

"I know. I know."

"Well, anyway. I done the best I could. We all gotta go now. They not supposed to show up until tomorrow but—well, ain't none of us want to be here if they arrive early. Not be here after sundown. Not with that bunch."

And it was true. The sun was a sliver of peach above a hazy, wood-shrouded horizon. The five workers who were still within the grounds of Candles could not seem to take their eyes off it. Every action, every bit of packing, of locking, of hiding away, of whispering encouragement and support—seemed to be timed so as to fill the two cars and leave before those last rays of sun were exhausted.

Until finally they were in the cars, Ben driving one, Mildred the other.

It was she who leaned out the window and shouted above the chugging motor:

"I'm sorry to leave you here like this, Ms. Gavin. But I have children. We all, all of us, are part of families."

"I know. I know."

"I want you to have this though—"

She was leaning out still farther, and offering something silver and shining to Margot.

Finally, Nina could see that it was a cross.

Margot took it, squeezed it, and put in into her purse.

"God be with you. God be with both of you."

And then the cars drove away.

And then the sun set.

And then the two of them were alone.

Waiting for writers.

"Well," said Nina after a time, "what do we do now?"

Margot thought for a time, then rose.

"Come on."

"Where to?"

"We talk to Amidon. And find out what's really going on."

"How do we do that, Margot?"

"We Skype with him."

"You can barely remember to keep your cell phone powered. Do you really knowhow to Skype?"

"Yes. Had to in the museum job. And now, even out here, both Amidon and Goldmann working together have put together an impressive display of technology in the music room. Come on. You'll see."

Nina followed, up one flight of stairs, around a corner, down a corridor, and then another.

Finally, Margot opened a door.

And the old Candles music room smiled back at them.

"This is one of my favorite rooms. Nina. It always has been, even from the first time I came here with Goldmann."

Margot switched on a standing lamp that was just inside the doorway.

Nina could see the yellow glow emanating from inside before she could see the room itself.

"Oh my!"

"Yes. Isn't it wonderful?"

And it was.

The first thing to catch one's eye was the harp, golden, shaped like angels' wings, standing exactly in the center of the room, forming the sun around which various planets— grand piano, smaller spinet piano, violins mounted on walls, pictures of opera houses and composers—had been frozen in their rotation and now stood ready for some final concert which would probably never come.

The two women entered and padded like cats, their shoes scuffing on a worn hardwood floor, their hands not daring to touch the instruments, their mouths turned respectfully away, for fear of careless breaths clouding enamel and gold finishes.

"Our music room."

"It's incredible."

"Yes. Yes, it is. But here is the most wonderful part. Over here, on this stand. Come, come this way!"

Nina followed, and found herself led to what easily could have been the most striking exhibit in this hall of dead sounds: a phonograph, its great curved bell yawning out over the rest of the room like some giant sea shell out of which, *if one leaned close enough*, thought Nina, *one might hear the roar of breakers, the comings and goings of the tide*. It sat regally on a square oaken box, which, like a desk upended, seemed to have been made specifically to support it.

"We can Skype over here; this is where we keep all the computers and modern things. But I insisted on the music room looking as it had. Okay, here we go."

Margot proved adept at modern technology, and within a minute the image of a smiling, business-suited Amidon Phillips was before them.

"Margot! You're a hard woman to track down!"

"Please let's not talk about that, Amidon. What the hell is going on?"

An elfin face on the screen smiled evilly, cirrus wisps of white hair raising slightly about the only slightly but still definitely Satanic and pointed ears:

"A coup, Margot! A wonderful coup!"

"But my vacation! My few free days!"

"Oh, it will be a vacation of sorts, I can promise you that!"

"I've brought my friend Nina up from Bay St. Lucy!"

"Yes, I've heard of her! The political revolutionary!"

"I promised her some days of rest! And now—"

"Now they will be days of discovery and pure fun, I promise you! Not to mention quite lucrative days for The Candles!"

"All right all right, would you just tell me what's going on?"

"Of course, of course. The bottom line of it is that one of my contacts called me several nights ago and alerted me to a possible business deal. And a very exciting one!"

"Go on."

"He had learned that a very particular group of artists had been booked into the Sheraton Inn Rosemont near O'Hare Airport, but that the leaders of the group, having done some advance scouting, were dissatisfied and might be persuaded to move elsewhere. Or be rerouted elsewhere, as it were. There was a bit of time before the convention actually began. So as it happened, I was able to contact these particular leaders and paint an enthralling picture of Candles. They seemed entranced. The long and short of it is that I persuaded them to change their venue and come to us."

"At the last minute? How is that possible?"

"It's possible because I offered to pay their airfare from Chicago down to Vicksburg, and arrange for a private jet to take them to Meridian Airport fifteen miles north of Abbeyport."

"Doesn't that cost a fortune?"

"It has cost something, yes, but our consortium can afford it, given the upside of the entire venture."

"That upside being?"

The smile eviled a bit more, eyes glinting brighter as they narrowed:

"National publicity, my dear Margot. And possibly a major contract with one of the major television studios based in Los Angeles."

"My God."

"Precisely my reaction upon first visualizing the potential."

"But, Amidon, don't you realize what's happened down here?"

A pause, a slight frown.

"What are you talking about, dear Lady?"

"The whole staff has quit! They've just driven off thirty minutes ago!"

"But why, for heaven's name?"

"Surely you must know that!"

"I have no earthly idea what you must be talking about!"

"Writers! The staff seems to think that you're sending writers to Candles!"

"And so we are!"

"But you know what happened last time! We're still dealing with the lawsuits. The police have refused to come out and provide protection for the physical plant, and they're planning to put up roadblocks so that none of the writers can get within five miles of the town itself. My God, Amidon, don't you realize? We're only four miles up the road from an elementary school. Children, Amidon!"

But the face on the screen only broke into a broad and strangely beneficent—for an agent of evil—smile.

"No no no no, you've got it all wrong!"

"How do I have it wrong?"

"Margot, those people who came in June were real writers—pornographic book writers, hard-bitten detective novelists, people who envisaged themselves Hemingways and Faulkners and Tennessee Williamses and—well, that sort. We knew what to expect from such reprobates, and we certainly got it. It was our fault entirely."

"No, it was your fault entirely."

"All right, blame accepted. But this! This will be entirely different!"

"How can it be different?"

"Because these people, these thirty people who are coming—"

"There are thirty of them? You're mad!"

"But they're NOT REAL WRITERS, Margot!"

"They're not—well, if they're not real writers, then what are they?"

"They're COZY WRITERS!"

Margot paused.

"What?"

"They're COZY WRITERS!"

Margot paused again.

Then:

"What is that?"

"They write cozy mysteries!"

"All right, that would make sense. But now you need to tell me: what the hell are cozy mysteries?"

Nina could not stop herself from interrupting:

"Okay, wait a minute, Margot. I think I know."

Amidon Phillips faced beamed out at them from the SKYPE screen:

"Oh, hello, Ms. Bannister!"

"Hello to you."

"Welcome to The Candles!"

"Thank you!"

"Will you be letting me have sex anytime soon?"

"Depends on the election."

"Well, I'm certainly doing my best to get as many women on the ballot as possible!"

"Then you might have some hope."

"Oh, I do hope so! Now, if you'll explain to dear Margot what cozy mysteries are—"

"I'll try. Margot, I think they're like Miss Marple."

"Agatha Christie?"

"Exactly."

"Thirty Agatha Christies are coming out here? I thought they all lived in England."

Nina shook her head:

"They used to all live in England. But in the last few years there's been a huge wave of cozy books that have gotten popular here in the United States. The heroine of the novel is usually an elderly retired lady, maybe an ex-librarian. She lives in a quaint little town, preferably New England. A murder happens and she solves it, because she's always just a little smarter than the local police, who are well-meaning and good-hearted, but stupid."

"Why are these books popular?"

"Because they have no violence, no sex, no bad words, and no naked people."

"Why are these books popular?"

"I don't know, Margot."

"They have no violence?"

"None."

"And yet they're murder mysteries?"

"I know, it's a little hard to grasp."

"How do people get murdered without any violence happening?"

"They get murdered between chapters, and then, when their bodies get found, the corpses are just lying there not doing anything. Except maybe with a dagger sticking out of them is all."

"And these books sell?"

Nina nodded:

"By the millions, from what I can read. The Bay St. Lucy library is filling up with them."

"Do you like these books?"

"Not particularly, but I check them out and read them at night to Furl. After a chapter or so, he goes right to sleep. But I think he mainly likes the cats."

"What cats?"

"Most of the cozy heroines own cats."

"Why?"

"I don't know. Cozy cat, you know."

"This is the strangest thing I've ever heard of."

Amidon interrupted:

"Strange or not, my dear Margot, it's a phenomenon that fairly screams to be exploited. And that's precisely what we intend to do."

"How?"

"The television contract, my dear!"

"I'm still confused."

"Then I shall set about enlightening you! Thirty of the nation's most successful cozy novelists are about to descend upon Candles late tomorrow morning, driving over from the Meridian airport in ten limousines. Once arrived, they shall set about conducting the business of the AGCW."

"The what?"

"The American Guild of Cozy Writers."

"Oh. And what kind of business is that?"

"Oh who knows? And who cares? But the important thing is that joining these ladies will be Sylvia Duncan of HBO."

"And she is…"

"An executive producer. HBO, Margot, has decided to tap into the cozy mystery craze itself. The network is planning to produce, next year, at least a dozen prime time hour and a half programs featuring a new cozy sleuth. That sleuth will be the creation of one of the writers you will be hosting. Sylvia Duncan will be doing interviews, talking to authors, negotiating—but the bottom line is that, at the end of the conference, the winner will be announced. The prize will be a contract worth millions of dollars to the lucky writer."

"My God."

"Yes, and it gets better. There is apparently a kind of rogue school among the newer cozy writers. They want to break free and, well, do the unthinkable. Or do what only a few years ago would have been deemed unthinkable. They are to the cozy world what Monets or Picassos were to the world of painting at one time. They want to break boundaries and see words in shocking ways."

"What do these people want to do?"

"They want to set cozy mysteries in quaint villages not in New England."

This caused Nina's mind to race, and her heart to skip a beat.

Almost immediately she leaned forward and blurted:

"Like Abbeyport!"

Amidon nodded:

"Yes. With scenes shot in Candles."

"What," Margot asked, "could Candles have to do with it? Candles isn't cozy!"

Amidon shook his head:

"It's only the heroine and her friends who are cozy, Margot. But the villain, either killer or murderer, always has to be obscenely wealthy—"

"—and live in a place like Candles."

"Precisely. And even if the plantation house itself won't be used in every episode, the production crew would have to have somewhere to stay. They certainly aren't going to hole up in quaint hotels in Abbeyport!"

"I'm beginning to see," said Margot, quietly.

"Yes, yes, isn't it wonderful! This could be a multi-million dollar venture!"

"All right. You're convincing me. But still—"

"But still what?"

"What are we going to do about the convention?"

"Why, host it, of course!"

"But the staff is gone! They thought they were going to have to deal with real writers, not cozy writers!"

"Margot, Margot, you still don't understand the beauty of this thing!"

"All right, enlighten me! Who's going to take care of these people?"

"Why, they themselves! Margot, these are thirty LITTLE OLD LADIES! Once they set foot inside the plantation house they'll want to do nothing more than start dusting, and cooking, and brewing tea!"

"They won't want marijuana?"

"They're sixty and seventy years old, Margot! They may have once known what marijuana was, but they've almost certainly forgotten it. The most they'll want to do is polish the silver and chat about the wall hangings. Margot, child, THEY'LL BE TAKING CARE OF YOU!"

Margot thought for a while and asked, quietly:

"So no sex raids into Abbeyport?"

Another laugh:

"The reason these little ladies don't write about sex, Margot, is that they do not wish to do the requisite research. Why, they'll probably be tucked safely into their beds by eight o'clock in the evening."

"I don't know. I still wish we had some—"

"You have a perfect situation."

"I don't know. Our cook spent most of the day in Abbeyport laying in stores, groceries, supplies—but we still don't have a lot of meat."

"Not to worry about. Most of these women will be vegetarians. Many will not even have teeth. If you have gruel, oatmeal—"

"Yes, yes, we have that."

"And tea of course. Tea is to Miss Marple what bourbon is to Faulkner."

"All right. We have tea, I'm sure of that."

"Then what more could go wrong?"

There was a pause for a second, while a silent alarm went off in Nina's brain.

There was that phrase again.

What more could go wrong?

They Skyped for perhaps half a minute more.

Congratulations were passed about like verbal cigars; money was counted; future publicity was listened to and read.

Then adieus.

And then a blank screen, and the near silent music room.

Then Margot suggesting that, since there was actually little more to do tonight in preparation, that the two of them should go downstairs and have dinner.

And then the rising, and then the making their way toward the doorway.

While, playing like a plaintive lyric from the old Victrola, came that same line:

What more could go wrong?

But it was time to do other things. First, Margot took Nina upstairs to her room. The door swung heavily open and the chamber smiled out at them, its dark green curtains, huge canopied bed, oaken rockers, and tapestried rugs—not to mention the armoire that seemed to enclose a slightly smaller room within its doors—all issuing at once a silently harmonious yet obviously deeply felt greeting.

Then downstairs.

Dinner.

The two women would not have to put up the fine china and dishware, as they had been warned by a departing staff to do.

Because the people coming to stay here tomorrow were not ruffians and lunatics.

They were cozy writers.

They would appreciate fine things.

Perhaps even write about them.

"Right through here, Nina. The staff apparently made us a lovely evening meal. All we have to do is heat it up."

Nina followed into the dining room.

"Oh, my!"

And worth an 'oh my!' it certainly seemed to be.

The table, the hutches standing by the walls, the serving trays.

A century of dining elegance.

Margot took two steps into the dining room, became a museum director again and said, quietly:

"The Havilland Dinner Service. Wheat Pattern."

Nina would have been content to stare out of the vast window, opening out onto the front lawn in twilight and count the kinds of things growing in a Fall Garden just beyond it.

But Margot circled the room like a bird of prey, all senses honed by the artworks spread out around her and visible through clear glass hutch doors:

"Dinner plates; pickle caster: Meridian Silver, Pin Inverted Thumb Print pattern; ruffled and quilted satin glass peach bowl; salad plates, cups, saucers, bread and butter holders, four each platters and serving bowls—there are, to the best of my knowledge, six complete Havilland Dinner Services in the world. The Chicago Art Museum has one."

They spent some time gawking as the room darkened and night fell on northern Mississippi.

Then they went into the kitchen, found the plates that had been laid out for them, and heated them in the oven.

Within half an hour, they had lighted candles at The Candles, pressed a button on the Boze radio to produce soft music, and sat down before a small tray of thin sliced ham, a tureen of turtle soup, a bubbling hot sweet potato casserole, a bowl of just out of the field salad—and two seductively glittering cut glass canisters of red and white wine.

Nina had a glass of the white.

After dinner they adjourned and went outside for Pernod.

An evil luxury.

They sat at a rain-stained wooden table square in the front yard, shaded by massive oaks through whose leaves the first evening stars had begun to twinkle. Their chairs rocked ever so gently on the soft turf of the lawn each time one of them happened to lift or set down one of her glasses.

They were seated perhaps fifty feet from the floodlit front entrance to the plantation.

"She is supposed to have appeared up there," said Margot, pointing to a balcony above the main doorway and sipping her smoky yellow drink, "while the plantation was burning and the union troops were standing around watching the blaze. Her hair was on fire while she cursed them. Burning-haired Sarah she is still called."

"What a story."

"Yes. Quite a tale."

Nina breathed deeply. She could feel herself relaxing.

Since the only entranceway to Candles now led in from the back, and dropped visitors near the rear porch, the old roadway up to the front had been overgrown by pines and undergrowth. Tree frogs sang in the dense foliage behind them as they sipped their drinks.

"So," said Nina quietly, "are the two of us going to be able to take care of these people?"

Margot shrugged:

"Shouldn't be hard. Thirty old ladies who sit around knitting and writing. They'll probably read a lot. And chat. It's like Amidon said: they'll be in bed by eight o'clock. If anything, it will be boring."

"Well. I came up here to rest."

"You should get a lot of that. I think I saw her, you know."

A pause.

Nina leaned forward in her chair:

"What?"

"I saw her."

"Who?"

"Sarah. Sarah Morgan."

"What are you talking about?"

"Flaming-haired Sarah."

"Yes, I know that. I remember the story, maybe because you just told it to me about a minute ago. It's the other thing I'm asking 'what' about."

"Me seeing her, you mean?"

"That's it. What are you talking about?"

"I was out here at dusk. I had drunk some wine…or maybe gin, or maybe both. Could have been both. It was a Sunday, and a group had just left. We were relaxing. Goldmann had gone inside to watch television. I guess I was dozing, or had dozed, whatever. But I sensed movement from the direction of the house. I lifted my head and saw a figure up there, on the balcony. At first I smiled and started to wave, knowing that it must be Goldmann. But then I saw more clearly. It wasn't Goldmann at all; it was a woman."

"A woman? Okay, but you're not going to tell me her hair was on fire. Because then I'm going to start to be really worried."

"No. Her hair wasn't on fire. But it was lush and red. She was dressed in—well, the clothes a woman would have been wearing in 1864. She was a strikingly beautiful woman with high cheekbones. She smiled down at me, and gave me a little wave. Then she turned, went back into the house, and disappeared."

"You dreamed it. You had a kind of fantasy. A daydream."

"Maybe."

"You never saw her again?"

"No. I went up there, to the balcony. But there was no one."

"And you're being serious now?"

"Yes, I'm being serious."

"Because when you drink gin…"

"I hadn't drunk that much gin."

"Then it was just a daydream."

"I suppose."

"Trust me. There are enough problems to go around. Something tells me we're going to start having them tomorrow. Little old ladies. We'll see. Anyway, Margot, I'm about ready to go to bed. It's early—but I'm a little old lady, too. So do you have anything to read?"

"We have a lovely library. You'll find anything you want."

"Wonderful!"

"You might start with this though. I found it lying on the balcony when I went up there to look for—whomever."

Margot reached down into her huge cow's belly of a purse. She wurgled in it for a while—wurgled being a word Nina had invented to signify what a woman did within her purse that was something between rooting and ferreting but neither one of these actions exactly—and finally took out a small sheet of what seemed exquisite stationary.

She laid it carefully on the table, so that it could be read in the flickering light of the tall white candle.

There were small tracings of the plantation's main buildings in each of the upper corners.

And on the page itself, in flowing script, was written:

"I feel that we have always been sisters. Welcome to my home. Which I shall never leave, no matter what happens."

It was signed:

"Sarah Morgan."

CHAPTER FOUR: ARRIVALS, THE FIRST WAVE

The following day dawned strikingly clear, bringing just a hint of fall and a hint of hurricane. The air had a sharpness to it that one might never have expected in late August, and the first light maintained that tinge of yellow that Nina always associated with trouble.

She and Margot rose, as luck would have it, about the same time. They met in the kitchen, made coffee together, and fried bacon. Margot did not know how to make grits, a shortcoming for which Nina had never forgiven her. But she could do eggs over easy, make toast, and set out a small carton of butter, proving that people from Chicago, if they did not understand civilization in its finest sense, at least were not complete savages.

At seven thirty, the first cars began arriving.

"What is this?" exclaimed Nina, hearing the crunch of gravel outside.

"I have no idea. They're not supposed to be here until ten o'clock."

Nina rose from the table, walked fast to the counter, stood on tip toe, and looked through the window.

"It's not," she said over her shoulder, "your guests."

"Then who is it?"

"It's your staff."

"My what?"

"Your staff."

"They left."

"Well, they're back."

And they were, arriving in four vehicles (two of them pick up trucks) instead of the two they'd left in, and spreading out on the driveway as though planning an ambush to be staged on the back porch.

"What's going on?" asked Margot, making her way to the door, opening it, and stepping out onto the porch. "Mildred?"

Mildred, who like each of the other eight or nine people with her, was unloading one of the cars, turned:

"Ms. Gavin! We had to come back! We're sorry, we really are!"

"Why do you have to come back?"

"Mr. Phillips, ma'am! He called the café late last night. Just before closing. Annabelle was just about to lock up when the phone rang."

"Amidon Phillips called Anabelle?"

"Yes, Ma'am, he did."

"What did he tell her?"

"The whole story, Ms. Gavin! He told how these people that's coming ain't really writers at all. They just a bunch of old ladies."

"Well, they're cozy writers. I don't know if they're all old ladies."

"They don't use no bad words?" she asked. "No fighting and killing? No naked people?"

"That's right."

"Who would write like that except for old ladies?"

Margot thought for a time:

"Well, you have a point there."

"Anyway, when we heard that, we knew it wouldn't be right to leave you out here. It'd be like making you run a rest home by yourself."

"Well, if you're sure—"

"It was wrong of us in the first place. We just got to remembering back in June—"

"I know. I understand how you must have felt. But what have you got there in the cars? What are you unloading?"

For the vehicles were in fact being quickly unloaded, a mélange of metal and cloth clattering on the gravel driveway.

"We called all the three nursing homes in town and made a deal to borrow some things they had in storage."

"What things?"

"Things you'll need for these old ladies, Ms. Gavin. Walkers. Chamber pots. Hospital gowns for them to sleep more comfortable in."

"Are you sure we—"

"Oh, yes, ma'am. Several of us used to work in such homes. It's hard work and you got to have the right equipment. Do you have enough blankets?"

"It's August, Mildred."

"I know, ma'am, but these old women get cold. Do you have cards?"

"Some. A few decks, I guess."

"Well, we brought some more. They like to play bridge and such games as that, the ones that's still able to see. And the ones that ain't senile."

So the unloading process continued. There were not quite enough walkers for each room, but there were enough crutches, and the younger people worked assiduously to make sure clearly labeled bottles of laxatives sat primly beside the toilettes in each private bathroom.

At one point during the process Mildred stopped Margot and Nina on the stairs:

"Have to tell you, too, Ms. Gavin, that we went by Abbeyport Methodist this morning."

"The hospital?"

"Yes, ma'am."

"Why?"

"Nurses, ma'am."

"Nurses?"

"Yes, ma'am. It's best to be cautious. You need professionals on hand if one of these ladies has a stroke or a heart attack."

"I suppose that's true."

"So two of them will be coming out at ten, when the ladies arrive. I figured you wouldn't mind paying them some overtime. Them and the ambulance driver."

"We need an ambulance?"

"You never know."

And so it went.

Candles underwent, in the next two hours, a kind of transformation, while Nina did what little she could, carrying walkers, arranging wheelchairs in the large game room, placing small miniature steps beside beds, and putting in plain sight diapers for those cozy writers who might prove to be incontinent.

At nine thirty these kinds of arrangements had to be put on hold.

The first members of the press began arriving.

In helicopters.

Two large bumblebee-like helicopters which, rotors chewing up the soft morning air and motors roar/clacking, set down in the West Pasture perhaps fifty yards from several outbuildings, whose last view of anything similar had probably been the first glimpse of Grant's army.

"Margot?"

Nina was standing in the driveway when the assault began, attempting to wrestle one last box of hospital gowns out of the trunk of a dilapidated Ford Escort.

"Margot?"

"Yes, I see them."

"What do we—"

"We go meet them. They're from the press."

"What press?"

"THE press. There's only one."

"What are they doing here?"

Margot, walking fast by the Escort and toward the pasture, simply shrugged:

"Sometimes I don't even know what I'm doing here. Come on."

"But I don't understand—"

"Amidon probably called all the media outlets in the state. Actually, he probably called all the media outlets in the world, knowing Amidon. These are the first to arrive."

The two women made their way through a crumbling fence which seemed to dissolve as they approached it.

They watched as two figures—unarmed, Nina noted with relief—emerged from the helicopters, and, bending low to avoid the rotors spinning over them and cow patties lurking under them, waved and smiled:

"Hello, the house!" shouted a young man.

"We're from WRGC," shouted a young woman.

They were glowing, radiant, blonde, well dressed, poster children of mass marketing. The woman looked like all of the women who bantered and made useless announcements from the sidelines of nationally-televised professional football games.

The man looked like she would have looked, had she been male.

"Ms. Gavin?"

"Yes!"

"I'm Tricia Lindenwood, and this is Chip Horagan! We do the nightly news!"

"How exciting that you've come," Margot answered. "Welcome to The Candles!"

Several photographers, Nina now noticed, had just emerged from the helicopter.

"You don't mind pictures?"

"No, no! Take all the pictures you want!"

The two landing parties, one coming west from Candles and the other east from the helicopter, met, embraced, shook hands, gushed, and in general rejoiced over everyone's existence.

Microphones were produced; cameras began whirring; an interview began, with Tricia and Chip alternately firing questions and Margot answering them:

"So are you excited about northern Mississippi hosting the AGCW?"

Strange, Nina found herself musing. *WRGC asking about AGCW.*

What had ever happened to words?

"We are thrilled," Margot lied skillfully, "that the AGCW is about to honor us!"

"Are you yourself a fan of cozy mysteries?"

"Oh, I certainly am!" lied Margot yet again. "I began reading cozies when I was just a little girl. Actually, Nancy Drew was my first favorite. But I was shy and books were my retreat. I discovered the Agatha Christie books in junior high school. Throughout all the following years I wanted nothing more than to secrete myself in my room and transport myself to some small English village where a little old lady was trying to piece together clues before the local constable could. When I think about it, I was the same way in college, and even up until today."

She's talking, Nina soon realized, *about me.*

There's no possibility on earth that Margot Gavin has ever read a cozy mystery.

She's talking about me, Nina Bannister.

"So, Ms. Gavin, who are your favorite mystery writers?"

Margot panicked.

So did Nina.

Who were some cozy mystery writers?

Which authors had most thoroughly impressed Furl?

"Well," Nina interrupted, "you were telling me, Margot, that you'd just finished a novel about a little old retired nurse in some quaint New England village—Maggie Maplewhite, in Seacoast Cove—and after the town miser had been found dead with a gunshot wound in his chest, she had to use her medical training to solve the crime, since the bumbling old police chief couldn't. It was called something like *Death Stares at the Stethoscope*. And there were lots of eccentric but lovable characters in it."

"Oh yes, that one! And what else had I told you about, Nina?"

"Well, there was…"

But the interview was ending.

More helicopters were arriving.

And horns were honking back on the entrance road.

Nina turned.

The first of a series of ponderous limousines was making its way over the bridge.

The Cozy Writers of America were here.

CHAPTER FIVE: THE MAJOR ASSAULT

By the time Nina and Margot had reached the driveway, the last of the limousines had parked and begun to disgorge its passengers.

All thirty of them, emerging from ten huge black shining cars.

"My God," said Nina, softly. "Who are these people?"

For they were not, in any sense, what she'd been expecting.

Nor were they the crowd expected by the staff, who were all standing on the back porch, open-mouthed and staring.

What all of the Candles had been expecting were frail little old ladies.

And, in fact, there were some little old ladies scattered through the bunch.

"That one," Nina whispered, "must be Rebecca Thornwhipple."

"Which one?"

"The short one there, getting out of the third limo."

"With the frizzled white hair?"

"Yes."

"What is she wearing?"

"A T-shirt."

"I know, but the thing printed on it—"

"Yes."

"Is that—"

"Yes."

"The male reproductive organ?"

"Think so."

Both of them stared for a while.

"A reproductor reproduction," said Margot.

"Yes. And it certainly stands out, drawn in red like it is."

"But what is that thing she's carrying?"

"A cat carrier."

"Wait a minute! Am I crazy? Look at them! What are they—I thought for a minute they were all getting suitcases out of the cars, but—"

"Cat carriers," said Nina. "Every one of them has a cat carrier."

"With cats in them, you think?"

"Betting on it."

Nina watched Margot and waited while her friend deduced the obvious.

"Thirty cats."

"Yes."

"We can't take care of thirty cats."

"You'll have to."

"Why are they all travelling with cats?"

"I don't know."

"Oh, my God! And just look at them! Those aren't little old ladies at all!"

"Well, except for the one with the penis on her shirt."

"Well, come on, we have to go and meet them. We're their hosts."

That was true, but it hardly seemed to matter, simply because the people milling in the driveway seemed more concerned about the names of their cats and the names of their characters than their own names. The cat carriers came forth from the limousines in a continuous and marvelously garish stream, onyx and pearl and filigree and black-satin and jewel-covered, as though they were the cats of sultans travelling in state and spread out across an oasis for the night. The felines' names were etched across the receptacles in which they travelled—wild, bizarre, non-earthly, supernatural and mythological names: Balthazaar, Plethorius, Cullegmugeon, Clawdius, Hisstoproprius, Edapuss, Deflepard—

—and as important to the writers as their cats were, their banners and posters, which were now being unfolded and held up to the light, so as to be checked for wrinkles, blemishes, or, Nina surmised in a necessary deduction, cat poop. Some of the banners contained pictures, some script, and some cartoon figures, but all bore the code: "The .... Mysteries."

The Sheila Hammersmith Mysteries.

The Griselda Hecubine Mysteries.

The Patty Parity Mysteries.

(Patty Parity, Nina assumed, must be a fighter for women's equality.)

The Olivia Smitherman Mysteries.

And on and on.

"This," Margot was whispering as they made their way through the crowd, "is my worst nightmare."

Nina looked up at her:

"Why?"

Margot shook her head.

"I'm allergic to cats."

"Really?"

"Stupid furry disgusting creatures. I start sneezing and their hair gets all over me and they leave little round turds on the rugs and—"

"Sssh."

"No I mean it. I just can't—"

"Get control of yourself. I think you have to say 'hello' to this woman."

And it was indeed a woman to be dealt with. Almost six feet tall, mannishly dressed, stentorian in posture and bearing—no, if the caretaker was the Scarecrow and the cook the Tin Man, this was certainly the Wicked Witch of the West. Not green perhaps, but—

—well, now that one looked closely at her, maybe a little green.

"Hello!" she said, extending a hand and smiling broadly, "I'm Harriet Crossman—you must be Margot Gavin!"

"Yes, I must be!" answered Margot.

If all of these characters are from The Wizard of Oz, Nina found herself asking, *then who am I?*

Dorothy?

No, she finally had to admit as she settled into shadows of the two women who towered around her.

Toto.

"Margot, it's so good finally to meet you, and to experience Candles! Mr. Phillips has painted an exquisite picture of both you and the establishment!"

"Well, Ms. Crossman, we're just more excited than I can say to have the honor of hosting you."

"The honor is all ours! I must tell you, the AGCW—oh, and I should tell you, I do serve as president of the organization—has convened in some absolutely dreary hotels and convention centers. But this! This is magnificent! Positively dripping with romance and intrigue. Why, I can already envision at least a dozen lovely murders after seeing only the exterior!"

"Once you get inside the place," Margot said graciously, "I'm sure more will come to you."

"I certainly hope so!"

"I'm sure of it. Well, to get on to more practical matters: we've assigned fifteen of our guest suites to your group. We're assuming people won't mind pairing up."

"Oh, not at all! We have some couples, of course, like Jim and Pat Hershey, the husband and wife writing team. There they are now, getting out of the car. Look at them: THEY ARE SO CUTE TOGETHER!"

Yes, they are, thought Nina, noting also that they looked a great deal like Roy Rogers and Dale Evans, except that they were dressed in matching blue blazers and had no cowboy or cowgirl gear on. But otherwise, dead ringers they were, looking for all the world as if they were eager to do nothing more than get inside and start a-baking or a-rodeoing."

"They will share a room, of course," said Harriet Crossman, as will several other of our authors, who are already paired up. But as for the rest of us, we'll be happy to choose roommates. And, of course, there are our little feline friends!"

"Yes there are!" said Margot, grinning broadly. "Does every writer have a cat?"

"Oh, of course! It's one of the marks of being a cozy writer! We don't absolutely require it in the by-laws, but it was for so many of the early years, when we were all just getting to know one another through Facebook pages. Well, at any rate, so many of the postings contained cat pictures, and then we started having the cats pose with copies of our books, and then various authors started taking cats to book signings, where they found that people were more interested in the cats than the books—so one thing just led to another—and now none of us will go anywhere without our little tabbies. I do hope you like cats?"

"Love them!" beamed Margot.

I'm about to get sick, thought Nina.

"Well, then, I don't know if you have a schedule set up for us—"

"Not a rigidly fixed schedule, no. But we generally serve dinner in the main dining room around seven o'clock. That will give everyone time to get into the rooms, unpack a bit, perhaps walk around on the grounds—"

"—and discover our first corpse!"

"Ha ha ha!!" fake-laughed Margot.

"Ha ha ha indeed! Oh, this is going to be so much fun!"

"I do hope so!"

"It will, it will. I do need to let you know: we shall have our first plenary session tomorrow, hopefully around nine. We'll need a large hall for that."

"Hopefully the dining room will suffice. We'll get all the breakfast paraphernalia cleared away."

"Good, good. Then a bit later, we'll be dividing into sub-groups and committees to do break-out sessions. The Guild has much business that must be taken care of in the most efficient manner possible."

Be quiet, Toto, said Nina to herself.

"What kind of business?" she asked.

Harriet Crossman, as though noticing her for the first time, glanced down and resisted the urge to pet her. Then she said:

"Well, our biggest concern remains the issue of standards. Thousands of amateurs are attempting to write cozy mysteries these days, and all of them wish to be a part of our guild, and have their books bear our trademark."

"And the books aren't any good?"

"Oh it isn't a question of that! Some of them are quite good! It's just that in so many cases they aren't cozies. There is a list of fifteen qualifications a text must have for it to be considered a cozy. Failing in any of these—well, to give you just a brief example: *War and Peace* is—I suppose you might say—'well–written,' if one has a taste for such things. But it could hardly be considered a cozy!"

"So you wouldn't accept it?"

"Of course not! Of course, the problem is—well, Mr. Tolstoy's piece of verbiage fails in so many obvious regards that it would hardly be an issue. But other works are more difficult. And there is always this pressure to expand our parameters. Make an exception here or there, allow into our little library of works a town that is not truly quaint, a sleuth who is not the proper age—"

"What is the proper age?"

"Sixty-five and up. Writers who are not perceptive enough to grasp that need to take their young women detectives and go elsewhere. If we start making these kind of seemingly small exceptions, then the floodgates of dilettantism will swing open and our literary civilization will degenerate into chaos."

"So this," Nina continued, wondering why she was speaking at all, "is what your meetings will be about? Choosing or rejecting new members who want to be cozy writers?"

"This is one of our issues. There are many others."

The cat carriers, by now, had all been taken out of the limousines and were being carried by their owners, in a small parade, in the direction of the main house. Several of the animals had begun to notice each other and were hissing and snarling, throwing themselves against the small wire doors of the carriers.

"Aren't they so cute!" said Harriet Crossman.

"The Hersheys?" asked Margot.

"No, the cats. I just love to see them interact!"

This is, thought Nina, *going to be a disaster.*

She was beginning to imagine the various ways in which it was going to be a disaster, when Harriet Crossman continued:

"Our biggest order of business, of course, as you undoubtedly know, is going to be the national television production. This will be a multi-million dollar affair. Each of our authors will be interviewed by the network representative—and by the way, Ms. Duncan hasn't arrived yet, I take it?"

"No," said Margot, shaking her head. "No, she's supposed to get here sometime tomorrow morning, I think about ten-thirty."

"Ah. Well, at any rate, her decision is going to be the making or breaking of one cozy author's career. But, of course, it will affect all of us. The national publicity connected with a major series of this nature will send sales through the roof. So we will be monitoring her interviews with great interest."

"I see. Well, you certainly have full plates and much work to do in the next days. Please don't hesitate to come to me or the staff with any questions. We're at your disposal, as is the entire plantation!"

"Thank you! Thank you ever so much! Well, now I must go fetch Hecuba and set about finding a roommate. Ta ta for now!"

"Ta ta!" answered Margot.

"Ta ta!" answered Nina.

Then:

Thousand one, thousand two—

Harriet Crossman out of hearing distance.

Margot, whispering:

"Nina, you've got to get into town. Take one of the trucks. I could send one of the men but I don't trust them. We've got no time, no time at all, and this is one errand that has to be done right!"

Margot had taken from her massive leather purse a ball-point pen and note pad, upon which she was madly scribbling.

"Take that red Ford pickup over there. The keys will still be in it. You can drive a stick shift, can't you?"

"I used to be able to. I think it will come back to me."

"All right then. Drive right into town until you cross Main Street. Take a right, go a quarter of a mile, and you'll come to Jarrod Wilson's General Store. Jarrod can get anything, and from any of the other stores in town, even the big Wal Mart on the Southside. He's become a good friend of Goldmann and me. Give him this note, tell him to put everything on our tab, and tell him he's got to hurry."

Nina looked at the note.

"Oh," she said, understanding now the importance of her errand.

"You understand?"

"I understand."

"Good."

So saying, Margot whirled and walked-ran toward the house.

The truck was old and ramshackle, and the gear shift was a stick extending up from the floor. But she'd driven such a vehicle when she was teen-ager, and had delivered prescriptions from the pharmacy owned by her father. It took only a short time for her to remember how the thing worked, and memories of her childhood and her parents came flooding back to her as she and the truck rattled across the entrance bridge over a small stream, then made their way out through the dense woods and turned onto the highway into Abbeyport.

She turned on the truck's radio, scanned the various channels as she had the day before on the trip up from Bay St. Lucy.

"What I hate—and I think the whole country hates—about the liberals is that—"

"Marsha, I think what these right-wing conservative groups have forgotten to take into account is that—"

Blaaah de blaaah de blaaah.

Until:

"One cautionary piece of advice for the people of south Texas and Louisiana: Hurricane Clarence is picking up steam, but he seems to have altered his course slightly. Rather than heading for Matagorda Island south of Houston, he seems to be making his way farther north and east, with probable landfall 34 hours from now in the area around Beaumont. At this point wind gusts up to—"

Keep scanning.

Beaumont.

That would be hard rain indeed for Bay St. Lucy.

But Beaumont was Beaumont and not southern Mississippi.

Nothing to worry about.

Not really.

And so she drove on, mind alternating between the hazy golden years of high school and the strange group that awaited her upon return to Candles.

Cozy writers.

Cats.

Well, at least they were not, as Amidon Phillips had said, real writers.

At least they were not Tom Broussard.

Thirty Tom Broussards.

No wonder the staff had quit.

Of course, it must be said, this group did not consist entirely of little old ladies, either.

But still, how much trouble could they be?

So pondering, she pulled into the outskirts of Abbeyport, drove past the obligatory fast food restaurants, turned onto Main Street, parked, located the black and red neon sign that said "Jarrod's General Store," and walked into it.

There was a musty air about it, and she savored the look and feel of the dark-stained hardwood floor, the copper ceiling, the slightly too close together aisles of disparate this and that, slightly related and barely useful but fun to look at that and this.

Power tools.

Plates.

A small display of clocks.

"Yes, Ma'am, how can I help you, Ma'am?"

A white-haired older man with a white apron leaned across the store's main counter and peered over his gold-rimmed glasses:

"Welcome to Jarrods'!" he went on, smiling broadly. "Whatever you want, well, we probably got some of it!"

Nina made her way around two aisles and approached the counter.

She took from her pants pocket the note Margot had scrawled for her, opened it, and said to the counter-man:

"I want four hundred and fifty pounds of cat litter."

He stared back at her.

Finally, he asked:

"I beg your pardon?"

She repeated:

"I want four hundred and fifty pounds of cat litter."

He continued to stare for a time, finally asking, quietly:

"What kind of a cat have you got?"

She shook her head:

"It's difficult to explain."

Another man approached from the back of the store and stood beside the first.

This man was a bit shorter, a bit ruddier, and wore no glasses.

But the aprons were the same.

"What's the trouble?" he asked.

The first man looked at Nina, then at his associate, and said:

"Fred—Fred's my brother, ma'am—this lady wants four hundred and fifty pounds of cat litter."

"She wants how much?"

"Four hundred and fifty pounds."

Fred stared at her for a time, then asked:

"What kind of a cat have you got?"

She shook her head again:

"It's difficult to explain."

The first man was speaking now, but, as the conversation wore on, it became a first-one-and-then-the-other kind of thing.

"This is not for one cat?"

Nina.

"No. Thirty."

Second man.

"You have thirty cats?"

"Not exactly. It's just that my friend Margot was not expecting—"

Both men leaned upon the counter, four eyes widening simultaneously:

Both said:

"You mean Ms. Gavin out at Candles?"

"Yes. She had a last minute booking by—"

The first of the two men shook his head:

"Doesn't matter. If it's Ms. Gavin and those artist people she brings in there—no, we've learned not to ask. There are seven places here in Abbeyport that sell cat litter. Fred here will take the truck. Give us half an hour and you'll have your four hundred and fifty pounds. Just promise me: you can't use cat litter to make methadone, can you?"

"I don't think so."

"No, I don't either, or the kids would have found out by now. Wouldn't be an ounce of the stuff to be had on the shelves. So then: give Fred and me half an hour, we'll have you fixed up.

She did.

And they did.

CHAPTER SIX: MARGOT AND NINA MEET THE COZY WRITERS

Her return to the plantation house was an occasion of great joy, even exultation, and, as she pulled the truck into the driveway, the cab was swarmed by people who seemed as though they might have been shipwrecked sailors clambering aboard a Red Cross relief vessel.

"Here! Give me that sack!"

"No, I need it for room fourteen, and I need it now!"

"I need two sacks! Two sacks!"

In little more than two minutes, the truck's back end was emptied of cat litter, and a dozen or so staff people had disappeared into Candles.

She got out of the cab, looked around, saw no one wandering the grounds, and assumed that the house itself had subsumed the writers who were to inhabit it for the next few days.

She wandered inside, looking here and there for Margot, and realizing that her search was likely to be fruitless.

There were a thousand places that Margot might be, and another thousand errands that her friend might be occupied with.

And so she simply wandered, turning down a corridor here and a passageway there, sighting now and then a cluster of writers who were wrestling luggage up flights of stairs and into half-opened doorways.

Finally, she turned a corner and entered a room at random, drawn at first by the strange and yet pleasant half-light emanating from it, and only aware some seconds later that it was a library.

Not a large room but an elegant one, with a reading desk sitting patiently at one windowed wall, orange glow of sunset filtered through the beveled glass.

She had taken two steps into library before she realized she was not alone.

A figure stood to her right. A man. Not a tall man, but still imposing somehow, with long black hair that swung in a kind of horse's tail back and forth over his forehead as he rocked back and forth. His attire matched his hair: black, leathery, and not to be trusted.

He had not, apparently, noticed Nina's entrance, for his attention was riveted to the books, which he was fingering, one volume at a time, while whispering:

"Crap."

The book back in its place.

Another book fingered.

Another whisper:

"Crap. Senseless crap."

The book back in its place again.

Yet another book out.

Another verdict hissed out: "Drivel."

Finally, he turned, perceived Nina's presence in the room, stared at her for a few seconds, and prepared to speak.

I'm not, she found herself thinking, looking forward to what he's going to say about me.

But he said nothing about her.

He asked, instead:

"So. Is it ready now, for God's sakes?"

She knew nothing to answer to this, and so said nothing at all.

He took a step toward her, glowering as though he had caught a prowler in the silverware.

"I asked you if it was finally ready! Is everybody in this house crazy? Or is it a house at all? Have I been taken by mistake to an asylum, and are all of you inmates?"

Anything to say to that? Anything springing to mind?

Nope. So why not just continue to stand perfectly still and be mute?

Why not indeed?

A silent, icy stare, followed by the same hissing tone that had been reserved only a few moments earlier for the books:

"I'm going to give you a few more seconds; and then I swear to God, I'm calling my agent. Do you want me to do that?"

Anything to say to that? No, so then—

—Wait!

There *was* something to say to that, after all!

"I don't care who you call."

And voila!

The perfect answer!

Of course, it was not exactly a conciliatory answer.

Because it changed the hissing into roaring:

"You don't *what*?"

"Care who you call."

The dark man before her suffered a minor stroke, got over it, found a few of his nearly paralyzed facilities again, got them together and made them ask:

"Do you know who I am?"

Nina shook her head:

"I haven't the faintest idea who you are."

The command of language had returned now, and he was even able to achieve the noble and straight posture necessary to accompany the anthem entitled:

"I am Garth Amboise!"

Nina nodded:

"Nice to meet you. I'm Nina Bannister."

Her reply had the effect of following "America the Beautiful" with a dirty joke.

A name such as hers—little rattrap thing that it was—had been inserted, WITH HIS, into the same five second span of time, as though her soiled underwear had been stuffed down into his gazpacho.

"I beg your pardon?"

"I said, 'I'm Nina Bannister.'"

"And why is this supposed to mean anything to me?"

And there it was again, a statement that simply hung in the limp library air and failed to invoke a response.

Just good old silence was probably the best thing after all.

And so the two of them stood there for ten eleven twelve thirteen seconds that seemed like forty-seven years and still counting until a door on the side wall that had hitherto been invisible sprung open and Margot sprung though it, saying:

"Mr. Amboise!"

Garth Amboise ripped his stare out of Nina's stomach, pulling several inches of entrails along with it. She watched blood droplets trickle over the carpet while he managed to turn his head and say:

"Please tell me that this horror story is ending."

Margot stepped into the room, nodded and said:

"We have your room ready."

He inserted the stare that had partially disemboweled Nina into Margot's stomach and allowed his voice to trickle over it like sulfuric acid.

The air between the two of them was smoking.

"It is, I trust, a private room?"

"It is."

"You knew of that stipulation beforehand, did you not?"

"We had a—"

"At least my agent assured me that you did. You must have. He wired you thirty-four hours ago!"

"There have been some breakdowns in communication."

"I think that is probably an understatement!"

"We're sorry for the inconvenience."

"As am I, I can assure you. Now, if you will have some of your people get my bags—"

"That's being taken care of as we speak."

"My God, something is actually being done right for a change!"

"Again, we're sorry if—"

"JUST SHUT UP! And stop your yammering! I don't care in the least what you're sorry about! Don't you understand that I have writing to do tonight? There are people in New York waiting for chapter—but why should that mean anything to you? I need to be taken to my room, I need to unpack, and I need to be undisturbed for the entire evening. Is that understood?"

"Yes. We serve dinner at—"

"You serve dinner in my room, or didn't my agent make that clear either? Fields, Edelstein and Morgan, they're the top agency in New York City. But somehow they didn't seem to make their wishes clear, now did they? All right, then I shall get down a few levels lower: ALL OF MY MEALS, BREAKFAST, LUNCH, AND DINNER, are to be served IN MY ROOM! Is that clear?"

At this point, Nina said something obscene.

It was under her breath, so that even she could barely hear it. It was also not a very creative obscenity, and could have been heard thousands of times every hour in any construction site, football practice, or teachers' grading session.

It was not a Penelope Royale obscenity.

Oh where, oh where, was Penelope Royale when one really needed her?

But it was the best dirty word—phrase actually, when one thought about it—that she could come up with, and she gamefully threw it out there into the room, where it disappeared.

"I think now," Margot was saying, "we are aware of all stipulations. We'll try to have your meal up around seven. Tommy here—"

She gestured to a young blonde boy who stood some steps behind her in the corridor.

"Tommy will take you up. The luggage should be there by now."

Garth Amboise did not answer, but simply strode across the room and disappeared behind the boy who'd been assigned to lead him.

For a while then, there was silence in the library.

This silence was broken by Nina.

"I hate him."

Margot nodded.

"I know."

Nina:

"I hate him so much. I hate him more than I hate Hitler."

"Well, Hitler was pretty bad," answered Margot.

"Not so bad, really, when you compare the two people. Let's go get a picture of Hitler, and I'll put it in my room, and—"

"Stop."

"Who IS that s—"

"Don't."

"Quit talking to me in these little one word orders of yours."

"You're not any good at swearing."

"Oh, but I can learn, I can learn."

"It's not worth it."

"All right, all right. Then who is that—that—that 'person who now occupies a position of low rank in my esteem?'"

"Come on."

Margot gestured.

"Come on where?" asked Nina.

"Let's go into the reception office. It's been the command center for the last half hour. It's where we've been checking everybody in, pairing up roommates, handing out keys, getting to know the guests a little bit—"

"—are they all like this?"

"No. Most of them are pretty nice, I think."

Nina followed.

In two minutes, the two women were seated in the small office space that served to check in guests, hand out keys, etc. Margot handed her a cup of coffee and a sheet of paper which she soon recognized to be the 'bio' of Garth Amboise.

"This came by special post last night, but I guess we were already asleep, so they just slid it under the door."

"Great."

"I don't know," said Margot. "If I'd read it, I might have refused to let the 'Pwoalpime' in."

"The what?"

"The 'person who occupies a low place in my esteem.'"

"Amazing how you got all those letters arranged like that in your mind."

"Well, I'm pretty special. There. Read it."

Nina did so:

GARTH AMBOISE

Garth Amboise, while still quite young, is succeeding in carving for himself a very special niche in contemporary American literature. Mr. Amboise has published more than a thousand poems in publications such as *The Kenyon Review, The Arizona Press, Tamarlane Monthly, The Oxford Review, The New Yorker, The National Review, Alaska in our Times, People Magazine, Ebony, The Frankfurter Allgemein, Newsweek,* and *The Readers' Digest.* He has won numerous literary awards, including The Henry Spencer Award for Best First Novel, The Elania Dusting Award, The Cincinnati Readers' Treasury Award, The John Deere Award, The Yale Writer of the Year Award, The California Psychology Best Creative Fiction Award, Dog Lovers' Monthly Award for Creative Prose in Support for Abandoned Animals, The Truett Spencer Award, The Amelia Earhart Award, The Bill Smith Award, The Lena Horne Award, The Andrew H. Perkins Award, The University of Texas Best Rodeo Fiction Award, the Paul Marten Best Novel to be Published by a Handicapped Writer at Georgia State Award, and The Queen Elizabeth II Award for Best Treatment of an Episode in English History (The Glorious Revolution). Mr. Amboise has also published more than two hundred novels, many of which have appeared on *The New York Times* Bestseller List. He holds six doctorate degrees, among them Ph.D.s in English Literature (Harvard), Chinese History (USC), Botany (University of the Bahamas), Paleontology (University of Berlin), Proctology (University of Singapore), and Oboe (Julliard School of Music)—a truly amazing set of accomplishments, given his age of twenty-six.

"So," said Margot, "that's the man who came to dinner."

"I don't care what he's accomplished," said Nina. "I still hate him. I hate him so much that—"

She was interrupted in what was certain to become a satisfactory stream of invectives by the entrance of Harriet Crossman, who crossed the small room quickly and embraced her, saying quietly but passionately:

"Thank you! Thank you so much!"

Nina allowed herself to be thus profusely thanked for a time, then finally pushed herself sufficiently free to ask:

"Why?"

"The litter! You got it here on time! No accidents, not one."

"Oh. Well, I do what I can."

"All of the authors have their own special blend of cat food, of course. But as for litter—"

"I was just glad to help," Nina repeated.

"And help you did, my dear. I will say though, that otherwise, The Candles seems perfectly suited for the cats. It was, clearly, originally built by a cat lover—or a cat-loving wife."

"How," asked Margot, "do you know that?"

Harriet Crossman gestured toward the corner of the small office.

"Look down there. That small board in the corner swings on hinges."

She took two steps, reached down, and pushed the panel, which did indeed swing open, then shut again.

"I never even noticed that," said Margot, quietly. "Are you saying there's one of those in each room?"

"As far as our writers have been able to tell. It's a marvelous thing; now the pussies can go visit each other."

I'm not, Nina found herself thinking, *completely sure that's a good thing.*

"And otherwise," Harriet continued, "I must tell you that you've done a splendid job in preparing for us. Every report I've gotten is favorable. The rooms are perfectly laid out, the pairings have been made, and all the writers are raving about the atmosphere of the place. We are so looking forward to the next few days!"

"Well," said Margot, "I'm glad to hear that. Unfortunately though, not everyone seems pleased."

"Not everyone?"

"No. We've just had a rather difficult conversation with Mr. Amboise."

"Oh God. That—well, no, I shan't allow myself to lose control."

"Nina and I have already lost control, so don't worry about it. Mr. Amboise does seem—well, different from the rest of the group, I must say."

"Of course, he's different! He's not one of us! Not one of us at all!"

"He has an impressive list of accomplishments."

"He has a massive ego, is what he has. And he's not a cozy writer!"

"Then what is he doing here?"

"He's here because we couldn't stop him."

"Why not?"

A frustrated shrug.

"His agents are the most powerful in New York. They were able to find a publisher for his one cozy mystery, and, being a name publisher, they insisted on his being admitted to the guild. As for the cozy, it's a dreadful thing, probably knocked off in a few days."

"But why," Margot asked, "would he want to even be here? He clearly doesn't like it here, nor does he seem to want to associate with any of the other writers."

"I think," said Nina, anxious to become known for something other than the acquirer of cat litter, "that I know."

Margot looked at her:

"All right, then why?"

"The HBO contract."

Harriet Crossman nodded.

"There you have it. Where there is prestige and money—big money—these types of sharks always show up."

"But still," interjected Margot, "I can't believe we're going to have to pamper him this way for days to come. Meals in his room! My God, I can't even imagine—"

"HELLO ALL!"

This greeting, dripping as it was with golden sunshine and wheat germ, came from a pair of plaid-shirted figures who were bursting in from the back porch, their arms laden with tins of something or other.

"We hope we're not disturbing you!" said the female of the pair.

"Not at all," replied Margot.

Female:

"We had to come down and tell you—"

Male:

"—that our room is just great. EVERYTHING, actually is just great!"

"Well we're glad to hear that."

"Please let me introduce to you," said Harriet Crossman, "Jim and Pat Hershey. They're rapidly becoming the best known husband and wife writing team in the cozy business."

"So happy to know you; glad you've come to stay at Candles."

Pat Hershey stepped forward, beaming—

—actually they both were beaming, but her beams seemed even brighter, more redolent of a noon-day sun to make up for the evening sun, which even now was disappearing.

No problem. She could light a large portion of the house, certainly at least this small reception area, by nothing more than the radiant energy being poured forth by the fifth generation dynamo which was her personality.

"We had to bring you these!" she exulted, holding forth her arms, upon which were cradled two-foot circular, plaid-designed tins.

The plaid of the tins, Nina remarked, matched the plaid designs of the Hersheys' matching long-sleeved shirts.

Somewhere upstairs, she told herself, were waiting other tins that resembled the designer jeans the chocolate pair were wearing.

Was she going to keep thinking of them as 'the chocolate pair?' Hopefully not.

"We brought you some cookies that we baked a couple of days ago!"

Or, maybe she was.

"How thoughtful of you!" said Margot, taking the containers that had been offered to her, then putting them on the counter behind her and taking two more from the male part of the pair.

Jim:

"We thought you might be so busy cooking for other people that you might appreciate it if somebody baked for you!"

"And we do! We certainly do! What did you bring us?"

Pat:

"Sugar cookies, chocolate chip cookies, ginger snaps—"

Jim:

—and teacakes. Our personal favorites!"

"We'll serve them for everyone along with dinner tonight!"

"Whatever you want to do," chimed in both of the writers in near unison.

How can they talk together like that? Nina found herself wondering.

This thought mysteriously transmogrified itself into an audible question, which came blurting out from her almost against her will:

"How can you write together? Isn't writing kind of a solitary, lonely thing?"

Their smiles, almost incredibly, broadened.

They both took one step forward and began answering, first one, then the other, in such a well-orchestrated back and forth rattattat that Nina forgot for a time to note which of the two was actually speaking at any given time.

"Our minds just seem to—"

"—think alike and when one of us has an—"

"—idea why the other senses it and types it—"

"—down on the paper even before the other one has—"

"—had a chance to tell the other one about—"

"—it but really that's the way it's always been in our—"

"—marriage and so why should it be any different when–
–"

"—we write?"

And for a second they just stood there beaming.

"That's amazing," said Nina, who actually was amazed and who'd never heard such a thing before.

"Jim and Pat," said Harriet Crossman, "write the Nancy Westmorland Mysteries. Their heroine is a retired librarian who lives in a small New England coastal village of around two thousand people. There is a curmudgeon of a police chief and half a dozen or so genuinely eccentric and lovable characters. Nancy loves to cook, the books are filled with yummy recipes. Murders begin around page sixteen—"

"Page eighteen in *The Crab-Claw Conundrum!*" interjected Pat.

"Yes, I'd forgotten about that one. But they *usually* begin to happen around page sixteen so that the readers don't get bored. After that, there's always one murder per chapter, and the killer is always a surprise-detestable villain who deserves to be imprisoned."

"Or executed," said Jim. "Many of our killers, at least when we project their futures, "are probably given lethal injections or, if they are originally from Utah, shot. But we don't take the stories that far and so no one really minds."

"The works are," said Harriet, smiling, "absolutely perfect cozy mysteries. We put them on the guild's website as examples to follow for young would-be cozyists just starting out in the business."

"You're so kind," said Pat, taking a step back. "Well, Jim and I should probably be running along now. We're up to chapter sixteen in our latest; we want to get this last murder committed before dinner, and write the final wrap-up on the fishing trawler."

Jim, in mock horror, held a finger up to his lips:

"Oops! Mustn't give it away now, Pat!"

She clapped both palms to her mouth and then took them down, laughing as she said:

"Oh, I did, didn't I? Now don't any of you tell!"

"We won't," said Harriet, still beaming.

"Well, at any rate, we hope to have the killer revealed a little later in the evening, and the epilogue done by bedtime."

"You should," said Margot, "have a quiet evening to work. I don't think anyone will bother you."

"Wish us luck then!" said the pair in unison as they exited the room waving.

"Good -bye for now!"

"Good luck!"

"Thank you, thank you!"

"Happy writing!"

"Happy…"

Etc. etc. etc.

Finally Harriet said, shaking her head:

"They are just so cute together."

To which Nina and Margot could only answer:

"Yes they are. Yes they are."

And the three of them continued to watch as Jim and Pat Hershey, arm in arm, made their way across the back yard.

Across the back yard, into the far south entrance, and gone from view.

"Frank and I had a wonderful marriage," Nina found herself whispering, "but even we didn't seem to think in unison like that."

"It's a gift," said Harriet. "I've been married twice, and—well, it's a gift. I just really don't understand how two people can—"

But she was interrupted by the opening of the entranceway door.

Tingle tingle tingle little bell.

And there, in the doorway, stood a figure of very different mien.

Sunshine replaced by darkness.

Exuberance replaced by gloom.

Health replaced by sickness.

It was a sad woman of indeterminate age, indeterminate hair, and indeterminate position in the world. A woman, actually, who seemed to deserve no position in the world. A short and mousy woman, bent slightly forward, overdressed in a trench coat which protected her from the rain that was not falling, but did not protect her from Harriet's rather cold stare.

"Yes? Can I help you?"

"I'm Molly."

"I'm sorry, I don't seem to be able to—"

"Molly Badger."

Upon saying which, she shrank back an inch or so and bent an inch closer to the ground, as though she were a poorly skilled but deeply driven boxer who had no choice but to remain eternally in the ring that was life, being pummeled, and watching helplessly as the blows landed.

"I wrote you," she said, almost inaudibly.

Harriet nodded, but the aloofness in her voice remained.

"Oh, yes. I do remember now."

"About coming. Taking part in the convention."

"I remember your writing, and I also remember quite clearly my answers."

Molly Badger continued to shrink, saying even more timidly:

"I know. I got the letters. I just thought if I actually came, if you saw how much I wanted to be here and to be one of you—to be a real Cozy Writer—"

Harriet shook her head:

"I'm sorry, Ms. Badger, but I must tell you that you have wasted your trip."

"Isn't there—"

"No. I'm sorry there isn't. It's as I expressed clearly in my letter: we simply do not have space to accommodate people in your—well, in your category."

"But I just want to learn."

"And that is an admirable goal. But it's not our job to teach you. There are courses that one can take—"

"I know, and I've taken them. Several of them. But they don't seem to do any good."

"Then I am deeply saddened. But that does not change the fact that the AGCW is not an instructional institution. We realize, of course, that there are any number of people in precisely your situation who would love to be members of The Guild, and to enjoy the privileges such membership affords. But the fact is that we cannot begin to accept all of you. If we did, our standards would—well, in short, it's simply impossible."

Helplessly, the woman turned and spoke to Margot:

"Isn't there—isn't there some place for me here? I won't be any trouble. I just want to listen, to soak in what I can. Ma'am, if you are the head of this Bed and Breakfast, don't you have some corner for Molly Badger to sleep in? I'll pay whatever you want. And I can help out! I can clean!"

Margot, almost mute, seemed to have nothing to say. She merely shook her head while Harriet continued to address the woman cowering before her:

"I'm sorry but this is not a decision for Ms. Gavin to make. I truly regret that you have been put to an inconvenience, and that you did not choose to believe my letters. But if we begin making exceptions for one of you, then we shall have to make similar exceptions for you all. And the standing of our Guild would plummet. Now I don't mean to appear rude, but I have a great deal of work to do, and I must ask you to leave."

"Yes. Yes, I understand. I'll go."

And, so saying, the woman made her way out through the doorway, across the broad, blue porch, and out into the yard.

When she was well out of earshot, Margot asked Harriet Crossman:

"Who is that woman?"

A shake of the head:

"Her name is Molly Badger. She began writing letters to me several months ago. I finally answered in terms that I hoped would make our position clear—for we get hundreds, even thousands, of such inquiries—but apparently she is simply more persistent than the others of her kind. It's very sad, actually."

"What does she want?"

"To be accepted as a member of The Guild, of course. And, of course, that's quite impossible. As is her remaining here at The Candles and being part of the convention."

"But we do have an extra room or so."

A violent shake of the head:

"No, that's not the issue. The issue is that she simply does not belong here. She's not one of us!"

"Why not?"

Harriet Crossman was silent for a time and then said, quietly but clearly:

"She is self-published."

Silence for a time.

"I'm sorry," Margot whispered, finally. "I didn't know."

"That's all right, Ms. Gavin. There's no way you could have known. But I suppose it's now time for me to be fully honest with you. The Molly Badgers of the world are one of the reasons that the Guild is meeting here at The Candles."

"How so?"

"Because, when we meet in the larger metropolitan hotels, it's very difficult to keep such people away. And the costs for security alone—"

"I understand."

"We thought, coming here, with the forests and the isolation—we thought we could use Nature itself as a buffer against self-publication. Obviously, we were wrong. But this is not a matter over which you should concern yourself further. If Ms. Badger should fail to take our warnings and leave immediately—we have ways of dealing with her."

The sentence, Nina thought, *had an ominous ring to it.*

But it was followed by a bright smile, a change in Harriet Crossman's demeanor, and the words: "Well, let's all try to put that behind us, and get on with more important matters. I shall see you, Ms. Gavin, and you, Ms. Bannister, for dinner!"

So saying, she turned and left the room.

In half a minute, she had disappeared into the plantation.

Margo hesitated for a time, to be sure she was out of earshot.

Then she whispered:

"Come on."

"Come on where?" asked Nina.

"Come on with me. We're going to talk to that poor woman."

"Why? What can we possibly say to her?"

"Just come on. You'll see. I think I saw our Ms. Badger go out and sit down by the old well in the back yard."

They left the office together, made their way across the porch, and headed out into the yard.

When they reached the well, Molly Badger was kneeling on the ground beside it, her forehead pressed against the moist, ragged bricks.

Nina could hear her sobbing.

Margot knelt and put her arms out; the woman hurled herself into the embrace, glad to have cloth and flesh to press against rather than masonry.

"I don't know, I don't know what they want of me," she said, gasping to get her breath.

"There, there—"

"Don't send me away! Please don't!"

"I won't," Margot said, consolingly. "I promise that I won't."

"Margot," Nina said quietly, "if Harriet Crossman insists—"

Margot shook her head:

"Harriet Crossman doesn't run The Candles. I do."

"Still—"

"No. We've never turned anyone away from here. We're not going to start now."

Then, to Molly Badger:

"I'm sorry that you're self-published. I truly am."

The woman looked up at her and shook her head:

"It's not my fault! I *want* to be published! Honestly I do!"

"I know. I know."

"And I can write! My style is as fresh and vibrant as theirs! I can do dialogue! I have believable characters!"

"Of course you do, my child. I'm sure you do."

"But—but all the real publishers, the ones that aren't vanity publishers, keep sending my manuscripts back."

"Why?"

A deep breath, another fit of sobbing, another deep breath, and then:

"My murder methods."

"Your what?"

"My murder methods. They say I have unbelievable murder methods."

Nina knelt, put her palms on Molly Badger's knees, and asked, quietly:

"What murder methods do you use?"

This, though, occasioned a stiffening, and brought about a look of instant distrust:

"No."

"No, what?"

"No, I'm not going to tell you."

"Why not?"

"Because you'll steal them. You'll steal my murder methods!"

Margot:

"No she won't, my dear. She's not even a writer."

"I'm just a retired high school principal," said Nina, consolingly.

The distrust continued:

"But everybody else here is a writer! Once I tell you how the murder is done, you might be tempted to tell the others. No. No, I've come up with perfect crimes. But the stupid publishers refuse to believe my murders are possible. So I self-publish, just so I can try to persuade people like Ms. Crossman to accept me."

"Where can we get your books, Molly? Are they in any of the big bookstores?"

A shake of the head:

"They're locked in a trunk in my attic. I don't want people actually to *read* them, because—"

Nina finished her sentence:

"—because then people would know about the murder methods."

"Exactly."

"Well," said Margot, "maybe just to get published you can use a more conventional murder method. A gunshot to the head, or a knife in the heart."

"But that would be selling out! *Everyone* dies from a gunshot to the head or a knife to the heart!"

"There's always poison," Nina said, trying hard to make the situation better, and saying desperately whatever came into her mind.

But Molly Badger was having none of it.

"There, you just said it yourself! There's *always* poison! Strychnine or arsenic or cyanide, cyanide or arsenic or strychnine! But my characters are important to me; I love them and I want to kill them in special ways!"

There was little to be said to that, and so the three women simply sat for a time.

Finally, Molly Badger asked:

"So—so can I stay?"

Margot nodded:

"Of course, you can stay."

Nina:

"How can she stay, Margot? Harriet Crossman will be livid."

"She won't know about it. At least for a time."

"How can you keep her from knowing about it?"

Margot straightened slightly and turned, pointing to the end of the south wing of the plantation.

"There's room at the end of one of the upstairs corridors that's set off by itself. We'll sneak Molly into it. Molly, just try to stay out of sight for a time. We'll have dinner sent up. Then, later on tonight, I'll try to reason with Harriet. Surely, if you promise not to bother any of the real writers—"

"But *I* am a real writer!"

"I know but I mean one of the published writers—"

"But *I* am a published writer!"

"I know but I mean one of the By Other People Published writers—"

"But *I* would be one of the By Other People Published Writers if they would just—"

"Just believe in your way of killing people, I know."

"Someday someone will believe it, I know they will!"

"And they will, my dear, I know they will. For now though, just go over there and walk through that far door. You see it?"

"Yes."

"Go up the staircase to your immediate right. You'll find a room at the top of the stairs. The door will be unlocked. Do you have bags?"

"I left them out by the main gate."

"Well, I'll have someone get them and bring them up to you."

"You're so kind! So kind!"

"I know. But now get off with you, before Harriet comes back."

"Thank you! I will be published. And when I am published, the book will be dedicated to you!"

"That will be my honor. Now go."

And with that, Molly Badger rose, straightened her shoulders and walked toward the building.

"I wonder," said Nina quietly, watching the figure disappear, "what her murder method is?"

Margot shook her head:

"I don't know. But you have to admire her. She believes in something."

"Yes. Even though it's only a murder method."

"Don't disparage murder methods. They've made many writers famous."

"And generals."

"Now you're being cynical."

"Am not."

"Are too. Come on. I have to find somebody to get Molly's bags. Then we have to see how dinner is coming."

And they did.

Then they did.

CHAPTER SEVEN: FOOD, WARNINGS, AND
SCREAMS AT MIDNIGHT

The Candles Plantation had grown to pride itself on many
things since being taken over by Margot Gavin and her
husband, Goldmann Bristow. But no aspect of the Bed and
Breakfast experience was more important to them and to
their entire staff, most of whom lived and worked near
Abbeyport—than food.

The men and women of Mississippi could cook.

Nina knew this, and, being a child of The Deep South
herself, had always known it.

But she was still somewhat taken aback when she walked
into the dining room, surveyed the tables elegantly laid out
with candles flickering radiantly and silverware glittering—
and made her way beside the long and sumptuously endowed
buffet.

Mildred and the others had done wonders, especially
given the fact that they'd all felt compelled to quit no more
than half a day before.

It was a southern feast.

There before her, simmering in platters warmed by small
gas flames, were all the great dishes of her youth, just as
they'd been prepared by her mother and her mother's mother
and all the mothers before that.

Fried chicken.

(Of course.)

Honey-glazed ham.

Veal cutlets.

(Choice of wondrously thick cream gravy or succulent
scented brown gravy)

Fried catfish.

(Not farmed catfish but catfish fresh caught out of the
magnificent Mississippi River and cooked in a special batter

whose secret ingredients no Yankee had ever succeeded in prying away from anyone living below the Mason Dixon Line.)

Golden fried jumbo shrimp flown up that morning from the coast.

Fresh lump crabmeat.

Oysters on the half shell.

And, of course, the side dishes.

New Potatoes.

Mashed Potatoes.

Fried Potatoes.

Squash.

Beets.

Black eyed peas.

Green peas.

Green beans in mushroom sauce with delicately breaded onion rings atop them.

And niblets of something else, a treasure that none of the northern-based cozy writers had ever seen before, and that elicited awed questions such as:

"What is that? I've never seen that before!"

"What are those things?"

Questions which made Nina, always proud of her heritage, smile as she said, in answer to whomever she could reach with her soft voice.

"It's fried okra."

"It's what?"

"Fried okra. And look, Mildred has done it just right. Just enough to make the okra bits crunchy like they should be."

"I see."

"Try it. Take some!"

And, of course, most of them, remembering okra as slimy and runny and squid-like, did not.

There was iced tea, there were urns of freshly-roasted coffee, there was juice, and, of course, there were decanters of white and red wine.

Nina watched as the cozy writers made their way up and back, along the buffet line, astonished at the huge amount of food that had been made available to them and certain that most of it would remain un-eaten, given what were almost certainly birdlike appetites of the ladies.

In this last, though, she was proven completely wrong.

The Cozy Writers ate like Teamsters.

They plowed through the chicken, gorged on the fish, shoveled potatoes of all kind on their plates, made mincemeat of the crab offerings, devoured the veal and sopped up the gravy with roll after roll after roll after biscuit after biscuit and then as though they had nothing better to do and an infinite amount of appetite to satisfy began to wolf down slice after slice after slice of apple, cherry and chocolate pie.

"My God," Nina found herself whispering to Margot, who was standing with her in an equal state of astonishment, "can these women eat!"

"We may," Margot replied quietly, "have to slaughter some of the cattle."

They were not forced to take such drastic steps for, after only an hour or so of feasting and drinking, the Roman Orgy was over.

Plates were removed from tables, some last cups of coffee or glasses of port or burgundy were poured, chairs were turned to face the dais, and Harriet Crossman had risen to address, for the first time this year, the plenary congress of the American Guild of Cozy Writers.

"Welcome, welcome, welcome to you all!"

Some shouts from the audience.

"Hear, hear!"

The sound of a few knives, a few forks, a few spoons, ratting on the tables.

"Tomorrow morning at precisely eight o'clock—for you all know, that as mystery authors we all value precision, else how could our lady sleuths outwit the dimwitted police and catch the careful but not quite careful enough murderers—"

Some laughter at this.

"—at precisely eight o'clock, I shall be calling into session the fifth annual national convention of the nation's most respected and august body of Cozy Mystery Authors!"

"Yes! Yes!"

Applause.

A bit of time for the applause to die down.

"And I am, of course, moved, as I always am, to be in the position to act as your leader. Your confidence overwhelms me; your trust brings tears to me. And, as always, I am struck to my core with feelings of insignificance in the light of the challenges facing me as your leader, as well as those facing you as members of the most rapidly rising literary genre in our nation today, if not in the entire world!"

"Up Cozies!"

"Yeah!"

"Huzzah!"

A bit more time for the rabble of shouts to abate.

Then:

"The tasks we face are enormous, and they grow larger and more menacing daily. You know, of course, what these tasks are, and you are as acutely aware of the threats surrounding us as I am."

A small hard object went whizzing through the air and struck the back wall of the dining room.

"They're throwing food," whispered Margot.

"It's just a biscuit," replied Nina.

"I know. But if they start with the gravy, I may have to intervene."

Harriet Crossman seemed not to notice, and continued unruffled:

"There is, of course, to begin with, the flood of self-published novels that fill digital space, and, unedited and unskilled as they are, give a terrible name to all of us and to our noble profession."

"Boo!"

"Down with them!"

"They should all go to Hell!"

"To Hell with the Selfies!"

Another biscuit went flying; Margot tensed visibly, but Harriet Crossman continued:

"We are, of course, pursuing legislation that would prohibit the publication of any work of fiction by any unauthorized—and so frequently unlettered—would-be author. But these selfies, even if they know nothing about the hallowed craft of writing, do know something about hiring lawyers, and they continue to insist that The First Amendment allows them to say anything they want."

"That's ridiculous!"

"You can't self-publish FIRE in a crowded theater!"

The speaker nodded:

"That is, of course, absolutely true. And we hope fervently that soon we can make the Federal Justice Department decree that no mystery novel can be published except by small independent publishers."

"Yes!"

"Take it to the Feds!"

"Put the Bozo Selfies in Jail!"

A time passed in order for some of the rancor to subside. Then:

"But that, of course, is material for our legal team. Remaining for us here, during these next days, is the daunting task of defining and maintaining our standards. Every month, every week, publishers such as those who make our own novels available, are deluged with thousands of manuscripts of Word files, all purporting to be cozy novels. And, of course, as I'm sure you know, only a small portion of this mountain of garbage is genuinely cozy material, just as only a small number of the authors have truly taken the trouble to read carefully through our by-laws to inform themselves about what a true cozy actually is."

"Idiots!"

"To jail with them, too!"

Harriet held up before her a sheet of single spaced typing:

"And here it is, of course, our constitution as it were, our rock, our foundation. The 'Rules for Cozies' sheet that all of us have memorized, and which, strictly held to, will make our genre the thing of rare beauty and value that it is and has long been."

Silence in the crowd.

An awed sense of reverence as thirty pairs of eyes stared at the document.

Harriet Crossman:

"The age of the heroine, the occupation of the heroine, the size of the cozy little town, the occupations of the eccentric and loveable characters who are friends of the heroine and who may be accused of but who cannot ever, of course, actually commit the murder, the method of the murder, the placement of the body, the time of day of the discovery of the body, the degree of bunglingness of the crotchety old police chief, the degree of stupidity of the deputy of the crotchety old police chief—these are not random elements."

"No! No, they're not!"

"Not random! Not random!"

Harriet, shaking her head:

"Far far from being random, they are as fixed and immutable as the chemical composition of a medical prescription or the core of an atom. They are never-changing values—we stretch them at our peril. And to disavow them, to look away from them, to stray from them—is to court disaster."

She paused for an instant to let this soak in.

Then she leaned forward over the pedestal and almost whispered:

"The Romans too thought themselves secure and impregnable. The magnificent Roman Republic. But then they began to turn away from the values and beliefs that had made them great. And what happened? Chaos. The Dark Ages. So now, ladies—and our two gentlemen—I stand here now saying: we have before us, to be acted upon by this convention, a manuscript submission set in—Philadelphia!"

Shocked silence for an instant, then several voices:

"What?"

"Philadelphia!"

"Burn the damned thing! Burn the manuscript!"

Arms raised, the speaker waited for calm.

When it came she asked:

"Does Philadelphia sound 'cozy' to you?"

"No!"

"Down with Philadelphia!"

Then, the small reed-like voice of white-haired Rebeccah Thornwhipple, who had seated herself at the front table:

"I was in Philadelphia once. I didn't like it."

Harriet Crossman smiled down at her:

"Of course, you didn't."

"I just wanted to come home."

The same smile from Harriet.

Other supporting smiles from around the room.

"And you did come home, didn't you?"

"Yes, I did."

"And there, living in that small town, you created your heroine. Sally Maplewhite, who has solved eleven murders in the past two years, despite being ninety-three years old and confined twenty-four hours a day to an iron lung."

"Hooray!"

"Way to go, Rebeccah!"

"Way to go, Sally!"

Thunderous applause.

Finally, Harriet:

"And yes, we admit, Rebeccah, that even among ourselves we have some disagreement. Several of your manuscripts we did have to reject as candidates for AGCW's Novel of the Year Award because of the intense nature of their erotic content."

The reed-like voice again:

"Ninety year olds can be horny too. And if the iron lung is big enough—"

A shake of Harriet Crossman's head stopped the argument.

"But enough of this for now. In our major morning session, as well as in our breakout session, we shall allow all voices to be heard. But now it's getting late. We've had a wonderful meal—and I think we should all give a huge round of applause to our hostess, the proprietor of The Candles—Ms. Margot Gavin!"

There was, in fact, a thunderous round of applause, and Margot could almost be seen to blush as she took her place at the podium and signaled for quiet.

Nina had no idea what Margot was going to say, but she was not at all surprised at the aplomb and confidence which her friend showed with even her first words. This was Margot Gavin at the microphone—tall, striking, highly articulate, and experienced in public speaking.

She said all the right things.

Then she went farther, and delved a bit into the history of Candles.

Then she went farther still.

She signaled for the lights to be lowered in the dining room, and when they were, she told the story of Sarah Morgan.

"You are all spending the next few days in a haunted plantation house!" she began, and she followed up with what Nina thought was a dramatic, detailed, and immensely moving account of burning-haired Sarah, who had perished in flames, and who still continued to haunt The Candles, refusing ever to leave, and appearing each time the plantation changed hands.

The room was silent after Margot finished.

She gestured for the lights in the room to be turned up again.

All of the cozy writers had their heads on the tables and were sound asleep.

All except Rebeccah Thornwhipple, who stood up, walked to the podium, and said, neck craning to look up at Margot:

"It was a good story, my dear. But it was a ghost story. It wasn't a cozy."

With that, the writers began to wake up.

In ten minutes the room was empty.

Margot's staff was as good at cleaning as they were at cooking, and there was very little left for Nina to do in the latter part of her evening except retire to her room, read (she read a Raymond Chandler novel, perhaps out of a strange sense of cozy defiance) and began, shortly after ten o'clock, to think about dozing off.

She was prevented from doing this by a knock at the door.

She got out of bed, crossed the room, opened her door, and stared somewhat groggily at two women who stood before her.

"Yes?"

"You're Ms. Bannister?"

"I am."

"And you're a friend of Ms. Gavin?"

"Yes."

"Then we need to talk to you. It's terribly important."

"All right; come in."

"No."

"What?"

"We can't. We can't come in."

The pair before her were an odd coupling. One was precisely twice as tall as the other, who came up barely to her belt. They were dressed in fringed leather vests, brightly-colored patchwork maxi-skirts, beads, bandanas, and other late Sixties regalia, making them appear to have stepped out of time and been shooped back half a century or so.

Though they were obviously a couple, they did not finish each other's sentences as the Hersheys had done. Rather, they spoke in short, distinct phrases, one at a time. After each phrase had been uttered, they looked around, three hundred and sixty degrees, up, down, in, out—as though worried that something invisible, hanging in the air, was about to spring into visibility and attack both of them.

"My name is Ruby Smathers."

Look around, look up, look down—

"And my name is Lacy Smathers."

Look over there! Look up there!

Nothing?

Well, not obviously.

Which is, after all, the most that any of us can ever say.

"Our cats are Mephisto," said Ruby the Tall, "and Lestat. You will get to meet them tomorrow."

"I look forward to it."

Lacy took two steps up the hall and stared at the doorway leading to the stairs.

Apparently nothing was there.

She retraced the two steps, then looked Nina up and down and said, quietly:

"If you survive the night."

Nina thought about that for a time, decided perhaps that *she* should look around her for a bit, and then responded:

"I beg your pardon?"

Both women looked at each other, then looked over each other's shoulder.

Some unseen force prompted Lacy the Short to break from their phrase-by-phrase formula and speak at length.

"We're cozy writers. We write the Hazeltine Winters mysteries. Hazeltine is a retired psychic who lives in a small cute coastal town in Massachusetts."

"I see."

"There was some trouble with the Guild, since our original town, Emerald Bay, had more than four thousand people. Harriet and several others said that we were treading dangerously near suburbia, so we had to change it. But that isn't the worst."

This was as much as either of the two sisters ever spoke without a thorough examination of the ether. This was done, along with a bit of smelling, and Ruby the Tall continued the tale:

"The worst is that we have a secret life, which we're trying to hide from the Guild."

"A secret life?"

"Both nodded, and both spoke simultaneously.

"WE WRITE PARANORMAL ROMANCES!"

This was said with approximately the same degree of guilt that might have accompanied the phrase: "We molest small children."

And it was followed by the original 'phrase by phrase be careful what creature is listening and what crevice it might leap from' format.

"We write them for a different publisher."

Look here, look there!

"But if Harriet would find out, she would still be upset. She wants the Guild's authors to maintain a kind of genre purity."

Is there something over there?

What about behind Nina, back in the middle of the room? No?

Well, not *now* anyway.

But that window—

"At any rate, our heroine—or Trope as we say in the business—is a vampire."

"And our Alpha is a Werewolf."

I must be dreaming this, thought Nina.

But no, the two women were there.

And nothing else was.

Despite the constant squints, stares, and investigations.

"We were the first to write about inter-creature sexual intercourse."

"But we can write these stories because we—well, we're different."

Oh really, Nina found herself thinking.

But don't be sarcastic.

That would accomplish nothing.

"We are ourselves psychic."

"We sense the presence of—well, of creatures unseen by everyone else."

"That's why we were so interested in your friend's story tonight."

"You mean," said Nina, "the tale of Sarah Morgan?"

"Yes! The other writers all went to sleep."

"Margot and I noticed that."

"Yes, that's because it's not really a cozy, you know."

"I know."

"To be a cozy it has to—"

"I'm becoming aware," said Nina, "of what makes a cozy."

"But we, being aware of the spiritual world as we are, were *very* interested, because—"

Lacy stood on her tiptoes before she continued; Ruby, listening hard and still looking around for hidden presences, scrunched down as though to be better grounded.

"Well, from the moment we entered The Candles we sensed the presence of the Beyond Earthly!"

"You mean a ghost?" asked Nina.

"Yes. Yes, definitely. But it's more complicated than that, much more!"

"How?"

Ruby took over the narrative, unscrunching a bit as she did so, thus allowing Lacy to come down from tiptoes, so as to maintain the two-woman height ratio that previously had been established.

"Sarah Morgan is here. Perhaps in the very room where you are sleeping. That's why we can't go in there—she would sense our awareness of her presence, and be resentful. The spirits don't appreciate mortals who show awareness of their presence."

"But Ms. Bannister," Lacy continued, "Sarah Morgan is not your chief worry."

"No?"

"No, Sarah is a benevolent presence. She wishes only to remain in her beloved home. No, there are other presences in Candles. We feel them constantly about us."

Ruby:

"And these presences are quite a different thing entirely."

"How? In what way?"

"They are demonic presences. Monstrous incarnations. They are evil, Ms. Bannister. And terribly dangerous!"

"Dangerous to whom?"

"Any human! They are Satanic Beings. Once they choose a victim—well, they might well tear him, or her, to pieces!"

Nina knew very little to say to that, except, finally:

"I don't really know what to say to that."

"Well, there is, we should think, only one thing to say. Or do."

"And that would be?"

"Go to your lovely friend, Ms. Gavin, and tell her of the threat. Tell her that the conference must be cancelled, moved to more hallowed ground!"

"All right, I see your point."

"No, that's just the problem: *you can't* see it! And by the time you do see it, it will be too late!"

"The problem is, Ms. Smathers and Ms. Smathers, that a great deal of money has been invested here. Very complicated plans have been made. The representative from HBO is flying in tomorrow morning. The Candles will make as much in the next three days as it normally might make in a year. And one cozy writer will become the recipient of a very rich, very lucrative, television contract."

The two women appeared horrified:

"You don't understand us, do you?"

"Well, I can see that you're worried—"

"You don't believe us at all!"

"I do believe you! At least, I believe in your sincerity."

Some hope seemed to creep back into their expressions.

"So—will you at least try to warn your friend? Make her aware of the dangers?"

Nina thought about this for a time and finally nodded:

"Of course. Of course, I will."

"Tonight? Now?"

"Yes. Right now."

"Oh, thank you! Thank you ever so much! Lives are depending on the two of you!"

"Yes, I see that; but, one thing I need to ask."

"Go ahead! Ask!"

"Why did this monstrous demon-like thing choose Candles?"

Two looks of astonishment:

"Why, the OPEN DOOR of course!"

"What door?"

"The psychic door, the spiritual opening, the cosmic crack as it were!"

"Opening? Crack?"

"Of course! It was opened by the benign soul of Sarah more than a century ago when her spirit took possession here; but it remained in place for all supernatural entities to use, despite what may have been her own wishes to the contrary."

"And so this demon…"

"Simply followed her inside, like a thief in the night."

"And why haven't any other ghastly crimes been reported? Why has this horrible thing been—well, inactive?"

Two shakes of two heads:

"And how do you know that it has been inactive? How do you know there have been no previous ghastly crimes? Given the demon's power and the intensity of its hatred…any body found would have been a horrible sight indeed. How do you know there were no unspeakable murders, that were simply covered up?"

"Well, I guess that's a point."

"So, do we have your promise?"

"Yes, you have it."

"You will go to Ms. Gavin now, and tell her of the dangers?"

"Yes."

"Wonderful! We shall go to our room and pack. It's our feeling that everyone may be safe for one night at least. If we can all leave by tomorrow morning, why—"

"Like I say, I'll do what I can."

"We can ask for nothing more! Good bye then!"

"Good bye!"

And the Smathers sisters disappeared down the corridor.

Nina waited inside her own room for at least five minutes, giving the women enough time to get out of the hallways and back to their own rooms.

Then she put on a robe and slippers, opened her door, entered the corridor, walked down it, and located Margot's room.

A sliver of light seeped into the hall from the base of the doorway.

Good, she thought.

Margot must be reading.

She knocked.

"Yes?"

"Margot?"

"Nina?"

"Yes, it's me."

"What is it?"

'Can I come in?"

"Of course. The door's unlocked. Just push it open."

Nina did so, and spoke to the figure lying in bed before her.

"I thought I needed to come and tell you something."

"What? What did you need to tell me?"

"The Smathers sisters are insane."

Margot answered immediately:

"I knew that."

"How did you know it?"

"Because all these people are insane."

"Oh."

"Anything else?"

"No."

"Well. Good night then."

"Good night."

So saying, Nina returned to her own room and went to sleep.

At precisely midnight—she knew this because of the chiming of a large gold clock on the dresser in her room—she was awakened by the sound of screams.

Horrible, piercing screams.

Coming from down the corridor where she had stood not two hours before, conversing with the Smathers sisters.

Aaaaggh! Aaaghh!

The screams were growing louder and were now being punctuated with the sounds of crashing furniture.

Terrible, piercing shouts as though someone were being ripped to pieces.

She lay for a while in the near darkness, aware only of the early fall moonlight seeping through the window opposite her bed—and of the awful carnage going on not more than three or four rooms away from her.

She was paralyzed.
"Aaaghhhh!"
Then:
"My God! My God!"
"Aaagh!"
"No! No!"
Crash! Crash!
There was a terrible urge to simply stay where she was.
Especially when she recalled the Smathers sisters' warnings:
Demonic Creatures.
Horrible deaths, bodies too mangled to behold.
She could stay where she was.
Why hadn't she taken the warnings seriously?
She had laughed the women off, called them insane.
And now?
More screams, screams growing louder, pitiable screams, screams of horror unimaginable.
Despite herself, she crawled out of bed.
Despite herself, she put on the same robe and slippers that she had worn to see Margot.
With whom she had laughed about demonic presences.
And now there were screams, unmentionably terrible screams, coming from—
—from where?
From which room?
Who was being victimized?
And by what?
She opened the door and stepped out into the corridor.
"What is happening?" she found herself saying.
There were other people in the corridor.
Other writers, most of whom she had not met.
They were all emerging from their rooms and staring:
At one door.
Room 216.
Two doors down and to Nina's right.
The screams intensified and now she thought she could hear cursing.
Guttural, vile curses.

They brought to her mind *The Exorcist*.

Everyone stood in the doorways, no one having the courage to take a step forward.

Only, of course, one person did have that courage.

Margot Gavin.

She had exited her room and was making her way down the corridor, a long white candle in her hand.

She glanced at Nina as she passed, whispering:

"The Smathers sisters?"

Nina nodded as she stepped out into the corridor and began to follow Margot:

"Maybe they weren't crazy after all."

"Maybe not."

"Whose room is 216, Margot?"

Margot was approaching the room now, and said over her shoulder:

"The Hersheys."

Oh God, thought Nina.

But that would be somehow demonically appropriate.

The best couple; the most loving; the most symbiotically unified.

That would be the first couple that a truly Satanic presence would wish to seek out and destroy.

Margot and Nina now stood before the door, others in the hallway a respectful—and somewhat safe—distance behind them.

"Margot—"

"I have to open it."

"Oh my God—"

"You don't have to look, Nina."

"No. I'll help. Whatever's going on in there, I'll help if I can."

"All right then."

The door was unlocked.

So Margot pushed it open.

The scene before them was ghastly.

Jim and Pat Hershey were in disarray, clad in torn underwear, their hair completely disheveled, their eyes wide with rage. They stood on opposite sides of the room, glaring at each other, their fists balled, their arms waving.

A small orange and white cat sat hunched in the corner of the room, terrified.

Both of the writers were screaming and cursing at each other, every other second grabbing whatever small object happened to be available at their arm's length and hurling it at the opposite wall.

The screams could be made out now:

"ARE YOU AN IDIOT! YOU IMBECILE! THAT COULD NEVER HAPPEN! NEVER IN A THOUSAND YEARS COULD THAT HAPPEN! WHAT IN……..NAME IS THE MATTER WITH YOU, YOU, YOU, YOU— YOU!"

"*YOU* ARE THE IDIOT! YOU CALL YOURSELF A WRITER! IT'S IMPOSSIBLE TO WORK WITH YOU!"

"YOU'RE THE ONE WHO'S IMPOSSIBLE TO WORK WITH! YOU MUST BE DRUNK! SHEILA WAS AT THE DAMNED PARTY HALF AN HOUR AGO, NOW YOU HAVE HER DOWN AT THE PIER!"

"BUT SHE'S *GOT* TO BE DOWN AT THE PIER IF SHE'S GOING TO SEE RAYMONDO DISAPPEARING AROUND THE CORNER!"

"IT'S NOT RAYMONDO YOU CRETIN! IT'S EDGARDO! CAN'T YOU AT LEAST GET THE NAMES OF THE CHARACTERS STRAIGHT!"

Margot stepped into the room and cleared her throat:
"Ahem."

Both of the Hersheys turned their heads, apparently aware for the first time that they were not alone in the room.

"Is everything all right?"

Silence.

Finally it was Jim who answered:

"We were writing."

Everyone in the hallway had now made their way into the room and were looking around with horror.

Pat Hershey, looking at Nina:

"Which is a better name, Edgardo or Raymondo?"

"Raymondo," answered Nina immediately, having no idea why she said so.

Pat glared at her husband and hissed:

"I told you! I told you!"

Then the two of them turned to the crowd and said, quietly:

"Maybe we should finish the epilogue tomorrow."

Margot cleared her throat again and said, hesitantly:

"Well, it does seem to be shaping up as a busy day."

"Yes," the Hershey's affirmed. "Yes, we'll finish tomorrow. "Sorry if we disturbed anyone."

Many answers from the writers:

"That's all right."

"Don't worry about it."

"Just the writing process."

"Love your cat."

"See you tomorrow!"

"See both of you tomorrow!"

"See you tomorrow!"

"Good night!"

"Good night!"

"Good night!"

"Good night."

And, after a time, the corridor was silent and empty.

Margot saw Nina to her door.

Nina went in and said:

"This is the worst thing you've ever done to me."

But Margot only shook her head and said:

"Not yet."

Then the two women went to their own rooms and to bed.

CHAPTER   EIGHT: PROFESSOR   BRIGHTON
DUNBURY

And so it came to pass that Nina Bannister awoke on the
second morning of the AGCW conference—in a haunted
room.

So it came to pass that she slid from her bed, took stock
of her reflection, threw on her Mississippi State Bulldog
sweatshirt—for the morning was quite cool for the last day
in August, and pondered what to do.

It was early. The world was in half-light, the sun having
not yet risen. She could see through the window on the south
side of the room that there was no activity on the porch or in
the yard, no movement anywhere that she could see, and no
sound other than the crowing of a rooster from one of the
barns.

She knew where the breakfast room was; she could hope
that some of the staff had already begun to prepare for the
morning's meal, had already put on a pot of coffee.

She might meet Margot bustling about.

On the other hand, she might meet some of the cozy
writers.

Not a pleasant prospect.

So she decided to do something quite different.

She would explore the forested part of The Candles'
grounds.

Why not go into the woods and watch the sun come up
through the thickly enmeshed branches of oaks and yellow
pines?

This proved to be a good idea.

She had no idea where she was going, of course; but she
had brought with her to Candles some good hiking boots.
The air proved deliciously fresh and pine-scented, and the

narrow paths seemed to beckon her, winding here and there, offering a new sight and a new smell every few turns.

In fifteen minutes she was completely lost, enveloped in the forest primeval, but not caring very much, and certain that she would be able to retrace her steps when she needed to.

Or *would* she need to?

Would she have to go back at all?

It had all seemed like such a good idea only a short time ago: she and her good friend merely hanging out in this marvelous old place, sipping coffee in the morning, wine or even cognac at night, chatting empty-headedly about this or that.

Chilling out.

And now this.

Thirty insane people screaming at each other about Edgardo and Raymondo—whoever they were—or sniffing the air for the scent of demons, or locking themselves in their rooms, or getting worked into a frenzy about the horrors of self-publishing.

All here, locked together, waiting for someone from the magic city of Los Angeles to come and make one of them famous.

Did she really want to go back to that?

Why should she not simply wander here forever in this forest? Perhaps she really had been transformed into a modern, though equally timeless, version of the Wizard of Oz, and these hard-packed Mississippi red dirt paths would soon turn to yellow brick roads and she'd never have to hear the word "cozy" again until she woke up where there's no place like (that is 'home') and Toto-Furl would be there playfully licking her cheek or pooping on the deck?

Why should she not be able to do that?

She had about decided that there was, in fact, no reason for her to go back, when she broke into a clearing and saw the Wizard of Oz himself.

He was seated beside a small emerald-like pond—at least the pond was emerald in color even if it was not a city—and he was fishing.

He was also petting the plantation dog Borg, who lay calmly at his side.

He was not the Wizard who appeared later in the film, but the old man who drove the Professor Miracle medicine show wagon earlier on, the one Dorothy stumbles upon after she and Toto run away.

He sat quite still, his back to her, obviously oblivious to her presence. He was fishing with a cane pole. She could see better now, for a sliver of sun had just appeared in the Eastern sky, and the small red-white bobber appeared quite clearly, no more than fifteen or thirty feet out in the lake.

Black frock coat, frumpy and equally black hat, graying hair falling in an unkempt way about and below his ears.

Yes, he was Professor Miracle, no doubt, later to become the ALL-POWERFUL OZ, and later still to be revealed as a complete humbug-master.

And his warm smile was exactly like the professor's when, hearing her take a step toward the lake, he turned and beamed and shouted:

"Well! Hello there, my dear! Another early riser, I see!"

Suddenly there came a mournful but chilling kind of wail from somewhere far beyond the pond.

"What is that?" she asked.

He smiled:

"It's a panther actually. Almost certainly a black panther."

"A black panther? In Mississippi?"

"Oh yes! One finds them in almost all areas of the country. Very rare, but very beautiful. Don't worry about this one though. He's miles away."

She continued to walk toward the pond, saying:

"Well, then, panther or not, good morning!"

"Yes, yes, it is definitely a good morning! Although I must say, there's something about the sky that disturbs me!"

She looked up and around.

Something about the sky disturbed her, too.

The dreadful yellow tinge had grown more pronounced, and it colored even the bright morning star that still hung in the West.

"They say," she said, "that a hurricane is heading toward East Texas."

He shook his head:

"Well, they may say what they wish. That's their prerogative."

"You don't believe them?"

"All I know, my child, is that 'the seller of lightning rods arrived just before the storm.' Lovely line, eh? Bradbury, of course. *Something Wicked this Way Comes*. And, of course, the original version of that title is in *Macbeth*. But wherever the line originates, it shows a startling amount of perception. I feel our lightning rod seller is just down the road a piece, and will be here before we realize it. Then will come the storm. Oh, let them blather about Texas if they wish. But the storm will come here, in one form or other. Please—come and sit beside me, and help me fish."

She was almost at the lake now, and there was a fallen tree trunk that seemed to have been made for a seat.

She eased herself down on it, then reached out to take the hand that was extending toward her:

"I'm Dr. Brighton Dunbury," the hand's owner said, cheerily.

No you're not! the shaker of the hand said mentally. *You're Professor Miracle!*

"Pleased to meet you!" said the shaker of the hand not mentally but audibly. "I'm Nina Bannister."

"Wonderful to meet you, wonderful indeed! Are you a writer of cozy mysteries? I don't believe I know your heroine or your charming small quaint village?"

Nina shook her head:

"No. No, I'm a friend of Margot Gavin. Margot and her husband run Candles. I came up from Bay St. Lucy for a va—to help her during the conference."

She could, of course, have said, 'I came for a vacation and ran smack dab into you loonies by accident—'

But what would that have accomplished?

And perhaps this man wasn't a loony at all!

"Are you a medical doctor?" she asked.

He smiled and shook his head:

"Veterinarian. My occupation has allowed me to calm our friend here."

"Borg?"

"Oh, is that his name?"

"That's what I was told yesterday when I arrived. They also said he'd been upset for months, not wanting to be around people. I do wonder what might have caused that condition."

"Apparently there was a convention of writers here in June."

"Ah! Well, that explains it then!!"

"Somehow you calmed him down though."

He nodded:

"I and this small apparatus."

He lifted his palm off Borg's head, where it had been resting.

In the palm was a small piece of metal that resembled an amulet of some sort. It was glowing green, and she could hear it emitting a slight buzzing sound.

"What is that?"

"You've heard of dog whistles, have you not?"

"Yes, they emit a kind of high-pitched tone. Dogs can hear them and we can't. But they drive the dogs crazy."

"Yes, they do. Well this little device—it's on the market you know, I didn't invent it—this device has the opposite effect. It's an anti-dog whistle. It calms dogs down. It actually—"

He was interrupted by the disappearance of the bobber.

"You've got a bite!" she said.

"Yes, yes, I certainly do!"

He jerked the pole, hooked whatever was at the other end of the line, and began to reel.

"What do you imagine I've hooked my dear? Trout, bass, catfish, shark, whale?"

"Or sunfish."

Which is what it was.

He held it dangling before them, and she admired, as she always did, the remarkable colors of the thing, the reasons for its name, the yellows and reds and deep purples that made it look like nothing more than the sunrise itself.

"What a thing of beauty, eh?"

"Yes, it is."

"Well, let's set about getting it back to its home!"

He deftly removed the fish from the hook that protruded from its mouth, and a second later he was flipping it back into the pond.

"That," he said, grinning, "was exciting, wasn't it?"

Nina nodded and said:

"For the fish, too."

He laughed:

"For the fish too! I like that! For the fish too. Ha!"

Then he re-baited the hook with a worm that he took from a red coffee can, re-cast his line, listened to the satisfying 'plop' sound, and asked:

"And what do you do, Ms. Bannister, when you're not helping your friend carry out her innkeeping business?"

"I'm retired now. I was a teacher."

"How splendid! And whom did you teach?"

"Mississippi high school students. I was an English teacher for a lot of years."

"Then I have met a colleague! I studied and taught classics for a time. I'm English, you know, born in London. I taught there for some years. But I tired of it. I had other loves—namely writing and, strangely, animals. I heard a kind of 'call of the wild,' as it were. I moved to Boston and studied veterinary medicine. And then I went further into the wilderness—namely the wilds of northern Michigan. I live in a small town there now, taking care of sick animals, and camping as much as possible."

"What do you write?"

He smiled:

"My mystery writing reflects my earlier classical training. Never lost that love completely, you know! I write the Drusilla of Sestos Mysteries."

"Drusilla of—"

"Sestos."

"I'm sorry, I—"

"I know, you've probably not heard of it. Possibly because it isn't very large. And also because it no longer exists."

"Where was it when it did exist?"

"About forty miles south of Rome. But it was destroyed by a volcano in 234 AD."

"I thought that was Pompeii."

"No, Pompeii's destruction came half a century later. And that wretched city got all the publicity. The tragedy of Sestos though was equally compelling. Wiped out completely. Dear Drusilla too. But I made quite a complete study of the lady earlier in my career. And finally, when I could no longer resist the urge to write fiction—something that someone might actually read, you know—I thought, why Drusilla is the perfect cozy heroine! She lives in a small coastal town—"

"With a volcano."

"Of course with a volcano, but also some charming sea vistas to look at…and she is the perfect person to solve mysteries, simply by dint of her occupation."

"Which is?"

"Drusilla is a seamstress! One of the few occupations open to Roman ladies of high rank and acute intelligence."

"She weaves."

"Yes, she weaves! But to the Romans, and to the Greeks, from whom they stole the imagery, weaving is also the ultimate mark of intelligence and artistry. One weaves cloth, of course, but one also weaves stories and tales. Homer's Penelope deceives suitors for years by weaving and then unweaving the burial shroud for Odysseus. Athena herself, the goddess of wisdom, is, as she tells Odysseus, the greatest of all weavers. Wisdom and lying are one and the same for the Greeks, and for the Romans after them—and for my Drusilla and—I suppose if we get right down to it—for me."

"Is Athena a character in your stories?"

"Of course she is! And she is my muse! I have a small image of her—actually a shrine one might say—and I pray to it daily before beginning to write. I also pray to the muse of course: Oh, sing in me, muse—which is what the Greek singer chanted before beginning his songs of Troy and the great battles and the great wanderings."

"You have a cat?"

"Of course, I have a cat! We all have cats. Mine is back in the room now, sleeping."

"His name?"

"Clawdius."

"That would fit."

The sun had risen now. They could hear bullfrogs croaking in the moss around the edges of the pond, and Nina found herself imagining them to be the incarnation of all the long dead singers and poets and cozy writers, chanting to the muse so that they could sing of Troy and Penelope and Odysseus and Miss Marple.

"Are you hoping," she asked, "to win an HBO contract and put Drusilla on weekly television?"

He merely smiled and shook his head:

"Oh no, that would spoil everything."

She looked at him and asked:

"Why?"

"Because it would mean success! And that would destroy my ability to write!"

"Why?"

"Oh, it would take the fuel away!"

"What fuel?"

"The, the…"

He shook his head, then thought for a time, and said quietly:

"I'm not sure about the other writers of fiction, my dear. Perhaps some do write for money. But there's so little of that commodity lying around, and so many writers trying to get it—that anyone who chooses the drudgery of fiction writing as an avenue for financial success, is surely an idiot."

"So why write? Do you want fame?"

An even more pronounced shake of the head:

"Fame is even in shorter supply than lucre."

"Then why write? What motivates you?"

"The same thing that motivates all fiction writers I imagine. Even though most do not realize it."

"And that is?"

"Spite, of course!"

"What?"

"Spite! I write out of pure spite! And had I not this wellspring of churning, spewing, bubbling, boiling, ever-regenerating, perfectly pure spite raging deep within me—why, I could never write a word. My fiction would be completely dead."

"I still don't—I mean—"

"I know it must be difficult for those of you in the outside world. But every time one of us receives a rejection letter—and we receive hundreds of them before we ever gain even the slightest glimmer of success—a grain of spite gets sown in the furrows of our little mental fields. Finally, there are rows of such spite seeds, and then more rows, and then complete fields, and then blossoming crops, golden in the sunlight, all bushels and bushels and bushels of complete spite, all of it dedicated to—to no one! To faceless people, editors who do not answer queries, agents who do not accept un-agented submissions, website entries that say, "We are no longer accepting submissions." We rage against all of these evil forces, and our rage generates power, and it's this power we harness in order to write. Reject me, huh! Well, I'll write another novel! I'll write a novel with one hand behind my baaack! And another one and another one after that. JUST TO SHOW YOU, TO SHOW ALL OF YOU! I'LL WRITE A HUNDRED NOVELS AND YOU CAN'T STOP ME!"

He had changed momentarily, Nina noted, from Professor Miracle/Wizard of Oz to the cowardly lion, raging and shouting, 'Put 'em uuup! 'Put 'em uuup!'

He was quite animated by this time, and he was forced to pause for a few seconds.

Finally, he was able to smile wanly, shake his head, and be his old self/selves.

"But, success? People telling you how they live for every word you write? How much they love this character or that? And what will the next novel be about and how they can't lead normal lives until it comes out and until they see the film of it and is it true that so and so is to play the starring role? No. Such success would be no more than a poison gas hovering inches above the typewriter. No writers could stand it. And most writers who do achieve it—well, you know, they attempt to commit suicide."

"They try to kill themselves?"

"No, they try to kill their characters. But the public will not allow them to do so. Sherlock Holmes was wished dead a thousand times by his creator. But England would have none of it; and so poor Conan Doyle was sentenced to life as a parrot, simply repeating again and again what he'd already said."

"And you don't want that for Drusilla."

"Of course not. My mysteries are published by a small house. I try various means to sell them and I fail. These failures enrage me, and I use this rage to write more books."

He was silent for a time, then he turned to look at the sunrise:

"I suppose," he said, "you must be sick indeed of hearing me ramble on."

"No. I just never thought writing would be like that. I did have one more question, if you don't mind my asking."

"Of course, I don't mind!"

"How did you get published in the first place? And, if your books don't sell, how have you gotten to be included in the AGCW, which only takes the top cozy writers?"

He smiled while he turned the bait can over and watched the worms crawl into ever deeper tufts of grass.

Finally, he said:

"Well, that was the influence of Harriet Crossman. I met her when I was living in Boston. I showed her my manuscripts. She found a publisher for them—she has many contacts, and called in a favor, I suppose. Then, since she was even at that time the most decisive force in the Guild, she used her influence to have me admitted."

"She must love your work."

He got to his feet, carefully wrapping the fishing line around the pole and securing the hook.

"That's possible," he said. "Or it might simply have been because for lo those many years we were sleeping together. So, ready? Let's go back!"

And he walked away.

CHAPTER NINE: FAME COMES A- KNOCKING!

During the mile or so walk back from the lake to the plantation house, Nina said little to the professor who walked in front of her, and spent most of the time thinking that it would be good for her to spend the entire morning locked away in her room, if for no other purpose than to imagine where and when and IN GOD'S NAME HOW??? did Professor Brighton Dunbury and Harriet Crossman become lovers?

But she was not to be allowed this luxury.

Much had been happening at the Candles.

In the first place, the cats were proving to be a problem. Unfettered access to every room and every corridor, such access granted by the ubiquitous cat doors carefully carpentered into the place by its original, obviously cat-loving builders gave them equally unfettered access to each other,

And after a few hours of such access, it became painfully clear to their owners, and much more painfully clear to Margot, that they all either hated each other or loved each other.

In various rooms or corners, on various counter tops, behind various chairs and sofas, under various beds—they hurled themselves hissing and spitting and clawing and tearing and ripping and spewing and yowling.

Or, in much these same areas, they made passionate love, assuming positions and postures that Nina, accustomed only to the celibate life lived by the confirmed bachelor Furl, would never have thought conceivable, except that she saw an example of it taking place just in front of the refrigerator when she went into the kitchen looking for Margot.

The same Margot who, at just that moment, happened to be coming out of the dining room.

Both of the women stared at the spectacle for a time.

"Would you look at that?" asked Nina, quietly.

"That's the most disgusting thing I've ever seen in my life."

"It's kind of educational though."

"What?"

"I mean, it's kind of like watching the nature channel. I really would never have thought—"

"Do you know this is going on all over the house?"

"In just this same way? I mean, with the same—"

"I DON'T KNOW, NINA! I'M NOT TAKING NOTES!"

"I'm sorry."

Margot was silent for a time.

They both were silent for the amount of time necessary for Hecubah and Driscoll (the two enamored animals in question) to consummate their relationship and wander woozily off in opposite directions, purring quietly and licking themselves.

"We are," Margot said, when it was possible to speak again, "going to have to have the whole place sanitized. Top to bottom."

"Well. You'll be able to afford it."

"It's not worth it. All the money in the world wouldn't be worth it. Just the cat hair alone—"

"I know. I'm a cat owner."

"You own *one* cat! *One*! I've been sneezing ever since I got up this morning! And last night—it was three in the morning, actually—two of them got into my room!"

"Were they friends or enemies?"

Margot shook her head:

"I'm not sure. I was half asleep, it was all so dream-like. But they broke a lamp."

"I'm sorry."

"You're going to be sorrier. I have a kind of difficult job for you; but you're the only one I can trust to do it."

"Is the litter gone? Because I'm not..."

"No, it's worse."

Nina was silent for a time, contemplating how this might be possible.

Finally she asked:

"What do you want me to do?"

"We're serving breakfast, you know."

"What do you want me to do?"

"Take Garth Amboise his food."

"No."

"Someone has to do it. He refuses to eat with the other writers."

"No."

"I can't trust any of the staff."

"No, I hate him."

"And *I* can't do it."

"Why can't you do it?"

"Nina, you know me. You know my temper. And you know how strong I am. I'd strangle him to death and then I'd rub grits in his hair."

"I have a temper too!"

"But you're weak! You're little and weak! He'd have at least a fifty-fifty chance against you!"

"So you're saying I can't kill him?"

"I'd really rather you didn't."

To this Nina had no answer.

She merely waited a while until Margot finally said:

"Listen: you've got to do this. I'll send someone up with you, one of the boys. No, two of the boys. One can carry the platter of food and the other can carry the box of stuff."

"What stuff?"

"All kinds of stuff has been coming in from publishers. Sweatshirts that say AGCW on them; commemorative plaques; there are even matching pendants and cat-collar attachments."

"There are what?"

"Little necklaces that go around your neck, and that have a gold charm or something that has AGCW engraved on them. Then there are cat collars to match with the same charms on them."

"And the publishers are contributing these gifts why?"

"Bribes."

"I don't understand."

"For post publication."

"I still don't understand."

"It's the HBO thing, Nina."

"Isn't it always?"

"Well, yes, I suppose you're right there. But anyway, once the TV series is made, every publisher and his dog…"

"—or cat."

"—or cat, is going to want to come out with a series of books based on the character. The writer will almost certainly get to choose who gets to publish the books. So all the publishing houses that put out cozies are trying to win loyalty. Anyway, there's like a Christmas tree of presents for every writer, and you might as well take Amboise his when you go up."

"All right. I'll do it, but I won't like it."

"Then, when you get back down, there's something else you have to help me do."

"What is it?"

"Somehow Harriet Crossman found out that Molly Badger is still here."

"How did she find that out?"

"I don't know. But she did, and she called me an hour ago. She's fit to be tied."

"What can I do about this?"

"Talk to her with me."

"Why?"

"You're a calming influence."

Nina looked at her for a time, then said:

"I'm boring, you mean."

"I did not mean that."

"What else is 'a calming influence' then?"

"I don't know, I just—"

"All right all right. Just point me in the direction of that, that—person of low esteem's room. I'll go up and wait outside the door until the boys arrive with the rest of the cr— stuff."

"All right. Oh, and there's one more thing."

"WILL YOU STOP SAYING THAT?"

"Well, there is."

"What is it?"

"Sylvia Duncan, the HBO representative."

"God, you mean."

"Goddess."

"Whatever."

"She's going to arrive around ten thirty. The first AGCW business session will last until ten. Then there will be a break, and we'll all be out in the yard to meet her limo when it arrives."

"And then everyone will surround her and kiss—"

"The ground she walks upon."

"That wasn't what I was about to say."

"I know what you were about to say, Nina. And shame on you for even thinking it."

"I've been around a lot of bad influences. So where do I go?"

"Up those stairs, turn left, and go two doors down. It's room 284."

"All right. And by the way—"

"Yes?"

"How are the Hersheys?"

Margot merely shook her head:

"Showed up bright and early this morning, first in line for breakfast, smiling, patting everybody on the back. Matching plaid shirts. I talked to Harriet Crossman about them. It seems it's common knowledge among cozy writers. They fight like cats and dogs when they're actually in the process of writing; but once the book is finished they're proud as punch of each other. Each one believes the other is as talented as Shakespeare. They can't stop heaping praise on each other."

"That's the weirdest thing I've ever heard of."

"Don't even think it. Now good luck with Amboise."

So saying, Margot turned and walked away, sneezing as she did so.

In five minutes, Nina found herself standing just outside of Garth Amboise' room.

She held a breakfast platter.

At her feet was a second silver platter, this one with a pitcher of steaming coffee on it.

Beside this platter was a cardboard box, approximately three feet high that held the presents Margot had mentioned.

These things had been left behind by the two boys, one of whom had asked Nina:

"Do you want us to stay?"

"No."

"We can, if you need us."

"You're minors. You don't need to see this."

"You're sure?"

"You have fine and productive lives ahead of you. Go now and live them."

The boys disappeared down the corridor.

Nina knocked on the door.

Silence.

No response from inside the room.

She knocked again.

A few sounds.

She waited, then knocked again.

Footsteps approaching the door.

She could run.

She could leave the damned presents and the damned food and the damned pitcher of coffee and just run.

But at that time she heard a key rattle in the lock.

The door opened.

Garth Amboise stood there, dressed in a black robe.

He stared at her.

It was the same stare Margot had trained only a few minutes earlier on the copulating cats.

It was a vicious stare, a disgusted stare, as though Garth Amboise were contemplating all of the evil in the world condensed into one small Bannister.

"Brought your food," she said.

He continued to stare.

"Here."

He took the platter.

"The white things are grits," she said. "If you're from The North , then you may not—"

"I know what grits are. I hate them."

"Sorry."

"What is this box?"

"Gifts. From publishers."

"Oh crap."

"Probably. But there's a collar in there for your cat."

"I don't have a cat."

"Forgot that. But you might want to put the pendant on, the gold one that says AGCW. It might impress Sylvia Duncan."

"All right. I'll put it on and wear it. When is Duncan coming?"

"I think Margot said ten thirty."

"Come and tell me when she arrives. My agents just called me; I'm first to be interviewed. After that I'm getting the hell out of here."

"I'll be up to get you."

He said nothing more but merely took the coffee inside, took the box inside, and closed the door, locking it from the inside.

Nina stared at the door for a few seconds, then whispered:

"Oh let it be poisoned."

Then she turned and left.

When she got downstairs, she saw Margot sitting in the far corner of the dining room, speaking very earnestly with Harriet Crossman, who seemed not at all pleased.

The dining room had been cleared of all culinary accoutrements and now served primarily for business reasons. Small groups were meeting in various areas, three and four cozy writers per group.

A large projector had been brought downstairs, and a light beamed from it.

On the opposite wall a huge, smiling, face was gleaming down on the participants of the meeting.

Nina stared at the face for a time, and then was aware of white-haired Rebeccah Thornwhipple, she of the erotic iron lung and the ninety-three year old protagonist, standing close by her side.

"Who is that?" she asked.

Rebeccah Thornwhipple answered with reverence:

"Oh, it's Jessica."

"It's who?"

"Jessica. Jessica Fletcher. From *Murder She Wrote*."

"What is she doing here?"

A shake of the white-haired head:

"Every culture," she whispered, "worships its own deity."

Then she toddled away.

By the time Nina had crossed the room, the conversation between Margot and Harriet Crossman had become quite intense:

"I thought I made our position concerning this matter quite clear last night."

"I know, Ms. Crossman, but it's simply not our policy—"

"Not your policy to what?"

"To turn people away!"

"Well you're about to turn more than thirty of them away! There's such a thing as principle, you know! We do not want to share accommodations with this woman. Or her kind!"

"But what harm is Molly Badger doing simply by *being* here?"

Several deep breaths.

For patience.

Finally:

"Ms. Gavin, you may or may not be aware of this. But both *Publishers Weekly* and *The New York Times* project, that by the year 2020, if current trends persist, more than a third of all Americans over the age of thirty-one will have published at least one novel."

"That does seem a lot, but—"

"One hundred million novels, Ms. Gavin. In a country in which fewer and fewer people are actually reading novels."

"But, if fewer people are reading them, then why are so many people writing them?"

"Because, given the quality of prose that is now being produced, it's so much easier to write a book than actually to read one! Don't you see that? And worse still, from our point of view: a huge proportion of these works will be murder mysteries."

"But why is that so bad?"

Frustration.

"Because, my dear Ms. Gavin, there are a strictly and tightly limited number of ways in which to murder someone. We try, as artists, to find more all the time, as God is my witness we do. We are always on the cutting edge; we are striving just as mightily as medical science only in reverse. But after a while, the supply of means simply runs out. People are killing other people by stuffing Christmas trees down their throats and, of course, that's just ridiculous—and CHAOS REIGNS! All because of the Molly Badgers of the world!"

Silence for a time.

Finally Margot:

"All right. All right. I guess I didn't realize the gravity of the situation."

"I guess you didn't."

"We'll go get Molly from her room and tell her she has to go."

"Thank you! Now perhaps we can get on about the business of the conference!"

And so saying, Harriet Crossman rose and left the table.

Molly Badger had been consigned to a small hidden room on the third floor of Candles (a floor seldom used except for the storage of unwanted furniture). It was almost invisible to one not already aware of its existence, its door blending into the paint of the walls and making it a better place for hiding than for living.

"Do you think she's in there?" asked Nina, as she and Margot approached.

"She would almost have to be. She's too frightened to come out and expose herself to the Published Cozy Writers during the day."

"Do you have a key?"

"Yes. We almost never go in here. It was supposedly used to hide escaping Confederate soldiers from the advancing Union armies. I can open the lock if I need to; but let's try calling out to her first."

Margot put her lips near the keyhole and whispered:

"Molly?"

No answer.

"Molly Badger?"

Some movement behind the door.

Then nothing.

"Molly! It's Margot Gavin and Nina. Your friends. Molly, you have to open the door."

Silence.

"Margot," said Nina, quietly, "you have to unlock it."

"All right."

The key was rusty, as was the lock.

Both screeched as metal scraped against metal.

Then there was a click.

"Open it!"

"All right."

Margot pulled.

The door came open painfully, hinges having not been oiled, obviously, for decades if not longer.

Before them they saw little more than a dark cell, no more than ten feet square. Along the far wall stretched a cot, upon which the blanket-enshrouded body of Molly Badger lay. On a shelf on the wall directly above the cot sat a glass vase, and in that vase a single red rose.

There was a reading table at the foot of the cot. A candle burned low in its tarnished gold holder, and, by the flickering light thrown by the small flame, Nina could see the book that Molly had been reading upon going to sleep.

The Diary of Anne Frank.

"Molly?"

Margot stepped into the room.

"Molly?"

No answer. No movement.

"Margot," Nina whispered, suddenly quite frightened. "Is she—"

But Margot merely shook her head:

"No. She's breathing."

"Do you think she took some kind of drugs?"

"I don't think so. There, look—she's waking up."

And in fact she was. She groaned a bit, stretched in the bed, finally opened her eyes, and managed a weak smile:

"Margot! Nina! You've come to see me!"

Margot nodded:

"Yes. Are you all right?"

"I'm all right. Just frightened."

"Of what, child?"

"Of the others. I'm afraid of what they'll do to me, if they find me here."

"They won't find you."

"I don't know. They hate me so much. They hate all of us. And why? Why could one otherwise civilized culture want so desperately to eliminate another, wipe them out completely?"

"I don't know. It's something I can't understand."

"Yes, so I'm a self-published author. But am I not still a human being? Does not a self-published author have eyes? If you prick us, do we not bleed? If you tickle us—"

"It's all right," said Nina, quietly but firmly. "We know the lines."

"I'm sorry. It's just that it seems so unfair. They think they're this Master Race of Writers, just because they're all in Kindle Select."

"I know," said Margot. "But Molly, I have to tell you—"

"I crept down into the kitchen early this morning, about 4 a.m., before anyone else was awake. I know I shouldn't have, but I wanted to see the world, the real world again. I found all of the presents that the publishers had sent. And— oh, this is so hard for me—"

"Go on, my child."

"I took something."

"What? What did you take?"

"I know I shouldn't have, but they all looked so lovely, lying there on the various tables. I took a sweatshirt. Look."

She reached under the cot and took out the shirt, holding it up proudly before her.

"It's blue. Pale blue. It has American Guild of Cozy Writers stitched across the front, in bold, black letters."

"It's beautiful, Molly," said Nina.

"Do you think I shall be allowed to keep it?"

Margot, consolingly:

"Of course. Of course, you will."

"Because—because whenever I wear it, no matter where I shall be. Even, *if* I shall b—I shall look down at these letters, and feel the blue sky above me, and the green grass spread below me—and I shall know that I too am a true Cozy Writer."

Nina tried to respond to this, but she was about to cry.

They were in silence for a time.

Finally Molly Badger said, quietly:

"It's the right size, too."

Again, silence for a time.

Finally Margot said:

"Someone must have seen you, Molly."

Molly Badger nodded:

"Yes. Someone did."

"Who?"

"The beauty queen."

Nina, who'd studied the list of cozy guests quite thoroughly, nodded and said:

"You mean Suzy Maples?"

"Yes, that's the one."

Nina looked at Margot:

"Suzy Maples writes the Chrissie Oakton Mysteries. Chrissie is young and beautiful, and takes part constantly in beauty pageants. All of the murders she solves take place at such pageants, and the victims are always beauty queens."

"That's good," said Margot, thoughtfully.

"Her cat is a beautifully groomed Siamese named Skipples."

"Her real-life cat?"

Nina shook her head:

"No. Her fictional cat. In real life her cat is a Siamese named Whiskers. I saw it earlier this morning having sex with that gray yard cat that the staff calls Sluggo."

"Well, that's not good."

"No, she won't be pleased."

"What was Suzy doing downstairs so early, Molly?"

Molly Badger was sitting up now, and she had reached back to take into her small hands the red rose that sat above her cot. Smelling it, and smiling, she said.

"I love this rose. It gives me courage."

"I know. But as for Suzy—"

"She was putting her makeup on."

"At four in the morning?"

"She said it takes her a long time to do it. She has to start early."

"I see."

"Anyway, I'm sure she saw me. She asked who I was. I told her. I didn't say I was self-published, but—they know. They always seem to know. Anyway, she said some vicious things to me, words I can't repeat—and then she went back to doing her nails."

Margot nodded:

"All right. She must have called Harriet Crossman."

A look of fear came into Molly Badger's face.

"So they know? They know I'm here?"

"I'm afraid they do."

"Then they'll be coming for me."

"Not if we get you out quickly."

"Those sirens! Waa daa! Waa daa! Oh, I hate the memory of them!"

"It won't get that far. But you'll have to leave, Molly. I've asked one of the boys to get a car ready. He should be up here any time now. You can go down the back stairs."

"But where? Where can I go, Margot?"

"Why don't you just stay in Abbeyport for a few days. I know the name of a motel there."

"And they'll accept me?"

"Yes. They're good people, and brave."

"Oh, thank you! Thank you! Oh my God!"

"What is it, dear?"

"The sirens! I hear the sirens!"

"That's a fire truck, dear. Out on the road."

"It's so hard to tell the difference—"

"I know."

Molly Badger was standing now, and she put the book she'd been reading in a small suitcase that she took from beneath the cot, saying:

"I want to thank you so much for letting me stay here even for this short amount of time."

"I'm afraid it wasn't much—"

But Molly shook her head, saying:

"It was enough. I accomplished what I wanted to accomplish. Just being here allowed me to do that. And now I can promise you—I *will* be published!"

"Certainly you will, Molly."

"Not only that—but I'll be the one who gets the HBO contract!"

How, thought Nina, *in the hell are you going to do that?*

But she didn't say anything, and, if she had, she would not have included the 'hell' part.

(She was already thinking like a cozy writer.)

By the time Nina and Margot had reached the main meeting hall (secure in the knowledge that Molly Badger had been whisked down the back stairs and was now being taken safely into Abbeyport), the main morning's meeting had begun. The room was full, the beaming face of Jessica Fletcher was blessing the proceeding, and Harriet Crossman had just begun an address that began innocuously enough, but was to lead to trouble.

Nina and Margot stood in one of the room's corners while Harriet spoke, the microphone squawking a bit as she said her first words:

"Good morning!"

"GOOD MORNING!"

"I wish now to declare as open the first morning session of Year 2015's annual Congress of the American Guild of Cozy Writers!"

"HUZZAH!"

Upon saying this, she struck the podium with a solid brown wooden gavel, shouting as she did so:

"THE SESSION IS NOW OPEN!"

"Hear, hear!"

"Our first order of business though, I must warn you, is to be a difficult one. It represents a difficult decision on my part, and one that I have labored over quite intensely."

Silence in the room.

What is this all about? wondered Nina.

Harriet continued:

"As you all know, at ten thirty this morning a representative from HBO is going to arrive."

They knew.

More:

"The HBO representative is named Sylvia Duncan. She is said to be quite powerful in the organization. She will interview at some length any of you who wish your cozy series to be considered to be the basis of a new, nationally televised, mystery series. In short, from the pages of one or more of your novels, is to come the nation's next—"

She turned and pointed to the image glowing behind her, spread across the wall.

"—the next Jessica."

A kind of awed silence ensued.

"And yet—"

The awed silence transformed itself into a suspicious silence.

"…and yet, serious concerns remain as to which works, and which authors, the Guild itself is to put forward to Ms. Duncan."

Now there were a few shouts.

"What are you talking about?"

"What is this?"

Harriet, hands in the air:

"Please, please just let me speak. This is going to be difficult enough, without our interrupting one another."

"What are you talking about?"

"What the-------- are you talking about?"

First obscene word of the meeting, noted Nina.

Not really a 'cozy' meeting, one had to say.

Harriet:

"As most of you know, we have in recent years given the coveted GACW seal—as well as membership in the Guild—to works which stretch the boundaries of what might truly qualify as cozy mysteries. Let us be honest with ourselves. There have been some very bloody murders committed within our pages. Also—"

She looked down at Rebecca Thornwhipple, who was seated, as usual, in the front row.

"—though I am no prude, I do take grave exception to the level of eroticism that we have allowed to creep into some of our narratives."

"-------- you!" chirped Rebeccah.

The room gasped as one.

Harriet, though, continued:

"Now, now. I am not going to attempt to pare down our membership, nor do I intend to lead a movement to purify our writing, and bring it back to the pristine state with which Agatha and Jessica began it."

Harsh voices now.

"See that you don't!"

"Down with Crossman!"

Crossman, though, was not to be flustered:

"It is my contention, however, that this convention should vote as a group on a certain list of titles that it will recommend to HBO. And that these titles be those which embody our rules of true coziness: charming villages—on the New England coastline whenever possible—genuinely lovable and eccentric, perhaps cantankerous in that we-love-them-all-the-same kind of way, characters: town barbers, crusty lawyers, elderly gossips, and here and there an attractive young couple engaged to be married."

"Boring!"

"Been done!"

"Also, that these chosen novels portray good, middle-class murders that even children can view and read about and talk about with their friends."

"Children don't read cozies!"

"To hell with children."

And with that, another biscuit went flying across the room, striking one of Jessica Fletcher's pearly white teeth before falling harmlessly to the floor.

Must have been left over from last night, mused Nina.

But, of course, there had been biscuits for breakfast, too.

"We want, in short, what we were raised on watching television and reading library books: good, straightforward knives and letter openers to the heart, and revolver shots—preferably one and perfectly placed—to the head. We do *not* want—and I'm not going to name authors' names here, or mention novel titles—men being beaten to death by kickboxers, their throats mangled by karate chops and their eyes poked out by thumb jabs!"

"All right, that's enough!"

A figure stood up in the middle of the audience.

Nina had not seen her before.

Though she wondered how it would have been possible to miss her.

The woman wore tight fitting black slacks and a tank top.

The latter was important because it showed off a chiseled and muscular upper body, biceps bulging, shoulders rippling.

The woman had short blond hair and ice blue eyes.

She spoke in an ice blue voice.

Everyone was instantly afraid of her.

Including Nina.

"We all know who you're talking about. Okay let's get it out on the table. I'm C.R. Wood and I'm a feminist cozy writer."

A woman just to the left of Nina muttered:

"As though there could be such a thing. The very idea!"

But she said this very softly.

"I write The Patty Parity Mysteries. Yes, I will admit it, Patty is a fighter for equal rights for women. And she's a body builder, as am I. And she's a trained expert in martial arts. She can kill with her hands and she can kill with her feet. And she does so, quite regularly."

C.R. Wood leaned forward and shouted:

"But she only kills when she's confronted by examples of sexist behavior!"

Harriet Crossman, attempting to be conciliatory, herself leaned forward on the podium:

"But C.R., in the last novel, Patty castrates a man with one karate chop."

"It's possible! I've done it."

An audible murmur ran through the crowd.

C.R. Wood glared at everyone in the room.

Then she sat down.

Harriet, shaking her head, continued:

"All right, clearly there are going to be some disagreements among us. But if we can just agree that what promotes best the well-being of the entire—"

She was interrupted by movement from the back of the room.

A door had opened, and in the doorway stood a radiant woman, beaming, dressed in white, and warming the entire room.

"I am," she said, "Sylvia Duncan."

No, you're not, thought Nina. *You're Glenda the Good Witch.*

Except you don't have a little crown.

It must be in a suitcase somewhere.

Everyone in the audience gasped.

They stared at her for a time, as though, despite her perfectly pressed business suit and crimson scarf, she was actually standing in the doorway completely naked.

She had so much confidence, of course, Nina found herself thinking, that she could have *been* naked and not worried about it one bit.

She continued:

"I am sorry. I was supposed to arrive an hour and a half later. I only realized my mistake a few minutes ago. I thought it might be all right if I just sat in on your meeting, perhaps got a few ideas about how your organization functions—

My God, thought Nina, *the last thing you want to know is how this organization functions.*

Harriet Crossman obviously thought the same thing.

Because after flustered apologies on both sides, a great deal of hand shaking and milling and stewing and standing up and sitting down and applause and 'My name is so and so and I write the such and such' and 'I'm so anxious to get to know you and to get to know you and OH WHAT AN ADORABLE CAT YOU HAVE THERE—"

For heaven's sakes, thought Nina, *at least keep the cats off one another for a while. Just a little while, anyway, until she gets used to the place.*

—after a few minutes of this kind of thing, Sylvia Duncan, who of course was not about to be consigned to the back of the hall as though she were just anybody—

—was at the podium, addressing the entire group.

"Well, Cozy Writers of America, I, as you know by now, I am Sylvia Duncan. I have the honor to represent HBO. We're always trying at our network to meet the ever changing demands of a diverse and highly intelligent viewing audience. Our attempts to recognize what's truly wanted out there, and what's being asked for, have led us again and again to the realization that cozy mysteries— wholesome mysteries with good well-crafted plots—are more in demand than they've ever been."

"Yes!"

"Yes!"

Sylvia Duncan smiled at these comments.

"We wish that we could make on-going television productions of all your fine novels. And perhaps, with time and luck, we can. But for now we must choose one of you. One series of novels that we hope will begin a—

And on and on.

She gave a brief succinct speech in which she said just about what everybody in the room already knew.

She was going to make somebody a millionaire.

And now it was time to begin the interviews.

And so she said, finally, after her preliminary remarks were finished and the true business to begin:

"Well, then. We're a bit ahead of schedule, but I see no reason why I should not begin the interview process. I'm to begin, I think, with a Mr.—"

She did not finish.

The screams prevented her.

Screams from a young woman—Nina recognized her as one of the cleaning staff—who was standing on the stairwell and pointing upstairs.

She was, that is, pointing with her right hand. Her left hand was pressed tightly over her mouth.

It came away, almost involuntarily, to let out more screams.

Heart-wrenching screams.

She continued to point, her arm swaying like a tree branch in the wind.

"Marjorie!"

Margot was walking toward the young woman now.

"Marjorie, what is it?"

Marjorie's reply:

"It's—it's up there! It's awful!"

"What is?"

"In the room! The blood! The blood everywhere!"

Margot spun, looked at Nina, and said:

"Come on!"

Then she walk-ran to the stairwell, Nina close behind.

It took them no more than a few seconds to reach the second floor.

Silence in the hallway.

They looked at each other.

"Any idea—" began Margot.

Nina merely shook her head.

The corridor loomed before them, rooms on either side.

"Which room was she talking about?" Nina asked.

"Obviously we should have asked her."

"Yes. Except for the fact that she's too terrified to speak."

"We may have to look in all the rooms," said Margot, quietly.

"We could do that," said Nina, quietly. "Or we could do it the easier way."

"What is that?"

"Check the room halfway down the hall, where the pool of blood is running out onto the carpet."

They both looked.

They saw the pool expanding, seeping under the door jamb, soaking the thin gray carpet.

"Oh my God," whispered Nina. "Maybe we should get the police."

"The police," answered Margot, "are in Abbeyport. Whoever's in there could be still alive."

The blood had formed a lake now, and had extended to the far side of the corridor.

"Come on," said Margot.

The world was silent.

Mid-morning. Early September.

Nothing moving in the deserted fields and outbuildings.

They stopped before the doorway.

The bottoms of their shoes were now soaked in blood.

"All right," said Margot. "Whatever it is, let's see."

She pushed open the door.

And they did.

"Oh my God."

"Oh my God."

It hardly mattered which of them had spoken first.

CHAPTER TEN: END OF A PRODIGY

When they re-entered the hall below them, the audience appeared as nothing more than a carefully detailed painting.

No one seemed to have moved.

No one was speaking.

Palms were still securely clapped over mouths.

Harriet Crossman remained seated in the first row.

Sylvia Duncan remained standing at the podium.

She moved aside just enough to let Margot take her place, and speak into the slightly braying microphone.

Margot's usually firm voice was breaking.

"I have—I have horrible news."

No sound, no movement.

Not even breathing.

"One of your colleagues, Mr. Garth Amboise, has been murdered."

Gasps from everyone.

"Ms. Bannister and I have just come from his room."

A few people began moving slightly now, leaning slightly forward on the tables in front of them, as though the news itself were magnetized.

"I know that I could spare you this, but I think you all have the right to know. The scene inside, I must tell you, is simply ghastly. There is blood everywhere. The sheets of Mr. Amboise' bed are drenched with it. The carpet of the room, the furniture. And his body—"

More leaning forward.

Everyone in the room breathing as one.

And finally Margot:

"His body is nude upon the bed. It has literally been ripped apart, his skin shredded."

She paused to let this seep in.

Then she continued:

"I was able to call the police a few seconds ago. I know James Thompson the Chief. He's a good man. He says help will be here in approximately fifteen minutes. He has asked me to advise you, all of you, simply for now to remain where—"

But it was too late.

The entire crowd of cozy writers had leapt to their feet simultaneously and were pouring into the aisles of the meeting room, stampeding toward the stairwell.

"Wait!" Margot screamed. "Stay here! You can't go up there! We don't know who did this! He might still be—"

But it was no use.

They were clawing at each other, tugging at each other, and forcing their way forward as fast as possible. Many of them were rummaging in large purses for their smart phones, ready to snap pictures to put on Facebook walls.

Some of them, Nina noted, had already begun to text.

"What is wrong with these people?" whispered Margot.

Nina could only shake her head:

"I don't know."

The stairway was now packed, and the clattering of feet could be heard upon the second floor corridor above.

One of the women who'd been forced to the back of the line bellowed to the crowd on the stairway:

"DON'T TOUCH ANYTHING!"

This same woman, coming abreast of Nina, asked:

"Did you see a knife?"

Numb, Nina could only shake her head.

But the woman continued her interrogation:

"Exactly what color would you say the blood was?"

Automatically, Nina found herself replying:

"Kind of—dark. Purplish on the sheet. But brighter red on the body."

The woman nodded.

"Good. That's very good. Was the corpse twitching around a little bit or was it still?"

Margot intervened at this point, shouting:

"What are you doing?"

But the woman merely replied:

"You can't get this kind of stuff from a library!"

Margot shouted even louder:

"A man has been murdered!"

"I know!"

Then, suspiciously:

"You aren't just staging this, are you?"

"I'm not what?" asked Margot.

"Just staging it. I know last year at The Love is Murder Conference in Chicago—"

"Of course, we're not just staging it! He's dead! He's in his bed and dead!"

"With his skin ripped off him you say?"

"Yes, yes, he's torn to pieces!"

"Was the skin ripped off in big, inch-long strips or was it—"

"Stop it stop it stop it!"

And so screaming, she pulled Nina away, to the back of the room.

The last of the cozy writers had made their way into the stairwell now.

The faint sounds of sirens could be heard coming out of Abbeyport.

"These women," said Nina, "are ghouls."

But then she was aware of the presence of two other women standing beside them.

The Smathers sisters, Ruby and Lacy.

One short, one tall.

Still looking around, sniffing the air, suspicious of the floor and the ceiling, steering well clear of the walls.

Ruby, from on high:

"We told you."

Lacy, from down low:

"You didn't believe us, did you?"

Ruby:

"We told you about the demons."

Lacy:

"But you did nothing! Now all this is on your heads. On both of your heads!"

Then the two sisters made their way toward the opposite door, saying, over their shoulders simultaneously:

"We don't need to go up there. We know exactly what it looks like."

And then they disappeared.

"They're insane," said Margot.

"Absolutely crazy," concurred Nina.

They were silent for a time.

Some of the cozy writers, having viewed the crime scene, had now descended back into the main hall and were walking up and down the aisles between tables, notebooks or apps in their hands, either writing dialogue to themselves or trying to tap descriptions into smart phones.

They wandered here and there, heads upturned or bent toward the floor, muttering:

"The room was in shambles. Peter lay upon the blood-soaked sheets, his skin quivering. Macy Maplethorp's mind raced: how had he come to be here? What was the mysterious phone call that he'd gotten?"

Or:

"Blood was everywhere, and, even in the half light of dawn, Starling Canterbury knew that the man's death had been almost instantaneous. And brutal. But who could have done it? Certainly Roger Saintsford was hated around the village, and certainly any number of his spurned lovers might have—"

"I cannot believe," Nina said, "that I'm hearing this."

"They're writing books about it."

"Margot, we have to get them out of that room! It's a crime scene!"

"And how are we going to do that? There are thirty of them!"

Margot shook her head:

"Besides, the police will be here soon. Come on, let's sit down."

They did so, at one of the tables in the center of the room.

"I can't believe the insanity of all this," Margot muttered. "I don't know who's worse: the insane Smathers sisters or the insane rest of the crowd."

"And yet, and yet—" Nina muttered.

"And yet what?"

"Margot, this just doesn't make sense."

"So what does make sense? A demon?"

"I don't know, I just—it's crazy! I took him his breakfast not more than two hours ago. He was fine then. I know he was fine because I remember so distinctly wanting to kill him."

"But you didn't."

"No, I'm fairly certain I would have remembered. My God, Margot, it's like we're in a cozy mystery ourselves."

Margot stared at her, incredulously, saying finally:

"Now *you* are sounding crazy! Just what about any of this is 'cozy?' We have musclebound women castrating male chauvinists with karate chops, cats humping each other all over the place, weird sisters smelling the devil, ninety-year-old women fornicating in artificial breathing devices—"

"Okay, okay, you're right."

"Where's the little village? Where are all the cute and eccentric characters?"

"All right, you've made your point already."

"This whole fiasco is as close to a 'cozy' as World War II was!"

They sat for a time.

More writers ambled past them, and they heard more dialogue, more description:

"Although Cecilia Phillips had seen almost everything in her seventy years as a Seaside Cove nurse, she'd never quite…"

"Word spread like wildfire through the streets of the charming New England village of Port Mariner. Eton Bransworthy, heir to the huge fortune built by his enigmatic—and often hated—grandfather had been butchered. Ms. Eleanora Stapleworth could not wipe from her mind the image of the blood, purplish on the body, brighter red on the sheet—"

"It was," Nina interrupted the writer who was passing by, "the other way around."

A woman looked down at her.

"Oh, you mean purplish on—"

"—the sheet, brighter red on the body."

"Well. Thank you."

"Don't mention it."

Finally the police arrived.

At least a dozen people entered the room, all dressed in various uniforms.

An older officer with white sideburns and a somewhat corpulent build, dressed in the light khaki and dark brown of a forest ranger, approached the table where Margot and Nina were seated.

"Ms. Gavin?"

"Yes, Officer Thompson. Thank you for coming. I've not seen you for a while."

"Not since the writers were here. You've got another bunch of them out here I see."

"Yes. We thought these would be different. But they're worse."

"We just got your call. Is the body—"

"Upstairs. Room 284."

"And the victim?"

"His name is—was—Garth Amboise."

"And how was he killed, Ms. Gavin?"

Margot shook her head:

"He was torn to pieces."

"Ma'am?"

"You heard me. He was torn to pieces."

"What tore him to pieces?"

"A demon," Nina found herself saying.

The officer stared at both of them, then asked Margot:

"Is she joking?"

But Margot merely shook her head and answered:

"I don't know. I really don't know."

Within thirty minutes, most of the necessary work concerning the crime scene and the mutilated corpse had been taken care of. The body was now on its way to the Abbeyport morgue, and policemen had replaced the cozy writers in Garth Amboise' room. Whatever *could* be found

in the way of fingerprints, murder weapons, ways in and out
of the room—evidence of any kind—*would* be found, at
least according to James Thompson.

Whom Nina found herself doubting, even as he stood
behind the same podium where only a short time ago Harriet
Crossman and then Sylvia Duncan had addressed the crowd
of cozy writers.

Now he was addressing this same crowd.

"All of you know by now," he said with a gravelly voice,
"that a crime has been committed here in The Candles."

Of course they know about it, Nina found herself
thinking. They've already written the first four chapters of it.

The officer went on:

"One of your colleagues, I believe a Mr. Amboise, has
been brutally murdered. We don't know precisely how he
was murdered. But the body was—well, it was mutilated.
We don't have any suspects as of now. Our men are going
over Mr. Amboise' room even as we speak, and whatever
evidence is there, we will find it."

He paused to let this sink in, and he looked carefully at
the faces spread across the room before him. Was he
thinking this soft and grave pronouncement would force an
admission from one of them?

No such admission was forthcoming, and so he went on:

"Given the nature of the crime, and the fact that the killer
is obviously still at large—and may still be hiding in or
around the plantation house itself—it would seem more
prudent, I'm sure you all agree, that this conference be
cancelled. We can take all of you into Abbeyport in police
vehicles. Our department will work with you to get you all
back to Chicago, where I'm told you departed to come down
here. Once back in Abbeyport we'll have to interview each
of you and get statements. None of you are suspects as such,
but we want to know what you may have seen or heard in the
hours before the crime, or whether any of you had talked to
Mr. Amboise. It may be possible to get you all on a flight out
before tonight. If that is not possible, we will try to find
motel space to accommodate you until something goes out
tomorrow."

He paused.

Harriet Crossman, who'd taken a seat in the front row, stood up and spoke:

"Officer, we thank you for your advice, and we appreciate the gravity of your task. But what you ask—and I assume all our coziests are in agreement with me on this point—is quite impossible."

He stared down at her, then at the other people in the room, all of whom were nodding in agreement with their leader.

"Hear hear!"

"No leaving! No leaving!"

"On with the conference!"

Officer Thomson could only shake his head:

"But Ms. Crossman, this is a crime scene."

To which she shook her head in return:

"No, Sir. Mr. Amboise' room is a crime scene. *This* is a hotel."

"I know, but—"

"When a crime is committed in a hotel, is the hotel closed? The entire hotel? Even if the crime is murder?"

"No, but—but you're all so isolated out here—"

"Would we be safer in New York City? Is anyone safe in New York City?"

Laughter at this and a few catcalls, a few shouts:

"Down with New York City!"

"Crime capital of the world!"

The officer's face was flushed now.

He continued, shaking his head:

"But you all must understand, we're going to have people here, going in and out, running tests—"

"Very well, then run your tests."

"But ma'am—"

She took a step closer to the podium:

"And there is almost certainly something that you, my dear officer, do not understand. And that is of the utmost importance to this conference. This is not just any literary conference, not 'Murder or Mayhem' or 'Love and Murder,' or any of those fun gatherings. No. Writing mysteries is not a game to us. Crime-Coziness is our life. Most of us may have had another profession earlier on in our lives, but by now we have almost certainly forgotten what it was, and without our cozies we would have no way at all of making a living in the real world."

The officer looked around the room, examined the faces of all the conference participants, then nodded reluctantly:

"All right, I can see that. I can believe that. But still—"

"There is vital work to be done here in the following days. Decisions to be made as to which of thousands of manuscripts and digital files may be awarded the coveted AGCW Medallion, signifying membership in our organization; publicity campaigns to plan and co-ordinate; kitten giveaways—"

The officer leaned forward as though he had not understood.

"Kitten giveaways?"

"Yes, most assuredly! Book giveaways stopped working for many of us long ago due to the deluge of self-published books on the market. So most of us have begun giving kittens to anyone who will also agree to take a book. And this requires a *great* deal of work and planning. There are shots to consider, methods of transporting the little animals––but animal husbandry has now become a part of the writing process, and we must all of us accept that."

"All right, I understand that, too. But still—"

"Still? Yes, then, still. Still there is the question of HBO. A series of interviews is about to take place this afternoon that may determine who is to be the next Jessica Fletcher!"

"The next who?"

"Never mind. Just believe me when I tell you that these interviews may well be worth thousands of dollars in television rights, millions if the series goes to a film version, and billions if it's picked up by YouTube. These interviews cannot and will not be postponed. Ms. Duncan?"

Sylvia Duncan spoke up:

"Yes?"

"You're going to be completing your plans for the coming season quite soon I understand?"

"Yes, next month."

"And if a decision is not made very soon, even in the next few days, on the Cozy project—"

"Then we'll have to cancel it. At least for the time being."

A burst of jeering from the crowd:

"Boo! Never!"

"Keep the conference!"

"Out with the police!"

"Keep HBO!"

"*I* am Jessica!"

"No, *I* am Jessica!

"No, *I* am Jessica!"

Harriet Crossman took another step forward and said, almost desperately now:

"You can't imagine what this means to us, Officer. You have a real profession. You have real criminals to deal with; we have to make ours up. And we have to give away kittens, and—"

"All right, all right, I understand. You do realize that I can make you leave?"

"And do what? Haul away thirty women—well, thirty eight and two men—well, one man now—by force?"

T. J. Wood, who, during the interim while the corpse was being removed, had oiled down her muscular torso and was now gleaming, rose, flexing, and said sternly:

"Try it."

The officer looked at her only for a moment before he said:

"No. We won't go locking up defenseless women."

The body builder stepped into the aisle, moving menacingly toward the podium as she asked:

"What did you say? Locking up *what* kind of women?"

He shook his head, clearly more flustered now, and corrected himself:

"We won't go locking up individuals who, despite coincidental differences in gender-related preference and diversity of muscular makeup, share equally a keen desire to defend their physical, mental, and emotional well-being."

He had clearly been forced at some time in his life to take a sensitivity training course.

"Well," said C.R. Wood, returning to her seat, "that's better."

"But, there's one other thing I've got to tell all of you!"

"What is it?" asked Harriet Crossman.

"It has nothing to do with the murder. But it's a vital issue all the same."

"What is it?"

The officer was still wary of C.R. Wood. After she'd clearly seated herself and become less of a threat, he said:

"Clarence."

Uh oh, thought Nina.

"Clarence."

"Who is Clarence?"

"Clarence, ma'am, is a hurricane."

A small voice from somewhere in the middle of the crowd said:

"That's the most ridiculous name for a hurricane I've ever heard."

The officer nodded but continued:

"That may be, but the storm itself is far from ridiculous. It was first projected to come ashore in Texas, but it's changed course greatly during the last few hours, and landfall now may be somewhere between Louisiana and Mississippi."

Bay St. Lucy, Nina found herself thinking.

My bungalow.

Furl.

But Furl was with Jackson Bennet's family.

He would be okay.

Was Bay St. Lucy being evacuated?

Nothing to do about it now.

Just wait and see.

"What does this mean," Harriet Crossman was asking, "for us up here in the north of the state?"

A shake of the head:

"Hard to say. But it could well mean heavy rains, even torrential winds. Possible flooding. Sometimes the storm spawns tornadoes. We're a good distance from the Gulf but a hurricane is not to be taken lightly. Not even one named Clarence."

Harriet Crossman to Margot, who was standing next to Nina:

"Ms. Gavin, I'd assume that the plantation has gone through hurricanes before?"

Margot nodded and said:

"Yes, it has."

Nina whispered:

"Is that true?"

And Margot answered beneath her breath:

"How should I know? But we need these people's money."

"Margot! Someone *murdered* that man!"

"*I* would have murdered him if I could have. And so would you."

"But I wouldn't," Nina said quietly, "have made such a mess of it."

"You're so picky."

"And also, Ms. Gavin," Harriet was saying, "I assume we have sufficient provisions here to last out a severe storm?"

This question Margot *was* certain about.

"We can feed an army for a month."

"Excellent. Well then. The decision seems to be made, Officer Thompson. We thank you for your concerns. And we shall, of course, answer any questions that we can relating to the murder. But for now, let us proceed with the business of the convention."

And they did.

CHAPTER ELEVEN: THE PERFECT MURDER

Things began to run so smoothly after that, that Nina almost forgot what had happened.

Or *had* anything happened?

Had she not, in fact, dreamed everything?

True, various police vehicles continued to come and go, and various uniformed officers kept going up and coming down the staircase.

But no one missed Garth Amboise in the least, and so there was no weeping loved one to console.

And the business that was being taken care of at various tables in the main hall and various plantation rooms and offices—this business seemed so important, that no one seemed to be able to think of anything else.

And then, of course, there were the HBO interviews.

These were taking place in the library.

Authors came and went, their books in briefcases or valises, along with pictures of the mythical heroines and seacoast New England towns that they wrote about.

She was, in fact, thinking about taking a nap, but she went to the reception office to check with Margot before doing so.

She found her friend looking down at a small pile of papers that lay on a table before her.

"Margot?"

"Yes?" came the answer, quietly.

"Things seem to be going on okay?"

Margot nodded but did not speak.

"I wondered if you needed me for anything. I thought I might take a nap."

The same mechanical nodding.

"A nap. Yes. A nap."

What was wrong with Margot?

"Margot?"

No answer.

The gaze was still fixed on the papers before her.

"Margot, what is it?"

Only then did Margot Gavin look up, take two long strides across the room, and hand Nina the letter that she'd been reading.

"This came in the early afternoon mail."

"What is it?"

"A letter."

"From?"

"Read it yourself."

Nina took the small sheet of stationary and read:

"Dear Ms. Gavin,

It *can* be done!

I have shown you, and I have shown them all.

Now I will continue to show them until they believe me!

Molly Badger

(Author of *The Perfect Murder*)

"Margot, what in heaven's name is this?"

But Margot merely shook her head.

"I don't know any more about it than you do."

"You think this is really from Molly Badger?"

"Who else?"

"But what does she mean, 'It can be done'? What is she talking about?"

"The murder."

"Garth Amboise' murder?"

"That's the only one we've had around here in a while."

"But Molly Badger couldn't have committed that murder!"

"I would tend to agree with you, since she's been in a motel in Abbeyport since early this morning."

"You're sure of that?"

"Yes. One of the boys just brought me this letter. He said he'd gotten a call from The Woodland Inn, which is the motel where I had Molly taken. A woman asked him to drive into Abbeyport. Said that it was very important. He did, and the woman gave him this letter, asking him to bring it out here and deliver it with the rest of the morning's mail. I asked him to describe the woman. He did. And it could only be Molly Badger."

"But—shouldn't you tell the police?"

"I've sent for Thompson. In fact, he's here now."

And that was true. Police Officer Thompson had just crossed the porch and was knocking on the door of the reception room.

"Ms. Gavin?"

"Yes."

"You sent for me?"

"I did."

"What is it?"

"Come in. Read this."

He did.

And he did.

He looked up, with precisely the same expression as Nina must have had upon reading it.

"What the hell is this about?"

"I don't know."

"Where did it come from?"

"A motel in Abbeyport."

"And this woman? This Molly Badger?"

"It's a complicated story. The main thing is that she wanted to stay out here and couldn't. I got her a room at the Woodland Inn."

"What's this line, 'It can be done!'? What's that supposed to mean?"

Margot shook her head:

"I'm not certain. But she may be talking about Garth Amboise' murder."

"What could she have had to do with the murder?"

"I don't know."

"Well, I don't either. But I'm sure as hell going to find out."

"You're going into town to talk to her?"

"Of course I am!"

"Then you need to take me with you. And Nina, too."

"Why?"

Margot was silent for a time, then said:

"Have you ever dealt with self-published authors before?"

He seemed taken aback.

He was silent for a time. Finally he said, pensively:

"She's self-published?"

"Yes."

"All right. Then maybe you better come along. But as for Ms. Bannister, why—"

"She needs to come, too."

"Why?"

"She's a calm—"

"Don't say it!" interrupted Nina.

Within minutes, the three of them were in a police car, heading into Abbeyport.

The Woodland Inn sat on the south fringes of the town. It was unpretentious, clean, and well run.

There were several cabins, each painted bright green.

The motel clerk told them where to find Molly's cabin, on the end of the row.

They walked to it and knocked.

Molly Badger opened the door.

She wore a black robe, but other than that, she was much as she'd appeared that morning.

"Good morning, Ms. Gavin."

Margot nodded:

"Good morning, Molly."

"I see you got my letter."

"I did."

"And I see you brought the police."

"Yes."

"Excellent. The police will, of course, have to be involved later on. As will various members of the media. I assume you haven't told any of them yet."

"Told them what, Molly?"

"Told them about Mr. Amboise' murder."

The police officer stepped forward:

"How do you know about that, Ms. Badger?"

A delighted smile exploded across Molly Badger's face, and she exulted:

"Why, I did it!"

Silence for a time.

Then:

"Ma'am, I'm James Thompson. I'm Chief of Police here in Abbeyport."

"So happy to know you, Sir!"

"Ma'am, I have to tell you, you shouldn't be saying such things lightly. This is a very serious matter."

"I know! I'm a very serious person!"

"But what I mean is—were you here in this motel room all morning?"

"Yes! It's a delightful room. Won't you come in?"

They did.

Molly Badger asked them to sit down. Two sat on chairs, and one sat on the neatly-made bed.

There was also a desk in the room. On it sat a laptop computer.

"I've made some tea; would you like some?"

They each accepted a cup of tea, which Molly poured, saying:

"Isn't this nice? I'm a *cozy* murderess!"

James Thompson took a sip of tea, then shook his head and said:

"Again, Ms. Badger"

"Oh, you can call me Molly! The whole world will be calling me Molly after the book comes out!"

Margot:

"Which book, Molly?"

"Why, *The Perfect Murder*, the one that I'm writing now. Well, 'dramatizing,' is perhaps a better word!"

"All right then, Molly," said James Thompson. "Molly, you need to be careful how you talk about these things."

"Oh, I'm always careful. I'm nothing if not careful."

"What do you mean by saying that you committed the murder?"

"I mean that I did commit it. That's what I mean by saying that I did commit it."

Nina had meant to keep silent through all of this, especially since no calming influence seemed to be needed at the moment.

She could not, though, and so, leaning forward, she asked:

"Molly, have you been here in the motel all morning?"

"Yes! I got here just after dawn. The nice boy dropped me off and the people in the motel office were waiting for me. You were so nice in making these arrangements, Ms. Gavin. I do thank you so."

"Nothing to thank me for, Molly."

"Oh, there definitely is. Most definitely!"

Then, to James Thompson:

"The other writers wouldn't let me stay in the plantation house with them. I'm self-published you know."

He nodded, and said quietly:

"I know that, ma'am. I'm sorry."

"Oh, it's all right. It's only a temporary condition, being self-published."

"I'm sure it is."

"And now it will all be different. For I've committed the perfect murder. Oh, I wrote perfect murders for years. And the publishers continued to reject my submissions, saying the murder methods were 'incredible' and 'unbelievable.' They even said that I was crazy."

Then, looking at Margot, she asked:

"Why *will* they say that I am mad?"

"That," said Nina quietly, "is a line from a Boris Karloff movie."

"Oh. Well, it doesn't matter. I'm *not* mad; I'm just cozy."

"Is there," Margot asked, "that much difference between the two of them?"

"What?"

"Nothing, Molly."

"And they will all realize that I'm a great writer, with wonderful murder methods that have never been written about before, not even by Agatha and Jessica and Janet and, well, not *any* of them. And they will publish my murders and, as God is my witness, I'll *never* be self-published again!"

Now I'm definitely going to be sick, thought Nina.

But she said nothing.

It was James Thompson who spoke, saying:

"The point is, Ms. Badger—"

"Molly, remember?"

"All right, the point is, Molly, the murder occurred at around ten o'clock this morning."

"I know."

"In Garth Amboise' room."

"I know."

"His skin was shredded, and his body mutilated."

"I know."

"How do you know, Molly?"

"Because I'm smart. I'm a genius, actually. I understand all about electronic devices. I was an electronics engineer, you know, before God came to me in a vision and told me that I was to become a Cozy Writer. That's the highest thing a person can be, you know—a Cozy Writer."

"I'm sure that's true, Molly, but the question is: how could you have committed this terrible, ghastly, bloody murder, if you were here all morning?"

"That's the question, isn't it?"

"Yes, ma'am. How did you do it?"

But Molly Badger merely shook her head:

"Won't tell, won't tell!"

Silence for a time, then Molly Badger held her index finger in front of her sealed lips and whispered:

"It's my secret. That's why it's the perfect murder method. No one can figure it out. Not ever. It's never been done before."

"Molly—"

"But if I told you now, then you'd simply take me away. And you would tell no one. You'd simply say that I was crazy. But none of the cameras would come. And I wouldn't be published, after all. And that would be so sad. All of those people would have died for nothing."

Something about this sentence froze Nina, who asked:

"What people?"

And Molly Badger looked at her:

"Why, the rest of them."

"The rest of whom?"

"The rest of those people out at The Candles. The writers. The ones who didn't want me. Oh, I'm not that vindictive. I'm not planning to kill them just because they rejected me. No, it's still sad, them having to die. And with so much blood."

She shook her head:

"But it's the only way, don't you see? The murders will keep happening. And HBO will be there to record it. And then I'll tell them how I did it. And I'll be the most famous murder mystery writer in the world. Because I will have committed—several times over—the most perfect murder in the world."

They all sat for a time in silence.

Finally, James Thompson stood up, gestured to Margot and Nina, and spoke to Molly Badger.

He said:

"Molly, will you excuse us for just a second?"

"Of course."

"We're just going outside a minute to talk about this."

"Help yourself."

They did go outside.

Margot asked:

"Well?"

James Thompson shrugged:

"Well what?"

"What are you going to do? Are you going to arrest her?"

"Arrest her for what?"

"For murder."

He seemed exasperated.

"Let me see if I've got this straight. I'm supposed to arrest this woman for the murder of Garth Amboise? She was here in this motel room, seven miles away!"

"Well, we don't exactly know that."

"No. But she was here early this morning and she's here now. So you're saying she just trotted up the road and murdered the man and turned around and trotted back?"

"No, she could have gotten hold of a car."

"So she drove out to Candles. Walked in, unseen by anybody, climbed the stairway, went in the room, tore all the skin off a man who was bigger and stronger than she was, went out of the door, then got back into the car she'd somehow gotten hold of, drove back to her motel room, and wrote and had delivered a letter saying she'd committed the murder."

Silence for a time.

Then Margot:

"I suppose that might be hard to prove."

James Thompson nodded, then said:

"The woman's obviously crazy as a bedbug."

"So what are you going to do about her? Take her in?"

"On what charge? Writing a letter?"

"But if she's crazy—"

He nodded:

"She's crazy all right. But that's not against the law, and, given that she's a writer, it's probably a help to her. No, the best I can do is this. We'll post an officer outside the motel here, to kind of keep an eye on her. We don't want her wandering off and maybe getting hit by a car. I'll send a court psychiatrist out her to talk to her. He can at least make a recommendation as to whether or not she's a danger to herself or anybody else."

"All right."

"All right."

It was not all right, thought Nina.

Nor was the weather all right, since the dark clouds heralding Clarence, the Cross-Eyed Hurricane, were beginning to roll across the sky.

None of these things were all right.

They were, in fact, all wrong.

But just how wrong—this she was yet to learn.

CHAPTER TWELVE: THE COZY WRITERS EXPLAIN
HOW THE PERFECT MURDER WAS COMMITTED

When the three of them returned to Candles, they were
met in the driveway by a fresh-faced young officer who said
to his superior:
"Chief, there's a bunch of people lined up to talk to you."
Thompson, who'd just gotten out of the squad car, used a
red handkerchief to mop the back of his neck.
"What kind of people?"
"The writers."
"What do they want to talk to me about?"
A shake of the head:
"I don't know. They won't talk to any of the rest of us."
"How many of them want to talk to me?"
"All of them."
"*All* of them?"
"Yes, Sir. That's what it looks like."
"Where are they?"
"They're all lined up outside one of the rooms that used
to be a kind of parlor."
"All right. Lead me to them."
They went across the porch and into the house.
Harriet Crossman met them in the corridor.
"Harriet," asked Margot, "what's going on?"
"The writers. Each of them has come up with the
solution."
Thompson frowned:
"The solution to what?"
They turned a corner and saw a line of people standing
patiently, most of them texting.
"What are they doing?" he asked.
"Oh, they're writing. It's such a unique experience
actually to have a real murder to write about. The fastest of

them should finish their novels any time now—they've been at it for more than two hours."

"This is unbelievable."

Harriet Crossman shook her head:

"No, that's the most unforgivable sin a cozy writer can commit. It has to be believable. That's why all of them are waiting to talk to you."

"Me? What do they want to tell me?"

"Why, the solution. The murder method. And, of course, the identity of the killer."

"But my people have been working for hours up in that room! I've just been in radio contact with my chief forensics guy—he hasn't come up with a shred of evidence!"

Harriet Crossman merely smiled:

"You policemen are always hard-working and sincere. But we all know you're not really very smart. Not when it comes to matching wits with a clever murderer. No, the only person who can really do that is a seventy-year-old retired woman."

"Ms. Crossman, I don't mean to be rude, but—"

"Please, Officer Thompson. So few 'teachable moments' such as this come our way!"

"All right, all right. I suppose I can at least listen to what they have to say. Who's first in the line?"

"I have the list written down here. First there's Rebeccah Thornwhipple. Her heroine is ninety-two-years old and still is able to—"

"Okay, okay, let's get on with it."

They made their way through the line, speaking to this writer and that, and trying not to disturb the incessant typing. Nina thought at first that the coziests were replying to them, but then she realized that they were only muttering out loud their dialogue before writing it down on paper, or, in this case, in digital space.

"Excuse me, ma'am—"

"Belinda Boxworthy sipped her second cup of tea, gazed out over the stormy New England coastline, and tried to see how Andrew could have brought the sixty razor blades—"

And:

"Pardon us, ma'am, while we get through here into the parlor—"

"Ms. Chutsworthy might have been old, but she was sly as a fox, and she knew that the police officer who had so discarded her theories concerning the mutilation—and the fiendish mind that had concocted it—was long on good intentions but short on brainpower! So as she walked along the deserted beach and saw clouds envelop the old Nantucket lighthouse—"

Etc. etc. etc.

Finally, they were seated in the parlor, a table before them and a huge picture window behind. Through the window, Nina could see gray clouds scudding over the sky, and rain droplets beginning to spatter on the glass.

"All right. Send this Thornwhipple woman in."

The small, white-haired woman entered and sat down.

"I'm Rebeccah Thornwhipple. The name of my heroine is—"

"That's all right."

"Her cat is named—"

James Thompson interrupted:

"I'm sorry to rush you, ma'am, but I believe you have something to tell us in relation to the crime that's been committed?"

"Yes, I certainly do."

"Well, then?"

"I know how it was done. And I know who did it."

"How do you know these things, Ms. Thornwhipple?"

A smile.

"Logic. Deduction. When one looks at the facts—I mean truly examines them—there is only one possible theory of the crime and one possible culprit."

"And who is that? Who did it?"

Rebeccah Thornwhipple turned, so that she was looking straight at Nina, and proclaimed:

"*She* did it!"

There was silence in the room for a time.

This is not happening, thought Nina.

It can't be happening.

But it was happening, of course. It was reality. And reality, as Nina had learned in recent months and years, could be utterly preposterous and still go on being reality, since God was the only true self-published writer, and the only one guaranteed to get everything into print.

And made into movies, for that matter.

"I'm sorry," she found herself stammering.

But Rebeccah Thornwhipple merely shook her head:

"It's no good, Ms. Bannister—if that really is your name."

"Of course, it's my name! It's always been my name!"

"We'll see about that!"

"We don't have to see about it! We already know it!"

"Nina," said Margot, "take it easy."

"But she's accusing me of murder!"

Rebeccah Thornwhipple continued to shake her head and smile:

"*I'm* not accusing you, my dear. The facts are accusing you."

"*What* facts?"

James Thompson leaned forward in his chair and growled:

"Yes, ma'am. What facts are you speaking of? Please explain this theory of yours."

A request to which the elderly white-haired lady was all too eager to respond.

"I believe, Ms. Bannister, you took the late Mr. Amboise his breakfast? I know because I saw you ascending the staircase, and then, some minutes later, two boys going up behind you."

"Right. One of the boys carried a decanter of coffee and the other a box containing some of the publishers' gifts: shirts, matching medallions and cat collar charms, things like that."

"And the two boys left before you opened the door?"

"Yes, I told them to."

"And why was that, my dear?"

Nina thought for a while, and asked herself:

I didn't really kill him, did I? I would have remembered, wouldn't I?

And yet it was starting to sound bad for her.

"I told the boys to leave because I wasn't really looking forward to confronting Mr. Amboise."

"And why not? Did you hate him? Did you detest him?"

"Of course not."

Hearing this, Rebeccah Thornwhipple settled back in her chair, folded her hands neatly in front of her, smiled an immensely smug smile, and said, softly:

"No. No, you didn't detest him, did you?"

"Of course not."

Then the woman sprang forward in the chair and shouted:

"Because you were in love with him!"

Silence for a time.

Several of the other writers had crowded into the room. Nina could hear soft voices murmuring:

"That's good!"

"I didn't think of that—did you think of that?"

And, in the midst of all this tension and shock, Margot began to laugh.

Actually cackle more than laugh.

Nina turned on her:

"What are *you* laughing at?" she shouted.

But Margot merely kept on guffawing, and trying to get her breath.

"You! Having an affair with Garth Amboise! Oh, my God, I think I'm going to die!"

Nina felt certain concerning the intensity of her anger, but somewhat unsure as to its object. She did not know, in short, if she were angrier at Rebeccah Thornwhipple for accusing her of murder, or at Margot for thinking it impossible.

"Why," she muttered, "couldn't I have an affair if I wanted to? I mean if a ninety-two-year-old woman can do it in an iron lung—"

"Now wait a minute," said Officer Thompson. "Ma'am, do you have any evidence to support the belief that Ms. Bannister here was having an affair with this man?"

A shake of the head:

"Logic, my dear officer. 'Once you rule out the impossible, whatever remains, however improbable, must be the truth.' I believe it was Janet Evanovich who said that."

"It was Sherlock Holmes," growled Nina.

But Rebeccah Thornwhipple merely smiled and shook her head:

"Try not to be angry with me, my dear. Surely you must have realized that these facts were destined to come to light in time. Why not simply confess everything now? The awful burden of the secrets you've been carrying around will be lifted, and you can tell your side of the story. He was trying to break off the relationship, wasn't he? He told you this when you delivered his food. You were outraged, but you acted calmly. You suggested one more act of passionate love-making. You told him it was to be a final good bye, but to yourself you meant it as a last ditch possibility to change his mind. So you entered the room with the breakfast dishes, tore your clothes off, had mad, passionate, stinking sex for half an hour, perhaps more. After it was over, you begged him to keep the relationship alive. You told him you would meet him anywhere in the country, anywhere in the world. But he refused. He refused! And so you attacked him! He was already nude, and his skin simply shredded beneath the incessant stabs of the foot-long butcher knife you'd brought inside the scrambled eggs platter."

The last sentence exhausted her supply of breath.

The writers jammed in the doorway were scribbling notes.

James Thompson was staring, open-mouthed.

Margot had stuck her head between her knees and was laughing convulsively.

"Be quiet, Margot," muttered Nina.

But Margot only shook her head and continued to guffaw in restrained gasps and sobs.

Finally, she regained sufficient self-control to ask:

"But Nina was with me for the entire morning. We watched the first business session together."

Another shake of the woman's head:

"Now, now. It's touching, Ms. Gavin, but it simply won't do."

"What won't do?" asked Margot.

"Ms. Bannister is your friend, is she not?"

"Yes."

"Could we not even say, your best friend?"

"Yes," answered Margot.

"Until now," whispered Nina.

Margot ignored this.

Rebeccah Thornwhipple leaned forward and whispered:

"Then isn't it time you stopped lying for her?"

Margot could only shake her head:

"I'm not—"

But she was interrupted:

"Everyone else in the room was worried about the meeting! No one was watching you and your desperately lovesick friend here! No one noticed when she slipped away. No one noticed her hour's absence, or the fact that she was covered with sweat when she returned."

James Thompson shook his head and said:

"Ms. Thornwhipple, it's an interesting theory, and, of course, we'll look into it."

"You're going to arrest her, aren't you?"

"We'll certainly keep close tabs on her."

"I would think so. And remember, I'm copywriting this plot."

"It's all yours, ma'am. I can promise you that no one in my department is going to submit it for publication."

"See that you do not."

"Yes, ma'am. But now if you don't mind—"

"I know. There are others who have theories. But just remember what I've said, and always remember P. D. James' immortal words: 'Once you eliminate the impossible, whatever remains, however improbable, must be the truth.'"

"It's Sherlock Holmes," said Nina.

Rebeccah Thornwhipple rose, took two steps toward the door, and smiled down at her:

"Don't be angry at me, dear. And do confess. You'll feel much better in the long run."

As she entered the doorway she was mobbed by other cozy writers, who embraced her and congratulated her:

"GREAT JOB!"

"NICE PLOT DEVICES!"

"CAN I USE THAT?"

After a time, James Thompson said to Harriet Crossman:

"Are they all like that?"

"I don't know."

"All right then, Ms. Crossman. I'll listen to these people, because it's my job to do so. But please tell them: if they have a theory of the crime, it needs to be based on hard, practical, believable evidence. Will you do that?"

"Of course."

Harriet Crossman went and spoke with the cozy writers who were standing patiently in line, some already finishing the novels they'd begun little more than two hours before.

She re-entered the room and said:

"They understand. Cold, hard logic."

"All right. Who's next?"

"These two ladies."

The Smathers sisters, Ruby and Lacy, entered the room.

"The killing," they began, "was done by a demon. He entered our dimension through a psychic rift in the cosmos which occurred when the ghost of Sarah Morgan returned to—"

James Thompson said nothing.

He merely rose, heaved a sigh, and left the room.

CHAPTER THIRTEEN: WITNESSES' ACCOUNTS, AND AN INTERLUDE WITH RED WINE

Nina was not booked for the brutal murder of Garth Amboise.

She was, however, invited to share the findings of Police Chief James Thompson concerning the psychological status of Molly Badger.

This conversation happened in the library where the HBO interviews between Sylvia Duncan and all interested cozy writers had been taking place during the day.

The interviews being over now, the small and intimate library was free.

The three of them—Margot, Nina, and Thompson—sat in green leather chairs, all contact with the outside world blocked by thick curtains.

Still, if the outside world was not visible, it was certainly audible, because the storm had arrived in earnest now, with driving rain and howling wind pounding on the Candles' walls.

"I want to apologize to both of you ladies for walking out on that group of people this afternoon."

"And I want to apologize to you," Nina said, "to you both actually, for murdering Mr. Amboise."

It was the first time she'd seen James Thompson smile.

"Don't give it another thought. I'm sure you were upset."

"At least we know," said Margot, "that it wasn't a demon. Although, Nina, you can be kind of demon-like at times."

"Damned straight."

Thompson:

"I can take all of that palaver. But when those two women started on about demons—"

Margot merely nodded:

"We heard the same story a little earlier in the day."

"I'll go back—I'll listen to all of them, because they're potential witnesses, and I've got to hear them out. But I have to take a little rest, I really do."

They merely sat for a time as the storm grew louder, and the entire house, despite its size, seemed to be shaking.

"I don't like all these people being holed up out here like this," said Officer Thompson. "I'd feel a lot better if they were all in town."

"They won't go, though," said Margot

And that was true.

So there was really nothing to do

Thompson finally continued:

"Since the two of you are already involved in this, I thought the least I could do was keep you informed on what we've learned."

"Thank you," said Nina, quietly. "We appreciate it."

"We were able to get someone from the city hospital to go out and talk to Ms. Badger at the motel. He's not exactly a registered psychologist, but he does have some credentials along those lines. We've used him several times in the past to get his feelings on whether someone is actually mentally ill or not, especially in cases where we feel the suspect might be a danger to self or loved ones."

"So what," asked Margot, "did this man think?"

A shake of the head:

"Well, before I get into that, I should let you know what we've dug up concerning her background. She's a genius, in a way. Great grades in college, especially in science courses. She worked for some years at a major communications corporation. But she was let go."

"Why?" asked Nina.

"We haven't been able to find out. The records are not clear. It may be the corporation just wanted to put the whole thing behind them."

"What whole thing?"

"Again, hard to say. But when an employee needs to be let go, well, sometimes there's no more than an amicable parting of the ways. Maybe an under the table final settlement. No risk of a lawsuit that way."

"All right. So she was let go," said Margot, "and we don't know why. Is she crazy?"

A shrug.

"All of these people seem crazy, as far as I can tell. But she apparently had a nice, lucid conversation with our man. When the subject of the murder came up, she refused to discuss it, saying it was not 'the proper time.' Otherwise, she seems quite calm, and he feels she's at no risk to hurt herself. Nor does she seem anxious to leave town."

"You don't think you should arrest her?"

A shake of the head:

"I can't see doing it. She's admitted to a crime she couldn't possibly have committed. Her version of things is no wackier than the Thornwhipple woman's, and we aren't going to arrest her. Or you because of her. No, I just want this damned storm to pass. Then I want to have a complete battery of lab tests done. Then I want these damned people out of here. Well, I've got to go now. I'll try to keep you apprised as to what's going on."

"Thank you, officer," they both answered as one.

And so James Thompson left the room, returning to his duties of hearing confessions, or at least alternative theories of the case.

He was replaced almost immediately, however, by a weary-looking Sylvia Duncan, who entered and said:

"I'm sorry to disturb the two of you. I'd just left a few of my notes over there on the desk. If I can get them, I'll get out of your way."

"That's all right," said Margot, gesturing toward the chair vacated by the officer. "Sit down, and join us."

"I don't want to be in the way."

"You're not in the way. In fact...wait a minute. I have an idea. Let me go get some things."

Margot rose and crossed the small library, while Sylvia Duncan sat and smiled at Nina.

"Ms. Bannister, we haven't really had a chance to talk."

"No, you've been busy."

"And so have you, murdering that man."

"So you've heard about that."

"Of course. In fact, Ms. Thornwhipple pitched it as her series proposal."

"Wow. Who's going to play me?"

Sylvia Duncan smiled:

"I don't know. Maybe Jennifer Anniston."

"In her dreams."

"Yes, you may be right. At any rate, I was very excited once I learned that you were here."

"Excited?"

"Yes, I'm a great fan of yours. I was and am a great supporter of the Lissie movement."

"Oh! Well, sometimes all of that, Washington and the rest—it seems like another world. I can't believe it all happened to me."

"But it did. And we have a good many new women in Congress because of it."

"I'm just—"

She was interrupted by Margot, who was re-entering the library with a bottle of wine in one hand and a small black box in the other.

"We're three hard-working women, and we've had a tough day. And we deserve these things."

Nina:

"What have you got there?"

The reply:

"A bottle of Chateau Margaux '86. Not really named after me, but close enough. If you'll reach into the cabinet drawer behind you, you'll find glasses.

Nina did, and did.

The glasses were distributed around the table. Margot had already uncorked the bottle, and so nothing remained except to pour the dark red liquid.

"Well, this is a treat!" said Sylvia. "What shall we drink to?"

"Not so fast," interrupted Margot, pointing to the small box, which she'd laid on the table.

"There's more. If we're going to be bad, why not be really bad?"

She opened the box, which revealed a dozen or so cigarettes.

"Oh, my God," said Sylvia, giving a small shriek.

"I haven't smoked in two weeks," said Margot.

"And I," added Sylvia, "in a year!"

"And I never," said Nina.

Margot:

"Well, we're not going to make a smoker of you, Nina. But you, Sylvia—"

"Oh, yes, yes, after today, definitely yes!"

And so the two women lit up, joyfully, conspiratorially, and blew out thick clouds of smoke which hung in the dark air of the library.

Then they all held the glasses of wine out over the table, while Margot asked:

"Now, what shall we drink to?"

Sylvia answered immediately:

"The end of the damned interviews!"

Both responded simultaneously:

"THE END OF THE INTERVIEWS!"

And they drank.

After which Margot asked:

"Were they really that bad?"

Sylvia shook her head:

"They weren't really that awful. They just all seemed to run together after a while. If I hear about one more quaint New England village or one more clever librarian—"

"I know," said Margot. "There does seem to be quite a lot of that floating around."

"Have you made," asked Nina, "your choice?"

"No, not quite yet. But I will. And I will soon, because I'm announcing it tonight after dinner."

"That fast?"

"It has to be. The schedule is very tight. I'm flying out of Chicago tomorrow afternoon for the coast, and we'll start initial production work later on this month."

"But you haven't," Margot asked, "made up your mind yet?"

A shake of the head:

"I've narrowed it down some, but, to tell you the truth, no one clear winner steps out to me. It's all like, been there, done that. There needs to be something unique about this show, and I haven't quite felt it yet."

"Well," said Nina, "it will come to you."

"Maybe. But now let's talk about something else."

And so they did.

In weeks and months to come, Nina was to remember the next moments, the next half hour, the next hour or more, as a kind of haze. She remembered that the storm raged ever harder outside and the walls could be heard shaking even more ominously; she remembered that the dim electric light in the library gave way to the glow of long white candles produced by Margot from some table or some desk; and she remembered that the first bottle of red wine gave way to a second, as the hours of tension dissolved into moments of lovely release, and the women poured forth their souls to each other, having found three islands of sanity in a cozy-sea of nuttiness.

The first to unburden was Sylvia.

She told about her early days in radio, and about the menial jobs she'd been asked to do, and which she'd performed with the earnestness and dedication that might be expected from any fresh-faced college graduate (She had, of course, mentioned which college, but, later on, Nina had never been able to remember it.). She went on to describe the slow growth of her career, the decision never to marry (though there had been offers), and the equally difficult decision to avoid as a matter of principle those sexual advances which might have meant faster promotions, but at dear costs. She talked about the move from radio to television, the first jobs of real responsibility, the thirty-hour days and nights, the pieces of pure luck, the men and women who were worth working with and why, the great moments, the not so great moments, and the terrifying moments which could have meant the end of everything—herself included—

—and that was the end of one bottle of wine.

The ashtray was beginning to fill up.

The storm raged outside.

Nina and Sylvia and Margot simply sat in the smoky and leather-colored library, surrounded by the friends that were old and musty books, sipping the old and musty wine, and, improbably, narrating their own lives as though it were a stormy night in the English countryside, and old Faversham was telling his favorite ghost story.

Next to come was Margot.

She described the youth of a privileged child, the years in private schools, the summers spent in Europe—

—and all of this took about a minute and a half.

Then her real life began.

It began at Berkeley, of course, and in the mid- sixties.

It began with the first protest marches, the rock concerts, the drugs, the arrests, the fervent hatred of authorities; then the affairs with various musicians, the harder drugs, the nights spent in jail, the visits by horrified parents, the decision to leave school, the decision to paint, the move to New York City, the loft apartment, the first wave of lovers, the second wave of lovers—

—and finally the first job at The Philadelphia Museum of Art.

Then the job at the Metropolitan Museum of Art in New York.

Then better and better jobs at the same museum, all of which Margot described with the brevity and casualness with which she'd talked of her youth.

Making Nina realize that her old friend, with all her ability and brilliance, would—if given a choice—still have preferred being transferred back in time, to the streets of Haight-Ashbury and the backs of vans painted with 'Get Out of Viet Nam' logos and the pot-reeking acres that were to house Woodstock.

And all that took a second bottle of wine.

None of them had a clear idea of what time it was.

Late afternoon, probably.

Dinner would have to be prepared, but, of course, dinner was being prepared.

Everything that was supposed to be done was being done. And so it became Nina's turn.

And since she was now living *The Wizard of Oz*, she had no choice but to admit who she really was.

She was not really Toto.

Furl was Toto.

No, she was Dorothy.

She lived on a farm with Auntie Em and her uncle and some hired men and a dog.

She had the most uneventful, middle class, perfectly prim and proper childhood that anyone could ever have imagined.

She told briefly of Frank, of meeting him in high school, of their marriage, of her first years teaching, and then more years teaching, and Frank's growing career as an attorney in Bay St. Lucy, of weekly bridge games with friends–

—and just as she was about to say, 'There's nothing more to say," Margot brought up Eve Ivory and the tale of the Robinson Mansion.

Well, yes, of course there was that.

Three bottles of wine was too much.

That would mean each of them would have drunk a whole bottle apiece.

Can't have that.

But maybe one glass out of the third bottle—

Which she accepted.

Then Margot brought up Helen Reddington and the Fabulous New York *Hamlet* production in little old Bay St. Lucy, and all of the things that had happened with that.

Well, yes, there was all of that.

Which Nina described in as much detail as she was able to remember.

But that did lead, of course, to the tales of Nina as basketball coach. And April van Osdale and the strange Max Lirpa and what had happened to the two of them.

Which Nina also described in as much detail as she was able to remember.

But that led to the tale of Aquatica, the huge off-shore oil drilling rig.

And Nina's role in saving the Gulf Coast of the United States.

Of this story there was simply too much detail to remember.

But she did what she could.

Not another glass.

Oh, all right.

And then there were the adventures in international art smuggling.

She had to talk a bit about those.

And the wonderful city of Graz.

And, of course, Carol Walker.

Where, she wondered, was Carol now?

Still on her estate, still watching the flowers dance on the Monet?

But then something had to be said about Washington. And about the Lissie movement.

And, of course, it was.

And then the third bottle was empty!

CHAPTER FOURTEEN: AND THE KILLER IS—

Five p.m. found her in her room.

She needed a nap.

She had needed a nap two hours earlier, but then there had been that letter from Molly Badger, and the ride into Abbeyport, and the strange interview.

Then she'd been accused of murdering Garth Amboise.

Then she'd gotten high on red wine with Sylvia and Margot—

—always something or other.

But now she was alone and exhausted, and there was nothing to prevent her from hurling herself, sweatshirt and jean-clad as she was, like a sack of wet cement on the wondrously thick bed comforter that subsumed her like a warm flannel bath.

There was nothing at all that could bother her now.

The storm raging outside.

The ticking of the standing clock.

THERE WAS NOTHING TO STOP HER FROM TAKING A NAP!

Except the knock on the door.

Knock. Knock. Knock.

For an instant she simply closed her eyes yet more tightly.

It would go away, wouldn't it?

It was a dream.

Who would be outside her door? Who would be responsible for the sounds that kept coming.

Knock. Knock. Knock.

It would not go away.

So she flipped over, sat up, stared at the doorway, stared through the doorway, and said in telepathy:

"Go and hang yourself. Go and throw yourself into the sea."

Hoping that the mental messages would penetrate wood, penetrate flesh, penetrate bone—

—death.

This did not happen.

Knock. Knock. Knock.

She would have to use a real voice.

This voice would say something so vicious, so cutting, so terrifying, that it would destroy whoever was standing out there.

And so she said:

"Yes?"

In a kind of lilting way that Nina had.

An answer came.

"I'm sorry to bother you, Ms. Bannister. May I come in?"

No no no no no no no no…

"Of course!"

And the door opened.

It was Harriet Crossman.

"I've disturbed your rest."

Well duuuuh!

"Not at all."

"I can come back later."

"No, this is fine. Come in. Sit down."

"If you're sure—"

"Of course. I'll join you. We can sit at that desk over by the window."

And, after a moment or so, that is where they found themselves.

By the window and not by the bed.

Which had been so wonderful, so delicious.

But here she was, sitting in a chair, listening to Harriet Crossman say:

"I wanted to apologize for this afternoon."

"For what?"

"Your being accused of murder."

"Oh, posh. I'm always being accused of murder. Don't think anything about it."

"Our members have such fertile imaginations."

"Well, that's one word for your members' imaginations."

"I know quite well you did not go into Garth Amboise' room this morning and have mad, stinking sex."

"Thank you."

"Because I know who did."

The storm.

The clock.

Two cats made their way in from one corner of the room, fought viciously for a few seconds of hissing and spewing and clawing and biting, then left through the small trap door on the other side of the room.

"What?"

"I know who had mad, stinking sex with Garth Amboise."

"Who?"

"Me."

"You!"

"Yes."

Well, what do you know about that?

Harriet Crossman.

The same person who had, lo these many years, been going to bed with Professor Brighton Dunbury.

The woman, Nina found herself thinking, *is a gerbil.*

"It was, in fact, almost exactly as Rebeccah Thornwhipple described it. I went up to his room between the end of breakfast and the beginning of the first session. I knew it would probably be no help because...well, some months ago, Garth had made up his mind. I was simply too old for him."

Be quiet, Stupid Nina, Smart Nina said to Stupid Nina.

"How did you meet him in the first place?" Stupid Nina asked, refusing the advice.

A shrug.

"In New York City, actually. Garth was there to accept some award or other. He was always winning awards, you know."

"I saw his resume."

"Yes. He has a splendid resume. It's such a beautiful thing. I fell in love with his resume, even before I ever came to know him. I have a copy of it, in my bedroom. I shall always keep it, along with a lock of his hair."

"Well, they can't take that away from you. Either of those things, actually."

"No. And I told myself that no one could take Garth, either. And no one could take him away from me. Except for Garth himself though. And he did. So I went to his room. And I threw myself at him. Gave myself to him, one last time. And do you know what?"

"No what?"

"He laughed at me."

"Son of a ...."

She hesitated, then said:

"... gun."

Harriet Crossman was obviously on the verge of tears.

"I was enraged. I've never hated another human being so intensely in my life."

Nina hardly knew how to phrase the next question.

She simply knew that it had to be phrased.

"So, did you..."

The woman looked at her in a puzzled way for an instant, then recoiled in horror:

'Oh, no! No, no, a thousand times no! I may have hated Garth at that moment, but I would never have murdered him. Even now, when I think of all that blood—that someone could have done that to him..."

Okay, said Nina to herself, *so you didn't kill him. Good. Why are you telling me all of this?*

"I don't know why I'm telling you all of this."

So, that question answered.

"It's just that I feel I can trust you. You're a kind of…"

If you say 'comforting presence,' I'll barf.

"…a kind of comforting presence."

"You're so kind to say that!"

"It's true, my dear. Already I feel so much better for telling someone about this."

"I'm glad that I can help."

"You are a help. A great help. Just to listen the way you do. I hope Officer Thompson is as good a listener, when I tell him my story."

"Are you sure you have to tell him?"

"Yes. Now or later. You see, I'm certain my fingerprints are all over the bed frame."

"Why would your fingerprints be all over the…"

"Don't go into it."

"Sorry."

Once again Nina found herself thinking:

Gerbils.

"And so I shall tell him my story. I can only pray he believes it."

"I'm sure he will."

"Perhaps, perhaps not. But there is one more thing. One thing that I must tell him, and that he absolutely must believe."

"What thing?"

Harriet Crossman leaned forward:

"Someone else had been in that room before me!"

I have, Nina found herself thinking, *an immense respect for Garth Amboise.*

Talk about a resume!

"There was a scent, an aroma."

"Perfume?"

"Yes. Garth would occasionally wear cologne, like when he flew to Paris to receive the Coco Chanel Award for Best

First Novel Promoting the Cause of French Fashion. But this was a woman's scent. Also I found, in the bed, a nail."

"A fingernail?"

"Yes, a long false nail. And it began to dawn on me: whatever woman had been there earlier in the morning could have come back. And with those nails…"

"You think fingernails could have done that much damage?"

"It depends on the woman. In one of C. R. Robertson's latest books, *Blood on the Glass Ceiling,* Patty Parity discovers a corporation in which men are being paid higher wages than women, even though they're doing the same job. She disguises herself as a secretary—long nails, lipstick, you know—succeeds in finding two of the chauvinist board members in a meeting room, and, when they make a pass at her…"

"I think I understand."

"Now I'm not saying it's a cozy novel. But it has sold a great many copies."

"I'm sure."

"There is talk of Patty Parity being played by Jennifer Anniston."

A thought appeared in Nina's mind, and she let it come out:

"Harriet, do you think C. R. Roberts could have been responsible for Garth's death? I mean, clearly he exploits women. He's every true feminist's worst nightmare. She's very muscular, but perhaps he might have found that attractive."

Harriet thought for a time:

"It's possible, but the body was all in one piece."

"I see."

"If it had been dismembered…"

"No, it was just a passing thought."

Harriet smiled and said:

"Well, you're not a cozy writer. No, I don't believe it was C. R. But I do believe a woman was there, and I believe she may have made love to Garth. If, spurred on by whatever passion, she was driven to come back…well, anything might have happened."

Harriet Crossman looked at her watch.

"My heavens, it's half past five. There will be dinner, then the evening session, and, of course, the HBO Award. Strange, isn't it? So very strange. It was to be a kind of crowning glory for the Guild, and a moment I would never forget. And now—now I can only think of Garth. He's gone. And I can only think the same thing, over and over. I can only think: I've never hated a loved one quite so much!"

"That's so moving."

"Good-bye for a time, Ms. Bannister. And thank you for listening."

And so saying, Harriet Crossman left the room.

Five minutes passed.

Harriet Crossman was definitely gone.

AND NOW THERE WAS NOTHING TO STOP HER FROM TAKING A NAP!

Except the knock on the door.

Knock. Knock. Knock.

For an instant she simply closed her eyes yet more tightly.

It would go away, wouldn't it?

Etc., etc., etc.

"Yes?"

An answer came.

"I'm sorry to bother you, Ms. Bannister. May I come in?"

No no no no no no no No no no no no no no No no no no no no no No no no no no no no No no no no no no no No no no no no no no No no no no no no no No no no no no no no No no no no no no no No no no no no no no No no No no no no no no no No no no no no no no No no no no no No no no no no no no No no no no no no no No no no no no no no No no no no no no no No no no no no no no No no no no no no no No no no no no no no No no no no no no no No no no no no no no No no no no no no no No no no no no no no No no no no no no no No no no no no no no No no no no no no no No no no no no no no No no no no no no no No no no no no no no No no No no no no no no no No no no no no no no…

"Of course!"
And the door opened.
It was Suzy Maples.
"I've disturbed your rest."
Well duuuuh!
"Not at all."
"I can come back later."
"No, this is fine. Come in. Sit down."
"If you're sure—"
"Of course. I'll join you. We can sit at that desk over by the window."
And they sat by the window and not the bed and—
—etc., etc., etc.
"I'm Suzy Maples. I write the Chrissie Oakton Mysteries. Chrissie is young and beautiful, and takes part constantly in beauty pageants. All of the murders she solves take place at such pageants, and the victims are always beauty queens. The cat is a beautifully groomed Siamese named Skipples."
"Your cat?"
"No, Chrissie's cat. My cat is a Siamese named Whiskers."
Oh yes, Nina remembered. *The one that was humping Sluggo, the plantation cat.*
Nina attempted to rid her mind of that image by looking more closely at Suzy Maples and noting how she was dressed:
She wore an Armani Colleziani sleeveless pique dress, over which hung a Helmut Lang 'eroded threads' sweater, the dress cinched at the waist by a liquid satin chain-embellished caviar-flash belt (from the St. John Collection). Underneath the dress, she wore (Nina could only assume) a Cosabella x Erin Fetherston unlined underwire bra, Wacoal 'retro chic' high cut briefs, and a star power by Spanx 'Lady Luxe' super slimming slip. Around her neck was a tasteful Etro double-sided floral/paisley scarf (white on dark green), and from her ears hung two Alexis Bittar 'lucite-dust' long-leaf statement aqua-marine earrings, which set off beautifully her delicately applied rouge (Koh-Gen do mai fan shi fresh-face cheek color Oro 2-Mandarin orange). Her

long fingernails were Deborah Lippmann 'Magic in the
Moonlight,' and from her wrists hung several bracelets,
among them a silver Vadri 'celtic knot' and a Nadri Pave
hinged open bracelet. Spaced among these charming
bracelets was an elegant watch (Kate Spade New York
'metro' crystal bezel heart dial watch 34 mm.) and several
rings, among them two Ariella collection mixed stackable
rings and Argento Viva hammered skinny rings. Her eyes
were shaded by Tom Ford 'celina' 55 mm. polarized
sunglasses (which Nina knew, from her trips to Wal-Mart,
sold for $3,678.00).

As headwear, she wore a striking lavender CGI infrared
Cole Gear beanie, and on her feet were two Valentino 'rock
stud' t-strap leather pumps with three-inch heels.

She wore Chantecaille hyra chic "Arctic rose" lipstick
and carried for a purse a Dooney and Burke nylon shopper
with braided handles.

Her scent was Hermes limited edition 24 Faubourg *eau
de parfume* edition numero 24.

"I love what you're wearing," said Nina.

"Oh, these old things."

"No, really, you look fantastic."

"That's so nice of you to say, especially since I've come
barging in here disturbing you."

"It's no bother."

"I just—well, I had to come and tell you. I don't hold it
against you."

"Hold what against me?"

"Murdering Garth."

"I didn't murder him."

"I know, that's what you have to say."

"But it's the—"

"No, you don't have to lie. He told me he was having an
affair with an older woman. A much older woman."

"Well, I'm not really that—"

"And he also told me he was going to end it. So I
understand. You were deeply hurt. I can only imagine what
it must be like to be your age."

"It's all right if you can take a nap every now and then."

Suzy Maples appeared not to hear this, and continued:

"I suppose by now you've figured out that I was having an affair with Garth, too."

As it was, Nina found herself thinking, the entire Daughters of the Confederacy was probably having an affair with Garth.

"I was in his room last night. This morning, really. We've been lovers for several months now."

"When were you there?"

"From about 2 a. m. until a little after 5 a. m."

"You made love for more than three hours?"

"Oh, no, we only had sex for a half hour or so."

"But you were there for over three hours."

"It takes me a long time to get undressed."

"Oh, I see."

"And then I have to hang everything up—"

"Yes, yes, I understand."

"It's not like it's all perma-press."

"Of course not."

"Then there's the makeup to take off."

"Obviously."

"And then, when we're through, I have to put it all on again."

"Well, that would follow."

That would also explain, Nina began to realize, *the scent that Harriet Crossman had detected.*

Hermes limited edition 24, Faubourg *eau de parfume*, edition numero 24.

And the nails.

Deborah Lippman 'Magic in the Moonlight.'

"I have to tell you that I thought about killing him. I really did."

"Why?"

"He was through with me. He told me so last night."

"What reason did he give you?"

"He was brutally honest, I will say that for him. I went with his last award. But he expected to get another award, so he thought he'd be needing another woman."

"I don't understand. What do you mean, you 'went with his last award'?"

"Atlanta."

"What about Atlanta?"

"A month ago. I won the Miss Atlanta Pageant. So of course, I had to write a Chrissie Oakton cozy, in which Chrissie won the Miss Atlanta Pageant. At the same time, Garth was winning the Atlanta Peach Award for Best Novel Featuring Globular Fruit. We met at a book signing. He asked me to go to bed with him, and since he was a writer, I said yes. But I found out he only wanted me for his second resume."

"Second resume?"

"Yes. He liked to have one woman for every literary award. And as long as his most current award was the Atlanta one, why, I was his most current mistress. I knew all of this, of course, but somehow I hoped against hope that he wouldn't win anything else for a long time. Garth was so brilliant though. You know, he had six doctorates and he was only thirty—"

"I know how old he was."

"Yes, and he'd published poetry in over a thousand—"

"I know that, too."

"He had the most wonderful resume. I loved to just touch his resume."

"Sure you did."

"Didn't you?"

"Thrilled me so, you can't imagine."

"But anyway he told me early this morning after we'd made love and I was an hour and a half into getting dressed again. He was expecting to win the HBO contract, and he would need a new woman to keep the resumes even. Probably a Los Angeles woman. I was so hurt."

"Well, who wouldn't be?"

"But now that you've killed him, it doesn't seem so bad somehow."

Nina had given up convincing Suzy Maples that she had not killed Garth Amboise.

In fact, she'd grown rather fond of thinking that she *had* killed Garth Amboise.

Killed him and cut off his resume.

But that was neither here nor there.

"Why," she found herself asking, "doesn't it seem so bad anymore, Suzy?"

She brightened.

"Because he was certain to win the HBO Award. Now that he's dead, I believe I have an excellent chance. I had a great interview with Sylvia Duncan. I can so clearly visualize Chrissy Oakton on television. Chrissie and Skipples."

If, Nina found herself thinking, *old Skipples isn't pregnant.*

But about this she said nothing.

"I feel myself getting so deeply into her character, her personality, her innermost being. She'll be played by Jennifer Anniston, of course. In the first episode, Jenn will be wearing a Donna Karan Collection organza trumpet skirt. The following week, when she wins the Seabreeze Cove Pageant—Seabreeze Cove is a quaint little New England—"

"That's all right, I can visualize it."

"Anyway, when she wins the contest, she'll be wearing an Akris Punto guitar print silk tunic. But later on, she'll change into—"

"You know, Suzy, maybe you shouldn't tell me."

Suzy Maples smiled.

"I understand. The suspense. You don't want me to ruin the suspense."

"That's it! I can just imagine sitting in my little bungalow, Furl the Cat curled up on my lap, watching Jennifer—"

"Jenn."

"—Jenn changing from one outfit into another—"

"And you'll be able to say to yourself, 'This is all happening because of me.' How is that going to feel, Ms. Bannister?"

"I can't tell you. I really can't begin to tell you."

"Ooooh, I was dreading coming to talk to you. But now I feel much better."

"Glad I could help."

"Are you going to be downstairs tonight when the big announcement is made?"

"Wouldn't miss it. And I'll be keeping my fingers crossed for you!"

"Thank you! Thank you so much!"

And, so saying, Suzy Maples rose and left the room.

To be followed, in precisely five minutes—

(How did they all manage to keep showing up in perfect five-minute intervals, as though they were German trains?)

—by Pat and Jim Hershey.

They knocked, she told them to come in, they did, they all went to the table.

And again and again and again and—

What if, once these two left, she just threw herself out the window and ended it all?

How high was this window?

She looked.

Probably not high enough.

And there were bushes down there to break her fall.

And it was raining, so she would get wet.

Better to just endure.

"We hope—"

"   that we're not disturbing—"

"—you but we wanted to tell—"

"—you how sorry we—"

"—are that you're suspected of murdering Mr.—"

"Amboise."

Pause.

"Thank you so much for being concerned."

"That's—"

"—all—"

"—right."

Amazing, she thought, *how they could do that.*

And those plaid shirts.

And those dazzling smiles.

"We thought it might help you to know that—"

"—we've come up with a theory of the—"

"crime. And we thought you might like to hear—"

"—it."

"Sure."

They both sat forward on their chairs.

"Pat, do you want to start?"

"Of course, Jim. Okay. We think it had to have been done by one of the cozy cat writers. We know this sounds crazy, but—well, what if some woman here actually was having an affair with him? What would you say to that?"

"I'd be shocked," said Nina, wondering for a time if she was the only woman at The Candles who was *not* having an affair with Garth Amboise.

"Of course, you would. Because you don't think the way mystery writers do."

"That is so true."

"But—well, Jim, you go on and tell her the rest."

"Sure, honey. Well, the way we see it, this mystery woman arrives in Amboise' room around 6 a. m."

Pat Hershey interrupted him:

"Five, darling. We said five."

He shook his head impatiently:

"No, six. Five would have been too early."

"Why would it have been too early?"

"It's still *dark* at five, anybody knows that."

"Dark or not," she asked, "what difference would it have made? And also, at six the household staff would have been up and running around the corridors."

"And you know this how?"

She stood up and raised her arms above her head.

Her voice was getting louder now.

"I know it because anybody with any common sense would know it; what's the damned matter with you were you raised in the wild?"

"I was *raised*, if you have to know, in a home where people made *sense* when they talked to one another!"

"Listen, if you're implying that I—"

Nina cleared her throat.

"Ahem! Listen, it probably doesn't matter so much about the exact time. At least not right now. If you could go over the basic theory. As it happens, I may know a couple of details that may be relevant."

"Of course, of course," said Jim Hershey, nodding. "All right. Then the basic problem that any good sleuth has to figure out, is how the killer got out of the room, since the door was locked from the inside when the maid arrived to find the body."

His wife stared at him for a time.

Then:

"What in God's name are you talking about?"

"The door, the one that was locked from the inside."

"It wasn't locked from the inside!"

"It most certainly was! That's why it's a locked-door-mystery!"

"The door was unlocked, you ninny! That's how the maid got in to find the damned body!"

"She got in by the window!" shouted Jim.

He stood up.

So did his wife.

They were glaring at each other now.

Pat Hershey spoke quietly, her eyes squinting, her lips tightly sealed together.

"We were in that room together this very morning."

"And there was a window."

"There was no window."

"Then how *did* the stupid killer get in?"

"By the secret tunnel!"

"The what?"

"The secret tunnel, Pat! We agreed not more than fifteen minutes ago that he got in by the secret tunnel!"

"I *never* agreed to that ridiculous notion!"

"Liar, liar, pants on fire, you *did*! You didn't want to at first because you don't have enough imagination to conceive of something like that!"

"A secret tunnel! How much frigging imagination does it take to conceive of a secret tunnel?"

"More than *you've* got!"

Nina tried to speak:

"I don't think there could be a—"

But she was cut off.

"You're not thinking, Jim, about what we actually agreed about not more than an hour ago; you're just spewing out those ridiculous ideas you had about how to write *The Jaded Juggernaut.*"

"All right then, if you're so smart, what did we actually agree on?"

"The woman arrived at five—"

"Six."

"FIVE DAMMIT OR SHE WOULD HAVE BEEN SEEN!"

"And what do you mean a woman? We said a man!"

"I never said that! How could it have been a man?"

"Because Amboise was gay!"

"That's ridiculous!"

"It's what you agreed to!"

"I was mocking you! I was saying, 'Oh, sure, Garth Amboise was gay, right'! Like, didn't you hear the irony in my voice? And besides that, there aren't that many men here!"

"There's me!"

"Sometimes I wonder about that!"

"What are you trying to say? Are you trying to say that I'm gay?"

"Well, Buster, if the slipper fits…"

"SHUT UP! JUST SHUT THE HELL UP!"

"YOU WANNA MAKE ME!"

"I think," Nina said, "if we could just get back to—"

But Pat Hershey had moved to the writing desk now, and was holding the neck of a porcelain vase.

Jim bellowed at her:

"So is that supposed to scare me or something?"

"IT'S SUPPOSED TO DO MORE THAN THAT, AUTHOR BOY!"

So saying, she hurled the vase, which missed her husband's head by inches and shattered on the wall behind him.

He laughed:

"Well, that's one murder method that clearly won't work! Just like all of your others!"

"You want me to find one that will?"

"You wonder what I want you to do?"

"Oh, yes, I'm dying to know what you want me to do!"

"ALL RIGHT THEN! I WANT YOU TO—"

The door burst open at that point and Margot stepped in.

"What's going on here? I was just coming up to check on Nina."

"The Hersheys," said Nina, "were writing together. They were telling me how the murder might have taken place. But somehow a vase got broken."

"It's a part," said Pat, quietly, "of—"

Nina finished the sentence:

"—of the writing process, I know."

Silence for a time.

Finally Margot said to Nina:

"Did you get a good nap?"

To which Nina answered:

"Shut up."

And then they all went down to dinner.

CHAPTER FIFTEEN: THE SINGING OF THE MUSE

Nina's mind was whirling as she began to follow Margot and the Hersheys down the stairs, as they all headed for dinner.

Two women had made love to Garth Amboise last night. Both were passionately in love with him. Both had been cast aside by him.

Both admitted these things.

Yet both denied having done the deed.

Still, if either had—

"Ms. Bannister?"

This from a rosy-cheeked young staff worker who was standing before her on the stairwell.

"Are you Ms. Nina Bannister?"

She thought hard about denying it but finally said:

"Yes, I am."

"The policeman, Officer Thompson."

"What about him?"

"He wants to see you in room 314."

"What about?"

"I don't know, ma'am. But he says it's important."

"All right."

The boy left and Nina climbed another flight of stairs.

In two minutes, she was knocking on the door of room 314, wondering whose room it was and what connection James Thompson might have to do with it. She was ready to knock, but her thoughts must have been audible from inside the room, because a voice said:

"Please do come in, my dear. The door is unlocked."

She pushed the door opened and entered a shrine.

The lights were down, incense was burning, and a small statue, perhaps a foot in height, had been placed in the center of the room and was surrounded by flowers.

"May I introduce you to the goddess Athena, Ms. Bannister? The two of you have much in common, especially in the area of wisdom."

This from Professor Brighton Dunbury, who, looking much as he had this morning at the pond, gestured toward a floral-covered easy chair.

"Please do sit down. You know Officer Thompson, I believe."

"Yes, of course."

Thompson was seated on a couch, Dunbury in a straight chair.

A coffee table sat between them and the chair Nina sat in.

It was on this small table that the incense burner sat.

"I asked the officer to come to my room, Ms. Bannister, because Athena and I have something to say to him. A tale to tell, as it were. Athena, as we learn from Book 13 of *The Odyssey*, is of all the gods and goddesses the best at the weaving of tales. But after he arrived, I thought it better to restrain myself until you came, too. I heard, you see, of the vile accusation that had been leveled against you—the theory that you had murdered Mr. Amboise."

"But I didn't—"

James Thompson interrupted her:

"That's all right, Ms. Bannister. Let's hear what Professor Dunbury has to say."

The professor smiled:

"Thank you, Officer. Well, it's rather straightforward, really. The fact is, Ms. Bannister could not have murdered the unfortunate Mr. Amboise."

"And you know this how?"

"I know it because I murdered him."

Shocked silence in the room.

Nina could hear the sound of her own breathing, and a soft hiss as the spray of incense floated upward.

"*You* murdered him?"

A nod.

"Yes, as a matter of fact. This morning at precisely ten fifteen."

"And what did you use to do this murder?"

"The same knife that I use for gutting fish. I simply— well, gutted him. As I'm certain the people at your headquarters have now ascertained. He was, you will admit, deeply cut."

"Yes, that's true."

"A veterinarian learns many things about how to inflict wounds. I simply used my expertise."

"And why did you commit this crime?"

"Oh, the oldest motive in the world. Jealousy. He was making love to Harriet Crossman, you see. Had just finished the act."

"How," asked Nina, "did you know that she had come up to his room at just that time? Surely she wouldn't have told you."

A shake of the head.

"The purest coincidence. I'd come up to his room to murder him. The fact that I saw her leaving only made it easier, more enjoyable."

"You enjoyed doing this thing?" asked Thompson.

A smile:

"Oh, eminently! After Harriet had left the room, I waited for a short time and then knocked. He shouted that I was to come in, thinking, I suppose that I was one of the staff and that I'd come to tell him it was time for his interview with Ms. Duncan. He was, I believe, first on her list to be spoken with."

"That's true," said Thompson. "We know that. Go on."

"And so I walked into the room. He looked at me with complete disdain and asked me what I wanted. I told him I wanted him to stop making love with Harriet Crossman; that she was much too elegant a woman for the likes of him—she comes from quite a wealthy and educated Boston background, you know, whereas he comes from nothing at all, except a wellspring of pure vanity. Well, at any rate I think he was astonished for a moment or so. Then he sneered. I remember him lying there on the bed, quite dressed and ready for the day, his watch, his jewelry, even the little gold AGCW hung around his neck—lying there and sneering. He asked me what his dealings with Harriet

Crossman could possibly have with me, and I told him that the lady and I had been lovers. In my mind were still lovers, and would always be."

Thompson:

"And then, Professor?"

"Then he laughed. Uproariously. The laughter began as a snicker and simply cascaded. Oh, it was quite unbearable, I assure you. At some points during his bellowing and guffawing, he managed to call me an old man, and impotent, and ready for nothing save a nursing home."

Silence for a time.

Then:

"At a certain point, I reached slowly into my jacket pocket. I could see him watching my hand. I suppose he expected me to extract something of sentimental value, an old photograph perhaps. At any rate, what I did extract was the fishing knife. Then I simply lunged. The first thrust carried deep into his heart. He was, I'm certain, quite dead instantly. I still remember the look of astonishment in his eyes. I'm not sure why I went on thrusting, and jabbing, and cutting. I suppose I was quite mad. The whole thing happened so quickly that he had no time to scream. But at any rate, after a minute or so it was done. Even though I'm in excellent condition for a man my age—all the hiking and camping you know—I was still quite out of breath. I sat there for a while, gaining my composure. Then I put the knife back in my pocket, went back to my room, and changed my clothes. There is a fireplace in my room, an elegant, even somewhat gentle touch. I succeeded in building a small fire with kindling that had been thoughtfully left there for the coming cold days of winter. In this fire, I burned the clothes I'd been wearing, and which were quite thoroughly soaked with blood. Then I went down to join the meeting. And I heard the announcement."

A pause, then:

"And that, my dear Officer, and my dear Ms. Bannister, is all there is."

Thompson stared at him for a time, as did Nina.

Finally Thompson said:

"That's a very convincing story, Professor Dunbury."

"The truth always is."

Thompson pursed his lips, looked down at his hands, and said, quietly:

"Yes. And when we finally learn the truth about this murder, I expect that it will be convincing, too."

Dunbury:

"I beg your pardon?"

"The truth, Professor."

"Why, I've just told it to you!"

"No. No, what you've done is weave a tale. Like you said your goddess there—what's her name?"

"Athena."

"Yeah, that. Like you said she was so good at doing. You've told a very detailed, very dramatic—pack of lies."

The professor simply stared for a time, then said:

"That is, of course, what Odysseus does upon his return to Ithaca. Interrogated concerning his origins, he lies splendidly. A wonderful story concerning murders and hatreds long past. None of it true. But the goddess overhears it and is delighted. Wisdom, tale weaving and lying are, to her, one and the same."

"And you lied so beautifully because you were afraid Ms. Bannister might be accused of the crime."

"Well, she was accused! I was there! I heard her being accused!"

"Ms. Bannister didn't commit this murder, Professor. And neither did you."

"And how may I ask—at least in my case—can you be so sure? What part of my story does not hold true, what part of the cloak that I have woven does not bear wearing?"

"Your cloak was fine, and your story would have been believable. Except for one thing. One thing I just learned from the Coroner's report, which was just faxed to me an hour ago."

"And that fact was?"

"The saliva."

Both Nina and Dunbury leaned forward.

It was she who asked:

"Saliva?"

"Yes, the saliva in his wounds."

"Something bit him?"

Thompson nodded:

"Yes, ripped him apart, actually."

They sat in stunned silence, while Thompson merely nodded, slowly, and said:

"I don't know what killed Garth Amboise. But it wasn't human."

CHAPTER SIXTEEN: I AM JESSICA!

He was ripped open.

By something inhuman.

Talk about a conversation stopper.

And Thompson's pronouncement did in fact stop conversation; killed it as dead as Garth Amboise certainly was, shredded it wide open, and tore it to pieces.

So for a time, the three of them just sat there, looking at each other in open-mouthed wonder, watching the shrine of the goddess of wisdom as it wheezed out fumes.

Professor Dunbury broke the silence:

"It is as though this house, The Candles, has become the House of Atreus."

Thompson:

"Pardon, Professor?"

"When Agamemnon returned from the Trojan War with a mistress, his wife, Clytemnestra, butchered him in his bath. The gods ordered her son and daughter, Orestes and Electra, to murder her as an act of vengeance. They did so, but then they were in turn attacked by the Furies."

Nina interjected:

"I remember them from mythology. Vicious demonic creatures, half animal and half woman, they tormented their prey."

"Yes, indeed, my dear. And it's as though poor Mr. Amboise has become one of their prey."

Nina listened to this, thought about it, and shook her head:

"Maybe but—"

Her mind raced back to the morning.

The pond.

Her first meeting with Professor Dunbury.

"You said what we heard was a panther?"

He nodded.

"Yes. Quite certainly a black panther."

Thompson:

"There are black panthers in these woods?"

A nod.

"They are rare, of course. But they exist. All the way down from Michigan. If the woods are thick enough."

James Thompson shook his head:

"No. I've lived here all my life. Hunted in these woods. Never seen such a thing."

Dunbury:

"Nevertheless, the thing we heard this morning was a black panther. I would swear by it."

"All right, so a black panther is out there roaming these woods. How the hell did it get into Garth Amboise' room?"

But to this question, Professor Dunbury could only shake his head:

"I'm completely at a loss, sir. It seems impossible."

"Completely impossible indeed. But I'll give you this, Dunbury: the Coroner's report stated that the saliva in question must have come from a predator."

And again, they could only look at each other.

Until Nina, remembering the people who'd come trooping through her room during the last hour, said to James Thompson:

"I've had a thought. It's a crazy one."

"It would have to be to explain this."

"All right. Can we three go downstairs and look at Amboise' room again?"

"Yes. If that would do any good. But I don't see any—"

"I'm not sure I can either, but it's the best I've got. And I'll need you to send one of your men to get a couple of other people, so they can meet us there."

"Sure. Which people?"

She told him.

Then they struck out for the room of the deceased Garth Amboise."

It had been cleaned completely since she remembered it. The sheets were gone, the bed bare, but large pools of burgundy stain still marked the carpet.

"No window," Officer Thompson was saying. Besides, we're up on the second floor. I don't see how anything that big could have gotten in."

"The storm's getting worse," said Nina, quietly. "Anything outside, anywhere near here, might have been driven in for shelter."

"Driven in where? Surely the thing didn't just come prancing in through an open door?"

"No, but—"

"Hi!"

"Did you send for us?"

And there in the doorway, beaming as usual, stood Pat and Jim Hershey.

"We did," said Nina.

"How can we—"

"—help you?"

"Your theory of the crime. I wonder if you'd go over it again, precisely as you told it in my room just a little while ago?"

They both stepped forward into the room.

"Sure, we—"

"—could!"

Pat Hershey said:

"You start, Jim!"

"Alright, honey. Let's go over it again. The woman arrives around six."

"No, we said five."

"How many times do I have to tell you this? Five is too early!"

"Okay, so you think it's dark. Who cares? Now, if you could talk about the theory again—"

"I will, if you'll just let me. The problem is how the killer got out of the room."

"Oh, we're back to this closed door stupidity!"

"The answer to that is the secret tunnel!"

"And I've told you and told you I've never agreed to that notion!"

"That's because you have no imagination!"

"I've got a lot more than *you've* got!"

Upon saying which, Pat Hershey ran to the far side of the bed and gripped a vase which stood next to the wall.

She raised it menacingly above her head, and was about to hurl it at her husband.

When, with a great groaning and squeaking of mechanisms, a panel opened in the wall itself, revealing a gaping hole.

That led, clearly, into a tunnel.

Finally James Thompson spoke, saying:

"Well, I'll be damned."

Pat Hershey put down the lamp, which, clearly, had triggered the mechanism, and said to her husband:

"You are *so* brilliant!"

Nina remembered what Margot had told her that very morning:

'They fight like cats and dogs when they're actually writing. But once the book is over, they're proud as punch of each other.'

And this book, to them, is over.

"Darling, you're the smartest man in the whole world; you're more brilliant than Shakespeare even."

"It was nothing, honey."

She put her arm around him:

"You're the most wonderful writer I know."

"No, you are!"

"No you are, Jim! And, my God, I want you so much right now!"

And so saying, she dragged him from the room.

Causing James Thompson to say:

"Look at the two of them. They really are cute together."

Nina glared at him.

Finally, Dunbury walked to the opening of the tunnel, peered into it, and said:

"It does lead down, probably to an opening out onto either another tunnel, or to the river itself."

Thompson joined him at the tunnel opening, saying softly:

"Rumor always had it that Confederate soldiers would make their way here, even after the place was in Union hands. The staff would hide them, maybe in tunnels like these. Escape tunnels. Now, if the animal were really seeking shelter, it might have made its way into the opening at the water's edge. It might have been attracted by smells and heat, and made its way up here."

"It would have been starved for food," said Nina. "The storm had made it impossible for it to feed."

Dunbury:

"How could it have opened the panel door? I ask myself."

To which Thompson:

"We know that the lamp triggered the door from the outside. But it's possible that mere weight would open it outward."

Nina:

"So that anyone—or thing—coming up from the inside would only have to push against it to make it open."

"And that," said Dunbury, "our animal, our panther, would certainly have done—sensing meat on the other side of the wall."

"All right, but then how—"

Thompson was interrupted by the door of the room opening into the corridor, and Margot and Mildred the cook entering.

They both stood gaping for a time at the tunnel's entrance.

Finally Margot stammered:

"What in God's name is that?"

Nina was about to answer but Mildred interrupted her, saying calmly:

"It's the old escape tunnel, Ms. Garvin."

"The what?"

"The old escape tunnel."

"You knew it was here?"

"Oh yes, ma'am."

"Then why didn't you tell us?"

"The girls was afraid you'd make them clean it."

There was little to be said to that. So Margot finally broke the silence by saying, quietly:

"You all better get downstairs. Especially you, Officer Thompson."

"Why, ma'am? What's the trouble?"

"Dinner's almost over. Sylvia Duncan has made up her mind about the HBO winner."

"Do you know who it is?" asked Nina.

Margot shook her head:

"No. But whoever it is, the others are going to tear to pieces."

"Margot," interjected Nina. "We think Garth Amboise was killed by a panther. Eaten alive!"

Margot merely shook her head, saying:

"He was lucky."

So saying, she turned and left.

The rest of them followed.

Dinner was chaos of course. The cozy writers all knew that the big announcement was imminent, and their minds were racing with fevered frenzy through the marvelous benefits of being rich and famous and going out and living in Hollywood and helping to choose the star of the new series and going to the Academy Awards program even though it was just TV and not movies, but, of course, there would *be* a movie and it would win the award for best writing and there would be the BIG SPEECH in which one said "I would like to thank everyone who helped me in creating this series, and I want especially to acknowledge my etc., etc., etc., and then there would be MILLIONS AND MILLIONS AND MILLIONS OF DOLLARS which could be used to fly to Aruba and the Costa Brava and all those places where one could just sit on the beach with one's laptop and write and drink Mai Tai's and never have to worry about paying rent or working a real job ever again.

There was a good deal of shouting in the room now as tension increased, and more hard objects—chicken wings, biscuits, oranges—were hurled seemingly at random targets.

"I told you," Margot hissed at one her staff members, "not to serve any more biscuits. Or chicken parts for that matter!"

The woman, obviously flustered, could only shake her head:

"We didn't at first. But they were throwing mashed potatoes."

Finally Margot was able to buttonhole Harriet Crossman, who was watching intently the scene before her:

"Harriet, can't you stop this?"

Harriet merely turned and looked at her, saying:

"Stop what?"

"Stop what's going on out there in my dining room!"

A shrug:

"Obviously, you've never seen a literary conference before."

"But the food?"

"It's not bad. We've had worse, although there have been numerous complaints about the fried okra."

"No, no, I mean *throwing* the food!"

"What about it?"

"Can't you make them stop it?"

Harriet Crossman thought about this for a time and finally said, quietly:

"I don't know. It's become such a tradition—"

"This is insanity."

But, after what seemed an eternity, dinner did actually end.

And it was time for the big announcement.

Nina and Margot were standing in the back of the room, as Harriet Crossman took the podium:

"Well we've had another splendid meal!"

"DOWN WITH THE OKRA!"

"NO MORE GRITS!"

"Now, now, other cultures other customs. But that's not the important thing now. The important thing now is the announcement that we've all been waiting for. The announcement that will serve as a kind of crowning star to our guild, and a vehicle to fame and fortune for one of our members. Ms. Sylvia Duncan of Los Angeles, as you know, has been conducting intensive interviews with each of you for the entire day. It was, of course, rather unfortunate that this work, as well as the other vital work that The Guild must deal with, had to be interrupted by the murder of Mr. Amboise. But we did not let that stop us. We marched on like troopers, and we will continue to do so until the conference officially ends in two days. Whatever remains, though, will be somehow anti-climactic. For the highlight of our gathering is before us now, at this moment. For a new Jessica is ready to be born—and I have the honor to introduce to you—Ms. Sylvia Duncan!"

Thunderous applause.

All writers on their feet, many of them holding cats high in the air now, so that the small animals could be visible to Sylvia Duncan, who, smiling, was taking her place before the microphone.

Finally, the bedlam died sufficiently for her to begin:

"I want to thank all of you, and, of course, all of your cats—"

HA HA HA! HA HA HA!

"For what has been an immensely enjoyable day for me. I've gotten to know so many people, both real and fictional. But you are all such fine authors that it's the fictional ones who stand out to me. And such a variety, a diversity, of characters! The whole of humanity is shown in your work and in your settings! Retired librarians, retired eighth-grade school teachers, retired high school teachers, retired nurses, retired dental technicians, retired housewives—and all of them working in places so different as a quaint seaside village of one thousand in lower Maine, and a quaint village of almost three thousand in northern Massachusetts. My mind, I must tell you, is spinning."

"BUT WHO'S THE WINNER!"

"WHO IS THE NEXT JESSICA?"

And of course the refrain:

"I AM JESSICA!"

"I AM JESSICA!"

"I AM JESSICA!"

But Sylvia Duncan merely raised her hands high over her head, and, laughing, continued:

"It may well be that several of you will become as well known as the creator of Jessica Fletcher. I fully expect our new HBO series to be wildly successful, and to spawn progeny!"

"UP WITH PROGENY!"

"HUZZAH FOR THE PROGENY!"

More from Sylvia:

"But, of course, all of this depends on our beginning. It depends on our choosing as our first cozy heroine a genuinely riveting character; a character who will make small retired old ladies around the world say, 'I can solve murders, too! I live in a quaint little ocean-side town and I'm smarter than our bungling police chief—bring on the next not too violent murderer—AND LET ME AT HIM!"

"YES! YES!"

"BRAVO FOR SYLVIA!"

"BRAVO FOR HBO!"

"BRING ON NOT-TOO-VIOLENT MURDERERS!"

"BRING ON THE BUMBLING POLICE OFFICERS!"

Another calming wave from Sylvia, who was actually beaming now, and whose radiant smile would have eclipsed that of Jessica Fletcher behind her, had that smile not been fifty times larger than hers.

"And so, dear ladies—and two surviving gentlemen—we shall bring them on! But first, we must bring on someone else. Someone who has created a truly spellbinding character! Someone who will blaze the trail of glory for all of you!"

"WHO IS IT?"

"WHO IS THE CHOSEN ONE?"

"TELL US! TELL US! TELL US! TELL US!"

"And so I shall! Esteemed members of The Guild of American Cozy Writers, the heroine of our new HBO series—is Ms. Nina Bannister!"

Complete silence in the room, which, for an instant at least, resembled the House of Wax.

Finally, several voices blended together and asked the same question:

"Who?"

"Ms. Nina Bannister!"

A pause.

Then Sylvia continued:

"I, as many of you I'm sure, are already aware of Ms. Bannister through her political activities and her creation of the nationally acclaimed Lissie Party. But after hearing of her exploits for the past months and years, her success in saving her home town of Bay St. Lucy from huge gambling and tourist interests, her role in protecting the entire Gulf Coast from eco-terrorists, her adventures in Austria and Washington—"

There were more voices now, and the writers had gotten to their feet:

"Austria?"

"Washington?"

"Those aren't cozy places!"

"And who is this woman, anyway?"

"She isn't one of us!"

"She's not even a writer!"

The coziests, outraged, had split into two groups now, one advancing toward Sylvia at the podium, and the other advancing toward Nina and Margot.

All of them were shouting.

To Nina:

"What qualifies you, of all people, even to *be* a cozy writer?"

Nina knew nothing to say.

She looked quickly behind her; there was no place to hide, no place to escape to.

"Come on, tell us! What qualifies you to be a cozy writer?"

"Well, I do have," she said, quietly, timidly, haltingly, "a cat. His name is Furl. He—"

But she was interrupted by shouts directed at Sylvia on the other side of the room.

"Who's going to write the scripts for the TV shows?"

"We've got the plots already, from Ms. Bannister's own real life exploits. As for the dialogue and description, we'll probably just hire Hollywood ghost writers."

This was precisely the wrong thing to say.

"GHOST WRITERS!"

"WHAT?"

"ARE YOU CRAZY?"

On the other side of the room, the group shouting at Nina had surrounded her and was closing in.

"Where do you live, anyway?"

She thought about lying, and saying:

'A little village on the Massachusetts coastline.'

But she did not.

Probably because she did not know the names of any little villages on the Massachusetts coastline.

Instead she answered:

"Mississippi."

Realizing how stupid that was, even as she said it.

The crowd reacted as though they were a small fire upon whom gasoline had been poured.

WHOOOSH!

"Mississippi! That's the WORST possible place for a cozy!"

A small voice did pipe up from the middle of the mob, saying:

"Well, except maybe for Arkansas."

But the blaze continued to roar, gaining in intensity and hatred:

"WHO ARE THE ECCENTRIC LOVABLE CHARACTERS WHO LIVE AROUND YOU?"

Desperately—for the ring of people around her had tightened, so that they were only a foot or so away—Nina pointed at Margot and said:

"Her!"

But this only made things worse, and the group continued to howl and scream:

"SHE'S NO MORE A COZY CHARACTER THAN YOU ARE!"

"FRAUDS!"

"NON-COZIES!"

"SEND THEM HOME TO MISSISSIPPI!"

"DOWN WITH THE LISSIES! DOWN WITH FURL!"

On the other side of the dining hall, Sylvia, who'd obviously not expected the degree of vindictiveness occasioned by her announcement, was trying to enlarge upon her vision:

"You see, we'll make each of the episodes be some kind of 'Change.' The first will be *Sea Change*; then the one in which she solves the actor's murder will be *Set Change*, because it has to do with the theater; then, when Nina goes back to teaching and becomes the women's basketball coach, the episode can be *Game Change*. Then—"

But these plans only worsened the rage and drew the crowd, which now was acting like a lynch mob, in closer:

"THOSE ARE THE STUPIDEST COZY TITLES I'VE EVER HEARD!"

"WHAT ARE YOU GOING TO PUT ON THE BOOK COVERS? THE BACK OF HER HEAD?"

Sylvia was growing desperate now, and Nina could see the look of terror in her eyes, as though she were a deer surrounded by savage wolves.

"But, but, listen, people will like the stories, I promise you, and we won't have to actually *go* to Mississippi to shoot the episodes, and, and—"

"STOP!"

Suddenly there was silence in the dining room.

One of Margot's staff was standing in the doorway, a horrified look on her face.

She attempted to speak for a second, but failed, her head shaking uselessly, an arm pointed downward.

Finally, she was able to stutter:

"C. R. Roberts, the body builder! She's down in the exercise room! There's a huge dumbbell on top of her!"

Shocked silence for a time.

Finally, Rebecca Thornwhipple piped up:

"Well, tell him to get off of her."

But the aide, growing more desperate, shook her head, saying:

"No, it's a weight! It's a—"

But Margot interrupted her, shouting:

"Come on! Fast!"

And she ran toward the doorway, Nina following as fast as possible.

The two women reached the exercise room just steps ahead of James Thompson, who'd heard the staff member's statement from a small room where he was seated.

"Don't go in there!" he was shouting.

But it was too late.

Margot had already entered the small exercise room, Nina one step behind her.

"Oh my God," she exclaimed.

For the scene was much as the earlier one had been.

Blood everywhere.

C. R. Roberts had been clad only in a tank top and shorts.

Those, and the gold AGCW medallion that still hung around her neck.

Now her body was soaked in blood, as was the bar of the huge weight that lay upon her.

Thompson moved on into the room, his firearm drawn and at his side.

Another officer followed, then another.

Margot and Nina stood rooted to the floor.

"It's just like before!" Nina found herself whispering. "She didn't even get to take off her neck ornament."

Margot nodded:

"She's ripped to pieces!"

"She didn't have time to get out from under the weight!"

Several of the cozy writers had made their way into the room, and Nina could hear them complaining:

"I'll have to add another chapter!"

"I can't add any more; I've already emailed *The Amputated Amboise* to my publisher. This will have to be a whole second book."

"But couldn't you just write a—"

James Thompson however interrupted them:

"All right; that's it! It's over! I want everybody out of this plantation!"

Harriet Crossman had pushed through the crowd. She asked:

"What are you talking about?"

"This convention is over! We're not going to take a chance on this happening again. I don't know how these people are getting killed, but it's got to stop!"

"What will you do with us? Where will we go?"

He merely shook his head:

"I've got two police vehicles parked outside now. More will be on the way. I'm taking you all into Abbeyport. We'll find room for you at local motels and B&B's."

"But our business committees! Our publicity campaigns!"

"They'll have to wait. You've got to go, all of you. And I mean now!"

"Can't we even pack?"

"No. I'll have some officers bring everything into town a little later on. The only thing important right now is getting you out of here. I have no idea what's going on, but something savage is on the loose. From what I've heard, the woman lying there dead and mutilated was an expert in martial arts. But this thing, or this man, or this woman, or whatever is doing these murders—ripped her to shreds before she could even try to defend herself."

"But, but—our cats?"

"The cats stay here for now. We can't take the time to find them all and get them in the vehicles."

"But we can't go anywhere without our cats! We're cozy writers!"

"I'm tired of arguing. Now—"

He was interrupted by another officer, a young man who came running into the room, open mouthed and wide eyed:

"Chief!"

Thompson straightened:

"What is it?"

"We just got a 911 call patched through to us!"

"That's all we need. What is it?"

"The call came from a woman who says she lives just a couple of miles from here, out on the Abbeyport Road."

"What's her problem?"

The young officer could hardly get his breath:

"She says she's just seen an animal!"

"What kind of an animal?"

"She doesn't know, but she says a huge flash of lightening came, and she was able to see this thing running through the woods near her house."

"And she doesn't know what it is?"

"No, Chief. The woman sounded terrified. She says it's like a wildcat but bigger, and black. It was roaring, and making these terrible noises. It was headed down toward Abbeyport, she thinks. She says—wait a minute!"

The officer put a walkie talkie to his ear and nodded:

"Yes, this is Abbeyport Police. No, go on, I can hear. What? You saw what? And it did what? Ok, where do you live? All right, we'll be right there!"

"What was that?"

"Another woman, Chief. Probably lives just up the road from the first one. Saw what must have been the same animal. Only this time it's worse."

"How?"

"This woman and her husband raise cows. The thing apparently went into their pasture and slaughtered a steer. She said they saw the whole thing, also in a lightning flash, and that it was sickening."

"All right. We've got no choice. We've got to try to find this thing and shoot it before it terrorizes anybody else. It's already been responsible for two murders. Whatever it is, it's dangerous as hell. We've got a lot of firepower in the vans. If we can find the thing, maybe we can bring it down! Now call into headquarters, tell them we're on the case. But tell them to send out here any available men they've got!"

"All right, Chief!"

Thompson turned to Harriet Crossman:

"We have to check this thing out. Maybe this creature, whatever it is, killed Amboise and this woman body builder."

"How," asked Nina, "could it have gotten into the house without anybody seeing? It clearly didn't come through the escape tunnel."

Thompson shook his head:

"I've been thinking about that. All I can say is, no, it didn't come through the tunnel we found. Maybe there are others. All I know is, something huge and vicious got into this exercise room and killed this woman. A few hours before, it got into one of the rooms upstairs, and it killed Mr. Amboise. Now something huge and vicious is rampaging over the countryside. I'm not going to take time to sort out the finer details; I'm going to shoot this beast first, and figure out how it did these killings later."

To Harriet Crossman:

"I'm sorry, Ms. Crossman, but we're not going to be able to get you all out of here as fast as I'd originally thought we could. But until that beast is caught, no one is safe. My advice is to be sure everyone is packed. Then have everybody stay together in the main dining hall."

She nodded:

"That's what we were going to do anyway. Something unspeakable has happened, and we've got to try to work together as a group and come to grips with it."

"I understand. I'm terribly sorry that these ghastly murders have happened, and that you ladies had to see these bodies. You're right, it's unspeakable."

"What is?"

He looked at her:

"The murders."

"What murders?"

"Why, the murders of Amboise and C.R. Roberts!"

"Oh that's not what I'm talking about at all."

"Then what are you talking about, for God's sakes?"

Harriet Crossman merely folded her arms and said, sternly:

"I'm talking about the choice of Ms. Bannister as the next Jessica Fletcher. It's unspeakable. Clearly nothing about her fits into the 'cozy' genre. If we allow this to happen, then all out work will be—"

But Thompson merely turned away in disgust, saying:

"You deal with that any way you want. But just keep these people together. And have them ready to leave as soon as possible."

Then, to the two officers who now were standing just inside the doorway:

"Come on, you two. We'll go out and rendezvous with the others. Then we'll go find this thing and kill it."

So saying, they left the room.

Nina whispered to Margot:

"Let's go."

"Where?"

"Somewhere to hide. Where's a place where these writers won't ever go?"

Margot thought for a time, then said:

"The library."

"Are you sure?"

"Yes. All they're interested in is writing books; they don't care about reading them. Now come on."

Nina followed, and in short order, they found themselves in the library, listening to the howling of the storm and the howling of the cozy writers who were bellowing horrible insults concerning HBO.

"Poor Sylvia," whispered Margot, who was trying to keep as quiet as possible, so that neither she nor Nina would be found.

"That's all right," said an equally frightened voice.

Both Margot and Nina whirled.

Sylvia Duncan was crawling out from under a table in the middle of the small room.

"Sylvia!" shouted Margot.

"What," chimed in Nina, "are you doing here?"

"I'm hiding. If I go out there, they'll rip me to pieces. Just like the other two were ripped to pieces."

That, thought Nina, *was probably true.*

She also thought back some hours, and remembered the glasses of wine the three women had drunk, when the world seemed still to make some sense, since only one person had been murdered and she herself was not hated by thirty cozy writers and Sylvia was not the devil.

"I'm still certain," said the devil quietly to Nina, "that you're the best choice to be our new heroine."

"Who would play me? Jennifer Anniston?"

"Betty White."

"Damn."

"Of course, I'm not certain it will happen now. If all of these writers are so dead set against it, then it may not make sense to proceed. I know I'm right though. Your adventures may go beyond the conventional cozy framework just a bit. But they have true social significance. They say important things about communities, and how communities work together."

"Maybe," said Margot, quietly, "you could tell them that."

Sylvia nodded, resolutely.

"You're right. I'm going to make one last effort. If they hate me, they hate me."

"That's the spirit! I'll even go with you. Maybe I can help."

"I would deeply appreciate it."

"Well, it's my B&B. I'm responsible for the safety of everyone here. Although I haven't been doing such a great job so far. Want to come with us, Nina?"

But Nina merely shook her head:

"I don't think so."

"Coward."

Another shake of the head:

"It's not that."

"You're not afraid of them?"

"I'm afraid of something. Just not them. They're not our problem. Not the biggest one, anyway."

"What are you talking about?"

"I just—I've got to talk to somebody. And here in the library is the best place to do it."

"Who do you have to talk to?"

"An old friend. One who always helps me."

"You're sounding crazy."

"No. For the first time, I'm sounding something other than crazy. Now go on out there, you two. Do the best you can. I'll be along in a little bit."

So saying, she turned and walked farther into the library, while Margot and Sylvia went to face the pack of angry writers.

And so, for a time, she tried to clear her mind.

The sound of the storm.

The sound of the shouting coziests.

The soft, not quite audible but always tangible, muttering of books.

Voices coming from the books.

She walked along the shelves.

Fine books.

Homer.

Shakespeare,

And of course Jane.

Jane Austen.

Her Jessica Fletcher.

"Listen, Nina, listen," Jane was whispering.

"You always forget. You're so caught up in the outer turmoil, that you always forget the most important lines of all."

"I know, Jane. Just tell them to me one more time."

"All right. They're from *Emma,* of course, my greatest mystery. And they go, 'A mind lively and at ease can do with seeing nothing. And can see nothing that does not answer.'"

"Yes. Yes, of course. And my lively little mind tends to be at ease when it should be working."

"Then put it to work, Nina. Put it to work like you always do. Those people out there need you."

And so saying, Jane Austen's voice disappeared.

It had to, so that Nina could formulate her own thoughts.

Ask her own questions.

A beast at large in the countryside?

Possible, but not likely.

Nothing about all of this was 'likely.'

It was all impossible.

Two mutilated bodies.

Perhaps someone could have come in and surprised C. R. Roberts, but that was not likely.

And Garth Amboise?

Still a mystery.

Nothing was making sense.

All right, then—forgetting Janet Evanovich and P. D. James and going right to Sherlock Holmes, eliminate what was impossible.

The trouble was though, *all* of it was impossible.

These murders couldn't have happened.

And yet they *had* happened.

All right, then if—

She was interrupted by the sound of the library door opening.

"Aha! I find here the next great celebrity! Congratulations, dear lady!"

She turned to see Professor Brighton Dunbury bowing low, his black flop hat almost touching the floor.

He straightened, and, smiling broadly, pronounced:

"So YOU are Jessica!"

She hardly knew what to say.

Finally, she did say:

"That doesn't seem very important right now."

"Really? Fame, riches, Hollywood, stardom?"

"No. I keep remembering what you said at the pond this morning."

"Ah, yes. You mean about the panther."

"No. About success. How it would keep you from writing."

"Certainly it would! But that is hardly a problem for you, is it?"

"Why not?"

"Because you don't write! The only person who can ever be sure of avoiding writer's block is someone who's never written to begin with!"

She thought about that for a while.

"Well, I suppose—"

Then she thought about other things.

The scene at the pond.

Everything that happened at the pond.

"You seem lost in thought, my dear Ms. Bannister."

"Yes. I guess I am."

"Much as I myself am, when I commune with Athena."

"Yes. Except I have another Athena."

"And that would be…"

But Nina did not say 'Jane Austen.'

Because her mind was still at the pond.

A mind lively, working at being not at ease.

"Professor, out at the pond this morning. So much happened."

"Oh, not so much, actually. We heard the panther--"

"Yes. The panther."

"And I caught a lovely little sunfish."

"Yes, there was that, but—but there was something else. Something that we're forgetting."

"We talked. I told you of my past. I spoke of Drusilla of Sestos. Of weaving and unweaving."

"Professor, you know that I'm a literature teacher myself. For years and years."

"I do know that. You told me. I was delighted to find that I had a colleague!"

"You talked earlier about *The Odyssey*, and about Odysseus, lying."

"And being loved for it by Athena!"

"Yes, but—I'm thinking about the other group of plays you mentioned. The House of Atreus plays."

"Ah, yes, wonderful works!" Dunbury shouted. "Clytemnestra murders her husband Agamemnon in his bath! She hacks him to pieces!"

"It seems a little like what's been going on here."

"You think one of the lady writers may be a vengeful Clytemnestra?"

"No. No, that's not quite it," said Nina. "It's not that easy. Clytemnestra may have stopped being human for a while—but she didn't turn into an animal either. Professor, you said the gods order Orestes and his sister Electra to murder their mother Clytemnestra in revenge for their father's death?"

"Yes, they did. And the pair obeyed their orders. Also in a very bloody fashion!"

"But then they were hounded," Nina asked, "by the Furies?"

"Yes, precisely. Until Athena herself intervened, and forgave them, and made the Furies harmless."

"Yes, I remember now. But Professor Dunbury, I don't think a panther killed those people. I don't know how I know that. But I do. Something far more deadly killed those people. But it all goes back to the pond. Something else that happened at the pond."

"But nothing else did happen! Nothing that I remember, anyway!"

"Yes, one other thing happened. The dog, Borg."

"The plantation dog?"

"That's the one. You calmed him down, remember?"

"Of course! He'd been upset by the writers some months ago. Poor fellow."

"You used a device on him."

"Yes, I did. But surely you don't think poor Borg did this!"

"You could make a device that would make him want to do it, though, couldn't you?"

"Well, yes, you could, by altering his brain waves, drive him almost crazy. Still, I don't think that he or any other dog would be able to—"

"No, they wouldn't. But the Furies would."

"My dear Ms. Bannister, I don't understand how—"

Her musings were interrupted by Margot, who burst into the library.

"Nina!"

She looked around:

"What? What is it?"

"Chief Thompson!"

"What about him?"

"He just called me on my cell phone. Actually, it wasn't him. It was a woman from police dispatch in Abbeyport."

"Fine, so I'll ask it again—what does Thompson want?"

"He wants us to drive out to the main road and meet him."

"Why, for God's sakes?"

"He says it's urgent! He's found something that might answer the whole puzzle!"

"Has he shot the animal?"

"The woman didn't say. But she did say that we need to go as fast as possible. Now come on: we can take the Volkswagen. I've got two heavy rain slickers in the entryway. Maybe we can make it to the car without drowning."

"All right."

And so saying, Nina followed into the small entryway/reception area.

Turmoil, turmoil.

The storm, terrible in its intensity.

Sylvia's voice in the dining room, trying to placate a sea of anger.

Chaos everywhere and yet—

—something about her was calmer than it had been.

Something was looking.

At—

At what?

A pile of boxes lying in a corner.

"Come on, Nina! Put this on! We've got to hurry! I don't know why, but the woman in the dispatcher's office said get there as fast as possible!"

The boxes.

Cardboard boxes.

What was wrong with the boxes?

They were the boxes that the gifts had come in.

Gifts from publishers.

Bribes.

All of the boxes lying there before her, with professionally-written return addresses on them.

O'Donnel Press.

Black Cat Press.

Leinart Press.

Except for one.

HBO.

Except that box, the one from HBO, had no address on it.

"Margot?"

"What are you waiting for? Come on!"

The return address was there all right: HBO, Los Angeles, Street Address, etc.

But no address.

"Margot, that box—"

"Come on!"

"That box has no address on it."

"Who cares?"

"But how did it get here?"

"I don't know!"

"And what was in it? Margot, what came in that box from HBO?"

"Some of the gifts, I suppose, maybe sweatshirts. But it doesn't matter now."

"Yes it does. I don't know why. But it's odd."

"Of all the odd things going on around here, an empty box is the one you choose to worry about?"

"I'm just—"

"Come on!"

And, so saying, Margot pulled Nina toward the door, somehow shucked her into a huge ill-fitting yellow slicker, and forced her to don massive overshoes.

"You ready?"

"Yes, but it's just so strange that—"

"Forget it and come on!"

Margot kicked open the door, and the two women lurched out into the midst of the storm.

The porch, the trees, the roofs, the outbuildings— everything was night-black over, obscured, rendered invisible by the rampaging winds, sheets of rain, and low-scudding clouds.

"This is awful!" screamed Nina, who was almost being blown backwards.

"Come on! It's not far to the car!"

She could hear rumbling thunder, and, from time to time, the world was illuminated by lightning flashes.

"There's the car! Come on! Just a little farther!"

"Margot, what could he have found that we need to see?"

"I don't know. But when the police call me and tell me to do something, I do it. I'm not like I was in the sixties!"

"It just doesn't make any sense. Like the boxes don't make any sense!"

"Will you forget about those damned boxes?"

"But how could that one box have gotten here without—"

"Forget it! Here—go around to the other side of the car, while I unlock the door!"

Nina did so, her feet overrun by a flood that was running through the driveway.

Margot pushed open the door from the inside and Nina stumbled in, wondering how the two of them were going to manage to navigate through sheet after sheet of driving downpour in the blackest of nights.

"All right, here we go!"

She turned the key; the engine sputtered, then started.

She gunned the accelerator, threw the gearshift into reverse, and, tires spinning in the mud puddle that had been solid gravel a day ago, jammed the car backward, turning it as she did so.

"Can you see, Margot?" screamed Nina.

"What did you say?"

"Can you see?"

"No, but I think I know where the road used to be."

"Maybe we should go back in the house!"

"With the writers?"

"Okay you've made your point. It can't get much worse."

"Hold on."

The Volkswagen lurched onto the driveway, then spun and careened its way into the surrounding forest, headlights boring a narrow tunnel of light through the pines and brambles that were now closing in on them, and the deluge that was pouring down around them.

"I don't know," shouted Margot, trying desperately to keep the car in some kind of path, "what kind of a panther they're going to be able to shoot in this storm."

"It's a goose," replied Nina.

"A what?"

"It's not a panther. It's a goose. A wild one."

"What are you talking about?"

"They're on a wild goose chase."

"How do you know that?"

"Because my mind was lively and at ease. All of our minds have been lively and at ease. Especially Officer Thompson's."

"You're not making any sense."

"No. For the first time, I am making sense. Oh my God, look!"

In front of them was the bridge, now overtopped by fast flowing water, but still barely visible.

"Can you get over that?"

"I'm sure I can. We had it worked on, remember?"

"Sure, I remember that's what you said, but—I can barely see where the bridge stops and the creek starts!"

"I know. When the rain gets hard enough, the river floods, and then everything else floods."

Nina could see that they were ten yards from the creek, which was roaring louder than the storm and the thunder.

Then five yards.

Then the bridge washed out.

It did so with a sucking sound, and then there was nothing but planks breaking apart, their jagged edges biting at the air above them and the water below as though they were sharks' teeth flashing in the Volkswagen's headlights.

"Oh my God!" shouted someone in the car.

It could have been either Nina or Margot.

No matter.

They were both thinking it.

"Back up, Margot! Back up!"

"I'm trying!"

But it was no use; the tires merely spun in water that was obviously deepening as the swollen creek reached out for them.

Then it was Margot's turn to scream:

"We're floating!"

"Get out of the car!"

Nina pushed the handle down and lurched against the car door, wishing she was heavier. The door opened with a sucking sound, and cold, swirling brackish water flooded into the passengers' side, covering her yellow galoshes, which peered back up at her as though they were faint yellow carp.

"Come on!" she heard Margot yelling from the other side of the car.

Then she was out of the car, shocked by the water that was now tearing at her, and soaking her jeans up to the knees.

"Get away from the car, Nina! Get away from the car!"

She was barely able to do so, grasping at the slender pine branches that, in turn, tore at her face.

She turned and watched, as the Volkswagen began to move, slowly at first, then faster, becoming after several seconds no more than a part of the rubbish and driftwood that was eddying fast toward a sharp bend in the creek.

"Come on! We've got to get away from here!"

"I'm trying, Margot!"

But it was almost impossible, for the water was getting deeper from second to second, and the downpour was so thick that it felt as though she were swimming. Rain and flood and creek water all became one, and would have swept her away along with the car had the trees not formed a kind of rescue net that she could pull herself along with.

Five yards back toward the house.

Ten yards.

Finally she could tell that the water was well below her knees now, and that the tall straight object she lurched toward, and finally grabbed, was not a tree trunk but Margot.

The two women held each other for a while, gasping, trying to get their breath.

"Your car, Margot!"

Margot, she could see, was shaking her head:

"To hell with the car! A couple of seconds more and we could have been in it!"

"Well, they say Volkswagens float!"

Another shake of Margot's head:

"I don't think 'they' know much about the Mississippi River when it floods. Look!"

Nina did so, just in time to see the roof of the car, now almost fifty yards downstream, disappear beneath the swirling waters.

There's very little to say, Nina realized, when watching a car one has just gotten out of, as it disappears beneath the swirling waters.

"Wow!" was all she could manage.

Margot was more practical:

"We've got to get back to Candles! Can you walk now?"

"I think so! We're farther away from the creek, and it's only ankle deep here!"

Each woman now had her arm around the other's waist, and, having no idea where any sign of a road was, they simply forced their way through the flooded forest, ignoring pine needles that tore at their faces and various scraps of flotsam and jetsam that pricked their ankles.

Finally there was a break in the undergrowth.

"There! There's one of the old barns! We're coming out of the woods and into the west pasture. The house is not more than a couple of hundred yards to the left! The worst is behind us!"

"Are you sure about that?" cried Nina.

"Yes, why wouldn't I be?"

"Look up! Look up at the sky just in front of us!"

"Oh my God!"

There was a lot of that being said these days, mused Nina.

For directly in front of them, out of the gray scudding clouds and frothing sky, a vertical black tube was dropping, as though it were a snake falling out of the sky.

Watching it created the same kind of effect as watching the car drown.

Very bad, but somehow fascinating.

The Nature Channel.

She had come to The Candles for a few days of rest and relaxation.

And she'd found herself slap dab in the middle of the Nature Channel.

Watching cats fornicate with intense passion.

And watching them fight, which was even worse.

Strange, she found herself thinking, *that standing here in this tempest, seeing a tornado about to strike the ground only a few hundred yards away—she was thinking about the vicious intensity with which cats fought each other.*

But those thoughts left her mind quickly, driven out by Margot's screams:

"It's a twister! Get down behind this tree trunk!"

And Margot, clearly not worrying about cats or cars, pulled her to the left, so that she was soon cowering behind the thickest pine available, and watching as the tornado sucked up the barn.

It did so with astonishing ease, just as the bloated creek had sucked down the Volkswagen, up down, up down, elemental forces running amok now, the barn swirling and twisting and rising, its shape nearly perfectly intact, as it simply disappeared into the sky.

And then the tornado was gone, having receded into the clouds as though they were its lair.

"Where is it?" asked Margot.

"It's gone! It's just gone!"

"So is the barn!"

"Da dum da dum da daah daah!"

"What are you humming!"

"The music from *The Wizard of Oz*."

"What?"

"This whole weekend. The handyman, Mildred the cook, Harriet, Sylvia, Dunbury—have turned into the scarecrow, the tin man, Professor Miracle, the Wicked Witch of the West, Glenda the Good Witch, The Wizard himself, and now the tornado. Margot, when that barn finally comes down, there's going to be a witch under it."

"You're crazy!"

Nina nodded:

"Or I'm dreaming. But there's no place like home. It's just that I'm not sure I'll ever get back there."

"You will. But come on; we've got to get back to Candles."

They rose and began to slog their way to the spot where the old barn had stood.

And then it came to her.

Jane Austen might have been standing there in the flood, smiling at her and nodding.

That was how it had happened!

"Margot, I think I know now!"

"What are you talking about? *What* do you know?"

"It's not the ruby slippers! It's golden instead!"

"Nina, what are you talking about?"

"The boxes! And an image I just thought about! From The Nature Channel! It was happening all around us. Nature, doing its thing—and we didn't realize it!"

"I hate it when you get like this! It's as though you were in another world!"

"No! Everybody else is in another world, a fake world. I'm in the real one. I'm the only one in the real one. Well. I and one other person."

"Will you tell me what you're talking about?"

But Nina merely shook her head:

"I've got to show you. But I think I can. Come on!"

And she strode off, Margot one step behind her, toward The Candles.

And to *The Solution*—

The Perfect Murder!

CHAPTER SIXTEEN: THE VOICE OF GOD

The situation back at Candles was much as it had been an hour earlier. Everybody seemed to be angry, and everybody seemed to be shouting.

It was hard to tell which of the two villains—Nina or Sylvia—was most hated.

Several of the writers had formed small groups and were discussing the possibilities of lawsuits against HBO. Or, of course, there was also the possibility of boycotts.

That was it! All mystery writers of the nation—or of the world—boycotting the new Nina Bannister series.

Even the sound of it—the Nina Bannister series—was ludicrous and insulting.

Of course, at the moment the Nina Bannister series was being completely ripped apart as a concept, the subject of that series was back in the entrance hall, talking with a member of Margot's staff about the mysterious box that had arrived with a return address but no address.

"Was this box delivered by the mail in just the same way the others were?"

"I don't know, ma'am."

"You didn't bring it in?"

"No, Ms. Bannister. It was one of the other girls."

"Which one?"

A shake of the head:

"I'm not sure about that, either. The boxes were arriving all morning, some of them by FedEx. I didn't sign for any of them, but other people in the staff did."

"And this box: do you remember what came in it?"

"No, ma'am."

"Okay, this is very important. Can you ask around and find out all you can about this box? I want to know who

brought it in and how it came here with no address on it. Can
you do that?"

"I'll try."

"Good girl. Whenever you find out, wherever I am, come
and tell me."

"All right."

And, so saying, the girl disappeared.

Nina threw herself into the dining room, ignoring the
hateful stares that were directed at her.

It was early evening, dark outside now because of the
storm and the twilight, and the chandeliers were glowing.

Dinner had not been served: no thought of eating, given
the rancor in the room.

Margot had disappeared somewhere, but that did not
matter to Nina.

She had to find Sylvia.

Where *was* Sylvia?

Ah, there, in the middle, of course, of a group of angry
people.

Hard to pry her loose, but necessary.

So Nina began to make her way through the crowd,
trying to remind herself that the stares directed against her
came from the fact that she was not even self-published.

She was non-published.

Of course, people here hated her!

Crossing the room was like walking out of the forest had
been, except that, rather than making her way through
floodwaters and pine needles, she was making her way
through bitter hatred and resentful jealousy.

But making her way she was, and Sylvia was now only
ten feet away.

Now only five feet.

When suddenly the lights went out.

Someone shouted:

"The storm!"

The entire room was black, illuminated only by flashes of
lightning that shone through the massive picture windows.

Even the screen which had glowed with the picture of
Jessica Fletcher was now dark.

There were small cries and orders and bits of advice everywhere:

"Somebody get a candle!"

"We need some light!"

"It must have been a lightning bolt!"

"Where are candles?"

"Doesn't The Candles have candles?"

One candle did appear though, just at that moment, in the doorway which led to the kitchen.

It was a tall white candle, and it was carried, of course, by Margot the Capable.

Whose voice resonated over the room:

"All right everybody, be calm. We have all the candles you need. Some of my people are bringing them now. The storm must have…"

But she was interrupted by another voice.

A voice that seemed to be piped in from speakers in each corner of the dining hall.

A voice which said:

"Please don't worry about the candles, Ms. Gavin. You won't need them for some time."

And at precisely that moment, the screen lit up.

Except on it was not the face of Jessica Fletcher.

It was the face of Molly Badger.

The image was in black and white, and showed no background, only the sad Badger face that Nina had come to remember from the small hideaway cubicle at Candles and the motel in Abbeyport.

The image was perfectly clear, however, as was the concerned voice:

"Margot?"

How could she see Margot?

"Nina?"

My God, thought Nina. *She must be able to see the entire room!*

Where was she?

How was she doing this?

And then, of course, the answer came: she could do this—whatever it was—because she was a genius at electronics.

"Margot! I can hear you—tell me what you're doing there!"

Margot stared at the screen, hesitated for an instant, and then said:

"Molly?"

"Of course, it's Molly! But tell me: why are you and Nina still there?"

"You can see us?"

"Yes, I can see all of you, and the entire hall. But don't worry about technical matters: just tell me what you two are doing there!"

"But Molly, where else would we be?"

"Out on the Abbeyport Road, where Officer Thompson told you to be."

"But how did you know—"

"Molly Badger, this is Nina. You didn't *listen in* on any call, did you? You *made* those calls!"

The image on the screen smiled slightly:

"Yes, that's correct. Nina, I'm so sorry that both of you are there. I wanted you to be somewhere else."

"Like out on the Abbeyport Road?"

"Yes."

"And that's why you were able to fake a call to Thompson and his men. And then a call to us. You somehow made him think—and Margot think—that you were the woman in the dispatcher's office."

"It wasn't hard, Nina. Not with my expertise. But you still have not told me: why did you not go?"

"We did go, Molly. Or at least we tried to. But the bridge washed out before we could get across it."

Silence, then a shake of the head:

"That's too bad. I'm genuinely sorry to hear it. I didn't want you to be in the hall. I didn't want you to see what may be going to happen next."

More silence.

Ominous silence.

It was Margot who spoke up:

"So there's no beast roaming the countryside, is there, Molly?"

The smile looming down on all of them changed slightly, though in precisely what way Nina would have found it hard to say.

The voice filtering down was softer, somehow.

"There are many beasts."

The storm roared.

Another lighting flash lit the hall.

"There are beasts almost everywhere. Some of them in us. Some we carry around with us."

Nina took two steps toward the screen:

"Molly, where are you?"

"It doesn't matter."

"You were not kidding this afternoon at the motel, were you? You really did commit the murder of Garth Amboise."

"No, I did not."

"All right. You did not. But you were responsible for it. It and the murder of C. R. Roberts."

"Yes. The body builder. I didn't truly hate her. I didn't hate the man Amboise, either, although he was in many ways a hateful man. But I felt nothing against them compared to the viciousness that has been directed at me. And now I must come to my main point."

She was silent for a time and then pronounced:

"Harriet Crossman."

It might have been the Voice of God, calling one of the sinners to judgment.

It repeated itself:

"Harriet Crossman."

Harriet, to her credit, did not appear cowed or terrified. She stood straight, in the middle of the room, and spoke up to the face staring down at her:

"I'm here, Molly."

At the precise instant she said this, a figure crossed the room and stood beside her.

It was Professor Brighton Dunbury.

He took Harriet's hand and held it firmly.

Then he said:

"*We're* here, Molly. Harriet and I. We stand, together, before you. What do you wish of us?"

To which the visage answered, funereally:

"Then I speak to both of you. And to all the other cozy writers. The seeds of your destruction surround you."

"What are you talking about?" asked Harriet.

"There is no place for you to go. The police are no help to you. And if you try to leave, you will be ripped to pieces, just as your colleagues have been ripped to pieces. Yes, they were indeed PUBLISHED AUTHORS. But that was little help to them, was it?"

Harriet bowed her head, stared at the floor, and said:

"No. No, it wasn't."

"Well, the same fate awaits you. And all of the rest of the writers."

Silence.

Only the sound of breathing.

Finally Molly:

"You will all be ripped to shreds. You will see your destruction coming. But that will be no use to you. For the forces that are to destroy you are those which you have brought to Candles with you."

The Smathers Sisters rose as one and said:

"It's a demon, isn't it? We've known all along: you've unleashed a demon!"

But Molly Badger merely shook her head and said, quietly:

"I am a demon."

And then, again to Harriet:

"I'll give you fifteen minutes. Then it will be midnight. If you are indeed true mystery writers, you should appreciate the scene, the timing. You will hear the clock strike twelve times. And that will be the last thing you hear."

Professor Brighton Dunbury took a step toward the screen and said, supplicating:

"Surely, my dear lady, there is something we can do—"

Molly Badger merely nodded:

"Yes. You can die."

And then the screen went black.

Leaving them all there.
Trapped in a huge house.
Escape impossible.
Police nowhere near.
All power gone.
Nina thought of Macbeth, and the witches' lines, the ones that had been quoted only that morning at the pond by Dunbury himself:
'By the pricking of my thumbs,
Something wicked this way comes.'

Something wicked was coming.
Coming to get all of them.
For a time no one said anything.
They were merely looking at each other.
Finally, Harriet said to the man still standing beside her:
"Thank you, Brighton."
"Why, for what, my dear?"
"For standing by me. For holding my hand like you did."
"I've always stood by you; and you by me."
"No. I let you down. I fell for that megalomaniac Amboise. You probably hate me now."
"Of course I don't hate you."
"I'm so thankful for that. And, Brighton?"
"Yes, my dear Harriet?"
"If we both have to die, I'd like it to be together."
"And it will be. Whatever furies this strange goddess sends to torment and ultimately devour us—they can never devour our love."
But, upon hearing this, it was Nina who stepped forward.
"That's very touching. I'm sorry to tell you, though, that you don't have to die. None of us do."
Everyone looked at her.
"I think," she said, "I've got it figured out!"
A voice asked:
"What are you talking about?"
"I know how she did it!"

Silence for a time.

Finally, Harriet Crossman stepped forward and said:

"But Ms. Bannister, how *could* you know?"

"The boxes."

"What boxes?"

"The ones that came from the publishers. The ones that were lying there in the entranceway, the reception office. One of them didn't have an address. It had a return address, but not a mailing address."

"What does that have to do with anything?"

"Just listen: the question is, how could the box have been delivered if there was no address? And the answer is, someone must have brought it in by hand and set it down among the morning's mail."

Silence for a time

Then Nina:

"I think I know who delivered that one strange box, and, more importantly, what was in the box. The murderer wanted us to think that the box came from HBO—but Sylvia, to the best of your knowledge, did HBO send a box of shirts or anything else out here as a gesture of good will?"

Sylvia Duncan shook her head:

"Not that I know of."

"No, of course you don't know of it—because it didn't happen!"

Harriet Crossman:

"Nina, are you saying that Molly Badger actually committed these two murders, by using what was in a box that she brought in herself?"

"Yes. Except, she didn't commit the murders herself. She had them done for her."

"Murder for hire? She paid someone to do it for her?"

Nina shook her head:

"No. It wasn't done because of money. It was done because of insanity."

"A lunatic?"

"Not one lunatic. That wouldn't have been enough."

"These people were killed, mutilated, mauled, by a group of lunatics?"

"Exactly."

"But that's impossible!"

"It's not impossible. It's simply all that remains when we've eliminated all the things that *are* impossible."

"Janet Evanovich."

"P. D. James."

"Josephine Tey."

"Tony Hillerman."

"Sherlock Holmes," Nina said. "But remember what Molly said: There are beasts almost everywhere. Some of them are in us. Some we carry around with us."

Then she looked at the entire group and said, quietly:

"You've all brought your own beasts here. Now you have to tame them. And I think I know how you can do that."

Margot stepped toward her and asked:

"Nina, I never seem to know what you're talking about when you're solving murders. But this time I have to tell you: you're not making any sense at all."

"It will all come clear in a very few minutes, Margot. Once I deduced WHAT WAS IN THE BOXES AND WHO BROUGHT THEM—and once I really thought about what the professor said down by the pond—and once I realized that the way Molly would get her revenge—and prove her genius and GET PUBLISHED was to go after everyone's pride, the very emblem of what must have seemed to her to be their arrogance—then I knew the answer. I knew how we will tame the beasts within us—and then we will wait for Molly Badger's call."

And she did.

And they did.

It was not a 'call,' precisely, but a reappearance, and it happened just as the standing clock in the corner of the dining room struck the first of twelve chimes.

The screen lit up, and there was Molly Badger's image once again.

Her face had no expression on it, as she stared across the room below.

She waited until the twelfth chime had sounded.

There was a scarcely audible rasp of static, and then came the voice:

"It's midnight. I hope you have all prepared yourselves."

Harriet Crossman:

"Yes, Molly, we have prepared ourselves. With Nina's help that is."

"How unfortunate that Nina should have to perish with you. She and Ms. Gavin are the only ones who've always accepted me despite—despite what I am."

Nina stepped forward:

"What you are, Molly, is a human being."

"But a self-published one."

"Self-published writers are still human beings."

"Not to Amazon."

"There is more to life, Molly, than Amazon."

"Yes, there's Barnes and Noble. But it doesn't matter now, dear Nina. None of it matters now. What will happen, what was fated to happen—will happen. And the time for that has come. I'm only regretful that you and your friend will have to suffer."

"No one is going to suffer. It's like Harriet said: we have prepared ourselves. We know of the furies you're planning to let loose upon us."

At this time, Brighton Dunbury stood up in the center of the room, and said firmly to the image:

"We know of these furies, my dear Ms. Badger. We had our own Athena here to tame them, just as the goddess tamed them in the myth."

A shake of the head on the screen.

"That's where you're wrong, professor. I'm simply too ingenious. I've proven it twice already; now I plan to do so again. In a kind of Grande Finale. When they find your bodies—and they will find them, sometime tomorrow, when I call both the police and the news media and the storm subsides enough for the cameras to get in—I will be recognized as having committed not only THE PERFECT MURDERS, but THE PERFECT MASS MURDERS!"

Nina:

"And then what will happen to you, after you admit all of this?"

A smile:

"I'll be taken away, probably. But I'll be written about. And I'll be famous."

"But you'll be in jail!"

"Iron walls do not a prison make, nor iron bars a cage."

Several voices in the room exploded as one:

"Tony Hillerman!"

"Simenon!"

"It's Richard Lovelace!" shouted Nina, losing her patience for an instant while someone from across the room shouted:

"Yes, it's Richard Lovelace! I met him once at a conference in Boston! He writes the Becky Althorpe mysteries! Becky is a retired female auto mechanic who lives in little seacoast village of—"

"Richard Lovelace is one of the seventeenth century Cavalier poets, you idiots! And he died fighting against the Puritan armies of Oliver Cromwell!"

Silence for a time. Then another voice:

"Who is Oliver Cromwell's detective?"

Nina shouted:

"He doesn't *have* a detective!"

The she regained her composure and said to the flickering black and white image:

"There won't be any mass murder, Molly."

To which Molly smiled, saying:

"Yes, there will. And it will start soon. No. Why wait? It's time!"

The camera panned backward, so that a small table appeared behind her, and on it a computer screen.

She turned and typed in some kind of command, then turned back, smiled, and said:

"Prepare to die!"

Upon hearing which, Nina merely said quietly:

"All right, Cozy Writers. Blow out your candles."

Everyone did so.

The room was in darkness, save for the glowing image of Molly Badger's face.

It continued to stare, without changing emotion.

Finally the image spoke:

"It should begin now. The first should be arriving."

Nina merely shook her head:

"Nothing will happen, Molly."

"It *will* happen! Just as it has twice before."

"No. Look."

Nina then nodded to Margot, who pulled the sheet off the large table in the middle of the room.

A pile of objects were glowing yellow, as though a nebula of stars had spawned on the table.

Around this nebula, spread across the room, more lights glowed yellow.

These lights were the AGCW pendants hanging from necklaces that all of the AGCW members had been given, and were still wearing.

Molly Badger stared at the room in horror.

"What is that? You've not…"

"Yes, we have. We realized, finally, what was in the box you left, Molly. It was the gold Guild pendants, and the matching pendants to hang on our cats' collars."

"But the cats should be—"

"The cats are here, Molly. All right, writers. Remove the shawls.

All of them did.

Revealing every cat that belonged to every writer.

Ezekiel lay quietly in the lap of Sarah Trimball, who wrote the Judy Finch mysteries.

Cardwin Cat lay quietly in the lap of Jessica Turner, who wrote the Celia McNaugton mysteries.

Roscoe lay quietly in the lap of Pamela Jane Sidberry, who wrote the Sarah Jane Dewberry mysteries.

And so on.

All of the cats in the room peaceful, all lying quietly— their collars having been taken off—in the laps of their owners.

Cozy, as it were.

But Molly Badger was horrified:

"Why aren't they doing anything? They should be going crazy by now, and ripping you all to shreds, just the way they ripped Amboise and the bodybuilder to shreds!"

"They're not going crazy, Molly, because we took their collars off. That's what you see there glowing on the table in the center of the room. Our pendants are glowing, too, giving out the signal that is supposed to be driving the cats wild, infuriating them, so they would attack whatever animal is wearing that wave inducer, or whatever you choose to call it."

"The transmitter."

"Yes. I should have put two and two together when Professor Dunbury told me about the device that had calmed down the plantation dog. An electronic device that sent waves into his brain, relaxing him. Of course, such devices could have the opposite effect. Of course, such devices could make cats go wild. Any human wearing the transmitter would be in terrible danger, because we all saw what a fight was like between just two cats. But you created something much worse. Amboise's pendant—the transmitter—going off silently, so that he was not even aware of it. Or of the faint yellow glow that it gave off to show that it was doing what it had been designed to do: attract and infuriate cats. They were all drawn to it like a male would have been drawn to a female in heat, only with ten times the hatred. Whatever was wearing it, they would tear to pieces. And they would have easy access, of course, because of the cat doors. I can only imagine the horror felt by Amboise and C. R. Roberts, seeing the animals pour into the room in a single line, then lunging—probably at the eyes first. Finally, all thirty would be there, ripping and tearing. Then, after enough time had passed and the ghastly deed had been done, you had simply to turn off the transmitter. The cats were at peace again, and would simply leave the room by the same cat doors through which they had entered. The victim was dead, and any blood that might have been found on individual cats was chalked up as a wound gotten in a single cat fight. A fight such as we all had gotten used to seeing."

There was silence for a time.

Finally, Molly said, quietly:

"Oh, what a world! My beautiful evil!"

"Molly," Nina said, "that's a line from *The Wizard of Oz.*"

The image stared back at her and finally said:

"What is that?"

"It's a movie."

"Is it a cozy movie?"

"No."

"Oh. Then I don't care about it."

And the screen went dark.

CHAPTER SEVENTEEN: DEPARTURES

The following day dawned clear in northern Mississippi, Hurricane Clarence leaving behind no more than flooded streets and wind-torn trees.

There was a vacant spot where once a rickety barn had stood in the far west pasture of Candles Estate, but otherwise the old plantation had suffered no damage.

So the building could continue to smile, as it always had, on guests arriving and leaving.

There were no arrivals today, and only departures, which were viewed by Margot and Nina as they sat at the table in the front yard, sipped coffee, and chatted with James Thompson in the late morning.

"So," Nina was saying, "Molly Badger is in Vicksburg now?"

The police chief nodded:

"She was flown out of Meridian on a special jet."

"And she's in jail?"

A shake of the head.

"No, she's in a luxury suite in the Riverside Hotel, which, I'm told, is one of the city's finest."

Margot put down her cup of coffee and leaned forward on the table.

"She's not in jail?"

"No."

"Why for heavens sake not?"

Thompson shrugged:

"We arrested Ms. Badger early this morning, about 2 a. m. She spent the night in our jail. We put her up before the judge at 8 a. m., told him what we suspected her of doing, and asked for an indictment. He just laughed at us."

"He laughed?"

"Yes. We told him that Ms. Badger had cleverly arranged it so that all thirty of the cats staying out at Candles were wearing special charms on their collars. That these were not really charms, though, but small electronic devices which, when triggered, would attract them to transmitters. That these transmitters were actually other charms being worn around the necks of cozy cat writers, such as Mr. Amboise and Ms. Roberts. That the brain waves of the cats were so heated up by the transmitters that the animals would go into a fury and try to destroy whatever was wearing the transmitters. That two cats fighting was a scary thing to see, but that the thought of thirty of them attacking any creature simultaneously was absolutely terrifying. That's what we told him."

"And?"

"Like I said, he laughed. He said that was the most ridiculous murder method he'd ever heard of and that we'd better go back to square one to solve the case. So we thought about it for a time and told him it was probably a panther, and it had been driven into one of Candles' escape tunnels by the storm. He said he'd never seen a panther in these parts, but that was at least a better theory than the one about the cats. And we let it drop at that. As far as the authorities are concerned, the case is closed forever."

It was Nina's turn to lean forward:

"But we know what really happened! It *was* the cats! There was no panther involved!"

Thompson merely shook his head:

"I understand your point, Ms. Bannister. It bothered me too for a time, knowing that Molly Badger was going to go free. I thought maybe if I came out and collected some of these devices, maybe rounded up some stray cats, maybe put on a demonstration for the judge—"

"Yes, yes...so why didn't you do just that?"

"Because I visited first with a lawyer friend of mine. I told him the whole theory."

"And?"

"He laughed and said it was the most ridiculous murder method he'd ever heard of, and that not even a mystery writer could think of anything so ridiculous."

"But, but—"

"So I pressed him. After he stopped laughing, I insisted. I said, well, just assume the thing was possible, and it happened just the way I said. What charges could Ms. Badger be tried on?"

"And?"

"He told me he couldn't think of any charges."

"But she committed murder!"

"No, she was in a motel room in Abbeyport when the murders happened."

"But she, but she—"

"She what?"

"She *incited cats*!

"Ms. Bannister, I and my lawyer friend did a check. There is no law in the state of Mississippi against inciting cats. There is a law against cruelty to animals. It's only a misdemeanor, though, and we can't arrest her for it, because she wasn't cruel to the animals."

"But she made the animals be cruel to people?"

"Which animals?" he asked, waving at the line of cozy writers who were now waiting to board limousines.

"Well, I don't know. I mean, are you asking which cats actually inflicted specific wounds?"

"Yes, ma'am. Even if we could put Ms. Badger up for trial, we would have to indict specific animals. We would have to prove that Hecuba or Ezekiel or Stanislaus or Pussywillow or whichever animal, actually clawed the jugular of Mr. Amboise open, and inflicted the fatal wound. And we can't do that for two reasons."

"Those being?"

"Well, first, we can't do it because, as you see, the owners are leaving as fast as possible and taking the cats with them."

Margot nodded:

"It's true, Nina. Harriet came to me early this morning and said the cozy writers had decided to cancel the rest of the conference. Each writer steadfastly denied that her personal animal was a murder-cat, but each writer also insisted on getting out of the state before any possible charges could be brought."

"All right, all right—but Officer Thompson, you said you couldn't indict for two reasons. What is the other one?"

"The other one is we don't have precedent. There is not, at least as far as a quick check can show us, any record of a house cat ever being executed for murder in the state of Mississippi."

He was silent for a second and then said:

"Now I'm not sure about Texas."

Silence for a time.

Finally Nina said, quietly:

"So she actually did it. Molly actually did it."

"What, may I ask?"

"She pulled off the perfect murder."

Thompson nodded:

"Actually, two perfect murders. But there's another aspect of the crimes that you have to bear in mind."

"That being?"

"The disagreeability index."

"The what?"

"How disagreeable the murder victims were. It may be different in other places in the country, but here in Mississippi we go a good deal easier on murderers who kill unlikeable people. From what I hear, this Amboise fellow was not likeable at all."

"No, he wasn't."

"And the Roberts woman apparently bragged about castrating men with one karate chop."

"Just sexist men."

"I know, but still—if you got an all-male jury—"

"I understand."

"Well. I have to go now. We'll all talk later."

"Thank you, Officer Thompson," said Margot. "I do want to—"

"Ms. Gavin! Ms. Bannister!"

Margot's words were interrupted by Suzy Maples and her cat. She wore an ebony black Calvin Klein open-front soft jacket and classic-fit trousers, suitable for traveling. Under the jacket, she wore a turquoise and black pleated-neck, arrow-printed top. Her feet were clad in Thalia Sodi Elina pumps, and she carried a Dooney & Bourke Lambskin Tobi tote in black, slung across her forearm. Burberry sunglasses topped her head, holding back her hair and ready to protect her eyes. Again Hermes limited edition 24 Faubourg *eau de parfume* edition numero 24 wafted across the lawn.

"You look marvelous," said Nina.

"Oh these are just some things I threw together for the trip. But Whiskers and I just stopped by to tell you how much fun we've had, and what wonderful hosts you've been!"

It was Margot who answered:

"You're so kind! I'm sorry about the two ghastly murders and the near mass murder of everyone."

Suzy Maples shook her head:

"We can't expect everything to go perfectly. But things are fine now, from what I hear. Everything except Whiskers here."

She pointed to the cat carrier.

Out of which Whiskers had just vomited.

"I can't imagine what's wrong with her!"

Morning sickness, thought Nina.

But she said:

"Probably journey-proud."

"Yes, I'm sure that's it! Well, thank you all again."

And, so saying, she left.

To be replaced at the table by the Smathers sisters.

Who, strangely, were not looking here and there, to the right and to the left, and everywhere in between.

Tall Smathers sister:

"My sister and I simply had to come by and tell you how much fun we've had!"

Short Smathers sister:

"Yes, it's going to be the basis of our next PARANORMAL ROMANCE!"

Tall Smathers sister:

"Our alpha male, who, you will probably remember our telling you, is a werewolf, is going to be spiritually invested by an ancient Egyptian mummy, who was three-thousand years ago the beautiful princess Isis. While he's unwrapping her in order to have sexual intercourse—"

Short Smathers sister:

"We were the first to write about inter-creature sexual intercourse, you know!"

"I remember you saying," said Nina.

Tall Smathers sister:

"While he's doing this, an army of pyramid-cats descend upon them and—"

Short Smathers sister:

"Stop stop, Sister! You mustn't give away the entire plot!"

Tall Smathers sister:

"Oh, I know! I always do that! Anyway, that wasn't the most important thing we have to tell you!"

"What is that?" asked Margot.

Both sisters at once:

"YOU ARE BEING DE-POSSESSED!"

Margot looked shocked for a second, then said:

"No, we're not! We've paid our bills!"

Short Smathers sister:

"No, no, not dispossessed; depossessed! The ghostly presence is about to take itself elsewhere! We feel it very strongly! And when it does, the demonic presence will accompany it. Your house will be un-haunted. We promise you!"

Margot merely smiled:

"Well, it's good of you to tell us. Thank you for your kind words. And good luck with your PARANORMAL ROMANCE. What will it be called?"

Both sisters in unison:

"*I Dismember Mummy*! There will be a Kindle version!"

"Wonderful."

"Good bye now!"

And so saying, the psychic sisters turned and left.

To be replaced by Rebeccah Thornwhipple.

White-haired, spry, and laughing-eyed as always, she tottled up to the table and sat in one of the vacant chairs, laying her cane on the ground.

She wore a sweater much like the one she'd arrived in, but the front of this one showed one end of an iron lung, with two pair of feet extending from it, and bright red hearts swimming in the air around it.

"I hope I'm not disturbing you ladies!"

The ladies laughed and told her that she was not.

She smiled.

"It has been such a pleasure staying here with the two of you!"

"The pleasure," said Margot, "was all ours."

"And it's a shame about Ms. Roberts. Mr. Amboise, too, but in his case—he was such a—I don't know precisely what word to use."

"No," answered Margot, shaking her head.

"Shit. He was such a shit."

Nods around the table.

Rebeccah Thornwhipple continued:

"And I must say, Ms. Bannister, that I do regret accusing you of murder."

Nina merely shook her head:

"I wouldn't think twice about it, Ms. Thornwhipple."

"Rebeccah."

"Rebeccah. No, I wouldn't worry about it. One gets accused of murder so often these days—"

"But it can be a bother, I know."

"Only if you let it."

"I am, of course, still going to write the novel."

"That's all right. I'm sure no one will connect the murderess with me."

"I'm using your name."

"Oh. What are you going to call it?"

"*Nina Bannister: Murderess.*"

"Well, okay, they might make that connection. Are you going to put in the mad passionate stinking sex?"

"Of course."

"What chapter will it be in?"

"Chapters five through eleven."

"What a charming tribute! And to think: whatever happens to me, the novel will endure, and I'll be remembered."

"Yes, my dear. It's the only kind of immortality we have. But wheels are already in motion for both the novel and the film version. I spoke with my agent this morning. He's already spoken with Betty White."

"Damn," said Nina, quietly.

"Oh, no, don't worry about it. Ms. White feels that the part should be played by a much older woman."

"Rebeccah," interjected Margot, who wished to change the subject because Nina's fists were clenching, "I'm glad you got a novel out of this, and I'm very proud that my friend will go down in literary history as a sex-starved homicidal maniac."

"It's the least I could do, given all your hospitality."

"But I'm sorry you didn't get the HBO Award. And I hope you and the rest of the cozy writers won't be holding it against Nina. After all, she won't be getting the award either, from what I've been hearing."

"I know. And as for who's going to receive it, here come the two people who might be able to tell us that!"

And she was indeed correct, for Harriet Crossman was approaching the table, arm and arm with Professor Brighton Dunbury, who shouted, breezily:

"Hello, the table!"

And the table shouted back:

"Hello, the Dunbury! Hello, the Crossman!"

Handshakes and hugs, laughter and frolic.

The two newcomers were seated, and Harriet Crossman said:

"Well, I've just had what seems to be the final word. Fields, Edelstein and Morgan have negotiated the contract."

"Fields," Nina asked, "Edelstein and Morgan? Weren't those Amboise' big time agents?"

"Yes. They all flew down yesterday to negotiate Amboise' contract with HBO. But then they found out he'd been killed and they found out how and they contacted Molly Badger and found out how she'd committed the perfect murder—two murders actually—and then they talked with Sylvia Duncan and all four of them called HBO and the long and short of it is Molly has the contract."

"Molly," asked Nina, "is going to be the next Jessica? Just like she predicted?"

"Yes, little Molly Badger. Apparently, she'd already written several novels with the same heroine—electronic genius Polly Nutria. They'd been rejected due to unbelievable murder methods."

"But since the methods have now been proven believable—"

"Exactly. Hollywood is clambering for more of them, and Molly is at the best hotel in Vicksburg, signing contracts"

"Fields, Edelstein and Morgan aren't concerned that she's not being prosecuted for the murder of Garth Amboise?"

"No. Apparently they didn't know what a terrible, selfish, arrogant, me-first person he really was."

"But they must have worked with him before!"

"Yes, but that was in New York City, and he just seemed to be like everyone else."

"I see."

Silence for a time.

Then Brighton Dunbury:

"Actually, I must admit: I owe Ms. Badger a great deal."

"In what way?" asked Nina.

"Well, I was resigned to having lost my dear Harriet. And after a great many wonderful years of being lovers."

Harriet blushed.

"It was completely my fault," said Harriet. "I was enamored by Amboise."

"And," added Nina, "his resume."

It was Brighton Dunbury's turn to blush.

"Of course, I have a resume too, my dear. But it's much shorter than Amboise' was."

Harriet chucked him under the chin and said:

"We'll lengthen it out."

"I shall look forward to that," he said, squeezing her shoulder.

"Oh, you're a very bad man!"

"No, I'm a very *good* man—"

Nina completed his thought:

I'm just a bad wizard.

But instead, he said:

"I'm a very *good* man; I'm just a bad cozy writer."

Brighton Dunbury and Harriet Crossman said their good byes and made their way toward the waiting cars. But they themselves were replaced by a beaming couple, who brought with them a large red cake pan.

"We've been in your kitchen all morning!" shouted Pat Hershey.

Her husband:

"We've baked our soft and chewy chocolate chip cookies. Just as kind of a thank you present for how gracious you've been to us!"

Margot stood, smiled broadly, and said:

"We owe both of you a lot. If you hadn't discovered the tunnel, there wouldn't have been a plausible theory of the crime, so that the case could be closed. And how wonderful to have the cookies! I love soft and chewy chocolate chip cookies, and I know my guests will, too. Could I possibly have your recipe for soft and chewy chocolate chip cookies?"

"Well, Jim and I have had a dilemma in our kitchen for a few months," Pat Hershey began. "A cookie dilemma. You see, I'm a fan of cookies that have a slight crunch to them. Meanwhile, my husband is a major fan of cookies that are soft and chewy. I'm talking completely soft and chewy with no crunch whatsoever. I've been experimenting with cookies over the past few months as I change up the ingredients, use different baking sheets, adjust the baking time Whatever I did, I noticed that every cookie that came out of the oven wasn't making Jim completely happy. Yes, he got his soft and chewy cookie after dunking the slightly crunchy cookies in milk. However, I knew that secretly he was craving a cookie that was soft and chewy without the use of milk.

"I'm excited to announce the dilemma has ended. How? I got rid of the brown sugar!

"I was craving cookies one night so I took inventory of the ingredients I had in my kitchen. I quickly realized that I didn't have brown sugar. After being worried for a few minutes, I decided to run with it and see what I could create without one of my favorite ingredients.

"After mixing, incorporating, and folding the batter, I noticed that it was light—not only in color—but also in texture. When trying to form balls of dough, the batter seemed to be a bit on the sticky side. I questioned it for a minute but then had the courage to put the baking sheets in the oven as, yet again, another experiment.

"I set the timer, walked away, returned to the kitchen, flipped on the oven light, and watched the cookies rise and turn a light golden brown. I cooled them on the cookie sheet and, while transferring them to the wire rack, decided to take a little nibble.

"Oh, my word! Mission *Soft and Chewy Chocolate Chip Cookies*—accomplished!" she exclaimed rapturously.

"I immediately began counting down the minutes until Jim returned home, as these cookies taunted me from the kitchen. When he got home, we sat down with a plate full of cookies and glasses full of milk. After his first bite, I tried to explain how I'd made them but was quickly interrupted by him as he closed his eyes, let out a sigh of relief and happiness, and said, "Please don't talk. These cookies need my full attention." Yes, they are that good! Words can't even describe just how *soft* and *chewy* they are." The blissful look on Jim Hershey's face echoed his wife's, as she described their cookie orgy in erotic detail.

"I now understands my husband's love of soft and chewy cookies," concluded Pat, recovering a bit from her trance-like state. "I don't think I will ever look at crunchy cookies the same."

Pat handed Margot a sheet of paper, saying:

"Here it is for you, Ms. Gavin, and all your guests—and, of course, our readers—to share!"

So saying, she handed Margot the following recipe:

Pat and Jim's Soft and Chewy Chocolate Chip Cookies

Ingredients:

1 cup (2 sticks) butter, softened
2 eggs
2 1/4 cups all-purpose flour
1/2 teaspoon salt

3/4 cup granulated sugar
2 teaspoons vanilla extract
1 teaspoon baking soda
2 cups milk chocolate chips

Directions:

1. Preheat oven to 375 degrees. Prepare a baking sheet with parchment paper.
2. Use a mixer to cream together the butter and sugar. Add the eggs and mix together. Pour in the vanilla and blend until combined.
3. Pour the flour, baking soda, and salt in a medium bowl and mix until combined. Slowly add the flour mixture to the butter mixture. Mix until combined.
4. Fold in the chocolate chips.
5. Use an ice cream scooper to form tablespoonfuls of the dough. Place the dough on the baking sheet two inches apart.
6. Bake for 8-11 minutes or until lightly golden. Remove from the oven. Allow to cool on baking sheet for 5 minutes.
7. Transfer the cookies to a wire rack and allow to cool completely.

And to the crowd assembled, Pat Hershey said: "Now just enjoy! And remember to buy and read our newest cozy *The Mystery of the Jaded Jambalaya!* Also remember that with every Kindle purchase of one of our cozy mysteries, you get a free recipe for one of our world famous pies! And we'll throw in a free kitten as well!"

With that, Nina noted that the limousines had been loaded, the cats stored, and the cozy writers were now standing in a ring in front of the vehicles, waving and shouting:

"GOOD BYE, NINA AND MARGOT! THANK YOU BOTH FOR EVERYTHING!"

To which Nina and Margot responded:

"GOOD BYE, COZY MYSTERY WRITERS OF AMERICA! COME AGAIN TO MISSISSIPPI!"

But Harriet Crossman, who'd joined the group now, shook her head, looking first at the crowd of writers and then back at the two women standing by the table in the yard of Candles.

"It was wonderful, it really was. But our hearts are with our characters, who all are at home in little seacoast towns in New England. And for true cozy writers—"

She stared at the group of writers now and said:

"ALL TOGETHER—"

And shouted in unison:

"THERE'S NO PLACE LIKE HOME!"

Then they got in their limousines and drove away.

And so Nina and Margot returned into the house.

Where they poured each other a glass of wine.

Then they retired to the rickety white table in the front yard.

Where they watched the sun set.

And where they chatted about this and that.

And where they planned the trip back to Bay St. Lucy (which, luckily, had been spared major damage by the hurricane.)

And where they saw suddenly, high above them, a tall red-haired woman appear on the balcony above the main entrance.

"My God," hissed Margot. "Do you see her?"

"Yes," said Nina, in astonishment. "I do!"

"It's Sarah. Sarah Morgan. But look!"

They looked and saw that the figure was holding a suitcase, and waving.

Then the balcony was empty.

"She's gone!"

"But come on! She left something on the balcony railing!"

Within a minute, the two women had entered Nina's room.

They rushed to the balcony that overlooked the lawn, on which they found a brief note, written on elegant brown stationary.

The note read:

"I'm going to a motel. I can't stay here anymore. These cozy writers scare me to death."

The note was signed:

"Ghost of Sarah Morgan."

They looked at each other.

Nina said:

"The Smathers sisters were right. You've been depossessed."

"No, we haven't! We paid every bill on time and we—"

But Nina merely took her arm and said:

"I'll explain it to you later, Margot. Now let's go finish our wine. We've got a trip to make tomorrow."

And because they did—

—they did.

EPILOGUE

The grand Mississippi loomed before Nina and Margot as they sat on top of the hill overlooking the ferry boat landing.

The boat approached. It was not, however, the ferry they'd ridden over on two days earlier, having been replaced by what seemed an exact model of a mid-nineteenth century steamboat.

"Would you look at that?" asked Nina. "We might as well be living in 1860!"

Margot nodded:

"Must be something the town's doing to boost tourism. Anyway, they're letting the chain down; we can drive on."

They did, and stood by the rail as the old craft chugged its way across the current.

Finally, as they were nearing the far shore, the captain came down.

He was dressed all in white, with frizzy white hair and sparkling blue eyes. He smoked a cigar.

"Did you ladies have an enjoyable time in Abbeyport?"

They each nodded.

"Well, that's good to hear. Did you go to the jumping contest?"

Nina: "What jumping contest?"

"Why, the frog jumping contest! I heard some joker put buckshot into one of the contestants. Did you two hear anything about that?"

They both shook their heads. The captain shook his, too, and threw his cigar butt into the river.

"Well, probably just a tall tale. You get a lot of those up here in Mississippi."

So saying, he turned and, with a wink of his eye, disappeared into the boat.

THE END

ABOUT THE AUTHORS

 Pam 'T'Gracie' Reese is an assistant professor of communication sciences and disorders at Indiana University-Purdue University Fort Wayne (IPFW). Nina Bannister was created while T'Gracie was a doctoral student at the University of Louisiana-Lafayette. She has happy memories of exploring Acadiana, dancing the Cajun waltz, catching beads at Mardi Gras and listening to French on the radio. (Geaux Cajuns!) Still, she also loves her new life in Ft. Wayne and enjoys getting to know northern Indiana. (Go Mastodons!)

Joe Reese is a writer and teacher. He's only partially responsible for the six Nina Bannister mysteries (co-written with his wife, T'Gracie), but he has to take full blame for *Kate Dee and Katie Haw: Letters from a Texas Farm Girl* and the play *Lunacy: A Play for Our Times*.

He and his wife have three children: Kate, Matthew, and Sam. The two of them now live in Fort Wayne, Indiana, where each teaches at IPFW.